Claudia

Other Books by
Mark A. Biggs

Above and Beyond

Operation Underpants

Whitakers's War The battle of the Atlantic

Books in This Series

Operation Underpants

Claudia

Claudia

Mark A. Biggs

mbkbooks

MBK CONSULTING

Copyright

A CIP catalogue record for this book is available from the National Library of Australia.

First Published in Australia 2017.

by

mbkbooks

MBK Consulting

5 Elizabeth Close

Drouin Victoria 3818

Australia.

www.mbkconsulting.com.au

Dedication

To my mother – Patricia Biggs

Acknowledgements

Thank you to those people who helped in the writing of Claudia.

Colin Chudleigh.

Colleen Crookston.

Sandy Komen.

Paul Smith.

Book Cover

Front cover Images: Pixabay Creative Commons CC0.

Cover Design by Craig Braithwaite – Aussiepics: www.aussiepics.com.au

Claudia

Prologue

Claudia

I watched in disbelief as Max reached across the table to the box housing the Janus Machine and ripped the mobile phone from its surface. Lifting his eyes, he looked at me and smiled, saying, 'Claudia, it was all a hoax.'

It was then that I realised the mobile phone had never been attached to a bomb; one supposedly concealed within the box. Max had threatened to destroy the Janus Machine if I did not reveal Olivia's whereabouts. Although I don't like to admit it, Max had ingeniously manipulated me. He had turned the tables. Kidnapping Olivia should have guaranteed us – the Russian Mafia – the ultimate weapon - but it didn't matter. Olivia might be free but the Janus Machine was ours.

Max unfastened the latches and lifted the lid, revealing nothing but a pile of old books. Seething anger flowed through my veins.

What! No Janus Machine!

'Where is it, Max?' I spat in fury.

How is it possible that two eighty-seven-year olds, Max and Olivia, had outwitted me, Claudia, a Brigadier, a Capi or Lieutenant, in the most powerful and influential of all the Russian Mafia Brotherhoods?

My task was straightforward. Follow Max and Olivia, two nursing home runaways from Australia as they made their way to the United Kingdom on a mission to retrieve the Janus Machine, a device hidden in the dying days of WW2. The primary objective of my task was to secure the device for ourselves but the overriding imperative was to prevent it from falling into the hands of the British Government. The stakes were high: billions of pounds in extortion money would be lost if we didn't succeed. For the British and other wealthy governments, thousands of lives were at risk.

Provocatively, Max looked at his watch, mimicking my actions of when I counted down for the explosion which should have killed Olivia. He said, 'The Royal Mail picked up a parcel a little over an hour and a half ago. By now, the Janus Machine is somewhere in Edinburgh and will soon be on a plane to London.'

The contemptuous senile old man! He will pay for this – I'm going to kill him this time.

Only seconds before, I had been the victor. It was a simple trade: the Janus Machine for Olivia. I had taken the precaution of holding Olivia at a different location so that when Max came to the exchange point, a farmhouse in Scotland surrounded by open fields, Olivia would be absent. Instead, he would watch a live video feed as we counted down to her death - a house that was slowly filling with gas. If he'd handed over the Janus Machine, I would then tell him where Olivia was. There was barely time to rescue her before an automated trigger device ignited the gas. It was enough. My plan ensured that Max had no time to cook up some cock-and-bull story, to stall hoping for a rescue mission. I'd not anticipated that he'd pretend to have concealed explosives in the box.

With Olivia free and the Janus Machine on its way to London, my retribution would be cold, swift and final. Max would cower before me; he would beg for his life before I extinguished it in an ecstasy of unrivalled pleasure.

As for the man who came with Max to the farmhouse, Jana, although I doubted that was his real name, I would let him live to tell the story of how I coolly eliminated – no, *executed* – Max. Fear of my name would spread: *Claudia, a cold-blooded killer*. I preferred it to *Claudia, the laughing stock*, outwitted by a doddering vicar and his nutty wife.

11

I reached to where the Glock pistol was holstered at my side and lifted it until the muzzle was pointing between Max's eyes. I pulled back the hammer, for no other reason than dramatic effect. The sound of it clicking into place sent a sudden rush of adrenaline surging through my veins. I quivered slightly as the orgasm from the anticipation of violence titillated my senses. I wanted, needed sex following a kill and this was going to be a pleasurable execution.

Max held my gaze, his eyes fixed on mine. I slowly squeezed the trigger; the mechanism that would bring forth his God.

Neither of us blinked.

But then something unexpected happened.

As I stared deep into the old green eyes, my mood mellowed. The rage I felt slipped away to be replaced by what?

Was it pity? No – grief. What was happening to me?

Without my permission, a tear formed and welled in the corner of my eye. Then another. I pushed them away but emotions that I had long forgotten surfaced. Staring into his eyes, I saw myself in the reflection. Not Claudia but Lucia, my real name: a fourteen-year-old girl, prisoner of the sex slave trade in the former Yugoslavia. Lucia stared back at me and I was transported to that time.

***

'You're my favourite, Lucia,' said Tamara, as she caressed and stroked my fine blonde hair. I felt the sweeping motion of the

12

brush pulling the hair softly against my scalp. In the mirror, I saw Tamara smiling and standing behind my chair, her body pushing against my back.

'We have some special guests tonight. They will want to take some pictures. Remember to be a good girl. You don't want Ivankov to send you away, like the other girls.'

'Just pictures?' I said.

'These are special guests, sweetie. You know I'm always outside and wouldn't let anything bad happen to you.' She ceased her brushing and, in the mirror, I watched as she gently leaned over and kissed the top of my head. 'Now get dressed, my little mouse, and make yourself beautiful.'

She placed the hairbrush on the dressing table beside me and turned to leave the room. On reaching the door, she paused. With her beautiful blue eyes and flowing brown hair, Tamara, the only mother I remembered, raised her hand to her mouth and in the reflection, I saw her blow me a parting kiss.

I'd been living there for so long that I no longer remembered my arrival or when I was given my own room. Unlike other children who were locked in their rooms, I was allowed to wander freely about the big house. I knew better than to ask where I was but I guessed, from what I had overheard, that the house was part of a large estate surrounded by a high stone wall with trees on the outside, their tops visible above the barrier. I knew that we were somewhere in Yugoslavia.

None of this mattered: my home was my prison.

To survive, I had learnt to smile, please and be pleasing. I had seen what happened to other girls when a guest complained, so I became a *special gift,* earning privileges in return. When I was alone in my room at night, I cried myself to sleep, wishing someone would come and save me.

At first, the tears were because I'd been stolen from my mother and wanted to go home. But then one day, I couldn't remember her anymore. Then the tears were for what they were doing to me and I cried to be rescued. But now I wept because I needed rescuing from myself. Sometimes, if a man or woman was gentle, my body screamed out in pleasure and desire. Afterwards, when they'd left, I floundered in the guilt of my own sexual feelings - despairing at what I'd become and what I would be.

'Please save me. Take me away from this place,' I whispered to myself, as Tamara pushed the door closed behind her as she left.

Through the window, from the gravel driveway below, I heard vehicles slowing and then stopping. I stood, left the dressing table and walked across to the window to look down from my upstairs bedroom. A white van stopped and I saw six children, mostly girls, but also a couple of boys, taken from the house. They were bundled into the back, to be whisked away to their new owners. It was a scene I'd witnessed many times. Watching it again, my senses were numb and my response emotionless.

When did I stop caring?

When new children arrived, I kept my distance; aloof, remote but not always a physical distance because sometimes the jobs I was given involved closeness or contact with them. But by never looking into their eyes, I learned to build a wall that protected me. I felt nothing but detachment, asking no questions and giving no comfort. I survived. Their future rested in their own hands, or in truth, on how they used their bodies.

As I turned away from the window, the scene drifted from my thoughts and I studied the garments in the wardrobe from which I could choose for tonight's *special guests*. I knew that I was expected to select my prettiest clothes; instead, I picked an old pair of blue jeans, a loose-fitting top and sandshoes. I changed into them, slinked over to the dressing table mirror and stared at the reflection. Gazing back at me I saw a girl, happily playing in a forest, then lying by a stream and frolicking with the animals. Imagining the sky as a beautiful rich blue and the grass a magical emerald green. Birds sang and I felt the warmth of the sun as it illuminated my face.

The fantasy was swept away by the sound of *tap-tap-tap* on the door followed by Tamara's voice.

'Don't be long Lucia, sweetie. Come downstairs when you're finished dressing.'

Tamara's footsteps faded and the silence of my room returned as she walked away down the corridor.

For a second longer I lingered, remaining motionless to stare at my reflection in the mirror. With no sound or movement, for the briefest of moments, the world was perfectly still. My delusion one of happiness. Turning from the mirror, I looked at my *pretty clothes* sombre in the wardrobe, awaiting my attention for tonight. Before putting them on, I returned once more to my reflection and escaped into my dream of happiness.

Gunshots! Yelling!

With curiosity, but not panic, I walked over to look out from the bedroom window. The van was still there but this time men were hurriedly pulling children from the back and ushering them towards the house. The commotion was coming from the far side of the driveway gates. Another shot rang out, causing more people to rush from the house. Some took cover behind stone artwork decorating the garden whilst others crouched behind the fountain, the central feature of the driveway and the entrance to the residence.

From my vantage point, I watched as an eerie quiet returned to the grounds which was suddenly broken by a deafening explosion. The bedroom window shook violently as the wrought iron gates that locked us away from the world danced upwards, spiralling toward the sky, leaving a fog of dust and dirt in their wake. Where these gates of hell had stood, the protectors of this underworld, armoured vehicles were now bursting in.

The sound of gunshots returned but this time they came from every direction. I remained motionless, frozen, a spectator to a gladiatorial battle. From outside of our compound, more vehicles entered the courtyard and armed military people spilled out in overwhelming numbers. A whooshing noise from the rotor blades of helicopters suddenly overwhelmed the scene. Looking up, I saw ropes being dropped and men in battle fatigues descending to the ground below. People in army uniform soon filled the area around our home. The sounds of gunfire drifted away and then almost as quickly as it all started, the outside became silent. Instead, the commotion switched to within the house; people were running and calling. I knew where they were heading: to the secret escape routes, a flight from justice. They would be gone before the victors crossed our threshold.

Turning back to the window, I watched police cars joining the swarm of military vehicles outside.

A car, memorably a red one, neither a military nor a police vehicle, entered the compound and stopped slightly away from the other vehicles. The door opened and I watched an older man and woman get out. They exuded authority; a man I'd seen issuing orders, directing soldiers during the fight, saluted them and pointed around the grounds and then towards the house. The aged couple nodded as the commander did so, and after a short conversation, they were left standing alone. They conversed and I could see, from the movements of their heads, that they were taking in their surroundings. Then slowly, the older man lifted his head until his gaze found my window and our eyes met.

I don't know how, but I knew that he had come for me and I would be safe.

***

Staring deep into his green eyes and with the Glock pistol pointed at his head, I was struck by the realisation - *It was Max and Olivia who came for me all those years ago.*

Age had taken a heavy toll on them, so much so, that I hadn't recognised either of them. But now as I looked into those eyes I was certain, although Max wasn't the name that I knew him by.

Rattled by my own feelings, I hesitated and then eased the pressure on the trigger of my Glock by relaxing the muscles in my finger.

I can't do it. I can't kill him but he mustn't know the truth.

Regaining my composure, I said in my overly polite manner, while trying to hide my ambiguity, 'You may have won but, tell me, what do you have to look forward to? Nothing! Max, you have nothing! Go back to where you came from and spend the remainder of your miserable life in a nursing home.'

I spoke those bitter words but inside I was being torn apart with feelings of despair replaced by a longing for the emotional emptiness of my life to end. It was the sound of my loyal henchman Semyon's voice that returned my focus.

'Boss, the diversion for our escape starts in two minutes.'

I hesitated, hoping that he wouldn't notice my distraction.

'Thank you, Semyon.'

It's important to act decisively and retain my authority. Nobody must recognise my temporary weakness, I said to myself.

Yet for reasons I was struggling to understand, I knew that I couldn't kill Max but nor could I leave him behind.

'I've changed my mind,' I snapped, 'I've other plans for you. Semyon, tie Jana up. Max is coming with us.'

'Where are you taking him?' I heard Jana ask.

'Sweetie, you will have to wait and see.

'Stand up Max,' I commanded, and with this instruction, I placed my arm under his shoulder and, with a gentleness that surprised me, helped him rise from the chair.

'I need to go to the toilet before we leave,' he said. 'You know what it's like for old men! And with all this excitement!'

'Sweetie, there is something about you that one can't help but admire, even if one of your legs is about to   fall off, we are leaving now! You can walk, shuffle or even crawl for all I care, but we are going.'

I escorted, half carried, him to the door which was behind my desk. Pausing, I looked back to where the Janus Machine box with its discarded mobile phone rested.

How am I ever going to explain this? Tricking me with the fake contents!

The building where we were hiding had been used by us as a safe house for over twenty years. It was perfectly situated on a slight rise in the middle of open fields, with one track in, and five hundred metres of unimpeded view of anyone approaching. It was only twenty minutes' drive from the Anstruther golf course, where we used a small sandy beach on the famous fifth hole, *The Rockies*, to smuggle people, arms and contraband in and out of the UK.

My masters will despair that I lost the Janus Machine. Compromising the safe house may be a step-too-far. Any more mistakes could cost me dearly and yet, here I am, taking Max with me. What plausible reason could I concoct for that?

With these thoughts swirling in my mind, I looked about for the last time. Passing Max to Semyon, I returned to the room and stood in front of Jana, still tied to a chair.

'Jana, sweetie. Unlike your little masquerade, we do have explosives and they are rigged to blow up and destroy this farmhouse. Vladimir, if you wouldn't mind sweetie, can you start the timer please?'

Vladimir answered with a nod of his head and left.

Saying nothing, I waited patiently while looking down at Jana. He didn't look up to meet my gaze, but stared straight ahead, staying mute.

About a minute later Vladimir returned.

'Done, boss.'

A sound filled the air.

Explosions, detonations.

Another noise.

Rotor blades. Our helicopters were coming to life.

This signalled that the diversions for our escape had started and it was time to leave.

'Jana sweetie, provided that your friends don't dilly-dally, you should be rescued, but this whole place will be flattened. Can I suggest getting away as quickly as you can? Oh, and I would watch the fireworks from a considerable distance! Until we meet again, *Proshchay* sweetie.'

CHAPTER ONE

The Escape

Inspector Axel

The phone rang. This time it wasn't the desperate Jana trying to discover whether we were going to make it to the village of Elie in time to save Olivia. It was Peta, the officer in charge, who telephoned about what we were calling the *Janus farmhouse incident.*

'Inspector Axel...sir,' she said. 'You will be pleased to know that we have Olivia. She's safe and I've rung Jana back to let him know.'

'Could you gauge Claudia's reaction when you told him?' I asked.

'No sir. I can only guess that she wouldn't have been happy. Max may be in real trouble now.'

'Okay Peta, great work. I was wondering, how did you get to Olivia in time?'

'We contacted an off-duty police officer living in Elie. Thank God, he was home and made it to Olivia with seconds to spare.'

'That's a blessing, excellent news. Where's Olivia now?'

'She's at his house, the off-duty policeman's, I mean. We have a car on its way to recover her. I suggest, sir, that you don't return to the farm but come to the mobile command centre which has been set up in Anstruther. We have live feeds coming in from the farm and have established communication with other security agencies.'

'Has anything happened since Olivia was freed?'

'Yes sir, Whitehall, the Cabinet Office Briefing Room or COBRA as we call it in the UK—'

I cut Peta off mid-sentence.

'Sorry, what's COBRA? I'm from Interpol in France, remember.'

'It's akin to the White House Situation Room in the USA.'

'Okay. I've got it. Go on.'

'COBRA was active because of the biological attack on London; they believe these terrorists are linked to that attack and are coordinating the overall situation now. We are running things on the ground but reporting back to them. We expect, sir, that the terrorists will attempt to escape using the two helicopters they have at the farmhouse. COBRA has authorised an E-3D Airborne Warning and Control System aircraft, an AWACS, from the RAF Base at Waddington to be their eyes in the sky. If the helicopters go airborne they will be tracked. They don't intend to intercept as they believe that the helicopters may lead them to those behind the organisation and, sir, they still want to retrieve the Janus Machine.'

'I take it that the AWACS will assume command if the helicopters take off? Is that right, Peta?'

'Yes, sir. But as I said, while they are in the air, we will still look after things on the ground. Inspector, their instructions are clear; if we are likely to lose them either on the ground or in the air, they will be eliminated. We can destroy the Janus Machine but under no circumstances can it be lost.'

'Understood. What about at the farmhouse? Has anything changed?'

'No sir, but we are expecting some kind of diversion before they attempt an escape. The consensus is they will use the helicopters. COBRA has authorised aircraft to shadow them from a distance and, as an added precaution, two Typhoon fighter jets from the Lossiemouth RAF airbase in Scotland are on standby. They are fuelled and ready to roll. If the helicopters head out to sea, the Typhoon's will be dispatched and instructed to intercept and destroy, even if we discover that Max is on board. The Janus Machine is the priority.'

'Are you planning to storm the farmhouse?'

Peta began to answer, then stopped and said, 'Wait, sir. Both helicopter motors have started and explosions have commenced in no man's land, the area between the house and the nearest cover.' There was a pause before Peta continued. 'They've detonated smoke bombs around the house. We've lost visual contact. This is it, sir! They're about to make a break for it. Inspector, the moment the helicopters leave the ground, we are storming the farmhouse.'

'Okay. Thank you, Peta. Be careful. The farmhouse may be boobytrapped. This is no ordinary criminal gang. Jana overheard Claudia telling Max that they have foreign government connections and you know what that means: significant resources, and God knows what they can call upon. Take great care.'

'Thank you, Inspector. You know what sir, it's quite possible the helicopters are themselves part of the diversion.'

'I was thinking the same thing.'

Peta paused and I heard only the sounds of the commotion on the line for a moment.

'The helicopters are airborne, sir.'

'Good luck, Peta. I'll be with you soon.'

When Peta hung up the phone I imagined what was taking place on the ground, in the air, and in her mind. I needed to be there.

'Come on Colleen,' I said to my driver. 'As fast as you can.'

Colleen glanced, or should I say glared, in my direction. Without her needing to explain, I was reminded that we were in a

26

1600cc buzz-box. It had no lights or sirens and my earlier insistence that she speed to rescue Olivia, almost got us killed.

'Safely… but as fast as you can,' I corrected.

It took seven minutes for us to reach Anstruther. Peta's mobile control centre was a medium-sized white van with Incident Control Unit stencilled on its side. Through the open back doors, I saw that the interior was filled with TV monitors, computers and an array of other fancy looking communication equipment. A satellite dish dominated its roof line and, inside, men and women wearing headsets sat at work stations. A large screen displayed live video footage of the ongoing operation at the farmhouse. The operator could switch between the cameras being worn by the officers involved in the manoeuvre.

Peta looked up from her seat, giving me a welcoming nod as I climbed into the back of the van. Colleen remained in the car.

'Good afternoon, Inspector. Shut the doors behind you, if you don't mind?' she said, politely but firmly.

I turned, realising that I couldn't reach the doors from inside. About to leap from the van, I heard Peta say, 'The blue button on your left. Push it and the doors will close automatically.'

I complied.

'Inspector,' said Peta, 'as you can see on the screen someone's been found. He's been tied up and appears to be on his own. Until we can establish who he is, I have told them to proceed cautiously. He could be a suicide bomber!'

'That's Jana,' I said with excitement rising in my voice. Regaining my composure, I continued, 'He's one of us. Ask your men for a situation report from him ASAP.'

'Ma'am,' said one of the men from his work station, swivelling his chair in Peta's direction as he spoke, 'The AWACS is reporting that both helicopters have been staying low and heading north about ten miles from the coast. They have changed course and are heading east, into the North Sea. They have also picked up two Russian TU-160 Blackjack bombers tracking from the north, on course for the Shetland Islands. The AWACS is wanting an update from the farmhouse.'

'A coincidence, the TU-160's turning up and the helicopters heading out to sea?' asked Peta, looking at me as she spoke, her face decorated with incredulity.

'I don't like coincidence,' came my reply.

'An update from the farmhouse please,' said Peta, 'and instruct them to speak to Jana, the guy you found. Tell them he's one of us.'

Via the monitor, we watched as one of the operatives spoke to Jana. Unfortunately, the sound feed was defective and we would have to wait for a radio message before we would discover what he had said.

Whatever Jana said created a flurry of activity.

The words that came over the radio were not what we wanted to hear. The farmhouse had been rigged with explosives and could detonate at any moment.

The situation report from Jana would have to wait until everyone was clear.

'Get yourselves out of there,' commanded Peta. 'As soon as you're safe I want to know if the terrorists have the Janus Machine and if they left in those helicopters.'

'And about Max?' I added.

'And find out about Max.'

As we waited for the team to withdraw from the farmhouse, Peta relayed what little she knew to the AWACS.

Their response was no surprise.

If the helicopters continued their flight into the North Sea, away from Britain, COBRA ordered them to be destroyed. The designated kill zone would be reached in five minutes at their current speed. The Typhoon fighters, on standby at Lossiemouth, had been launched and would be within missile range of the helicopters imminently.

Time has a habit of moving inexplicably slowly when in a hurry but all that we could do was watch and wait as our team evacuated the farmhouse. Inwardly however, I kept mumbling to myself,

Come on! Ask about the Janus Machine and Max as you withdraw. Surely you can walk and talk at the same time.

29

I knew better than to air my thoughts publicly. The rational and professional part of me knew that they would have asked, were it safe to do so. From the live video link, we could see our operatives and Jana enter the vehicles and begin speeding away from the farm.

'Ma'am,' the radio crackled. 'The Janus Machine is safe and is not on board either of the helicopters. Max posted it to London before he went to the farmhouse to make the exchange for Olivia. All the terrorist got was a box of old books.'

'Relay that message to the AWACS,' barked Peta, then added without taking a breath, 'I want to know where Max is and if the terrorists are on board those helicopters.'

'Max is with the terrorists,' came the reply. 'But Jana couldn't see the helicopters from where he was. All we can confirm is that they left the room together and then the helicopters took off.'

'Ma'am,' said the radio operator who was communicating with the AWACS, 'I've passed on the news about the Janus Machine and they are letting COBRA know; they will inform us if there's been any change to the plan. They also said, the Typhoon fighters will be within BVR, beyond visual air to air missile range of the helicopters, within four minutes.'

***

Claudia

Leaving Jana tied to the chair, I joined Semyon with Max and we made our way out of the farmhouse towards the awaiting helicopters. Max had developed an annoying and deliberate limp which was slowing our progress; a nuisance because we needed to be airborne before the fog from our smokebombs cleared.

'Max, sweetie, you are most exasperating. I spared your life so perhaps the least you could do is walk properly.'

'I'm aged, or would you believe - it's an old war injury. Or how about gout?'

'Sweetie, if that's the extent of your humour, it's pathetic. Vladimir, help Semyon with Max to my helicopter. Have the others been told that we are leaving?'

'Yes boss, everybody else is already on board and, as you ordered, Linda is waiting for you.'

'Thank you, sweetie. Do be careful with him,' I said, looking to Max. 'At his age, his arms may fall off. If he keeps up with that limp, drag him but try not to hurt him too much.'

'Boss,' said Vladimir, 'why are we taking him with us anyway?'

'I thought it might be entertaining to push him out of the helicopter. To watch as he falls in a five-hundred-foot spiral before hitting the ground with a splat.'

Vladimir sniggered and I looked at him with daggers as I said, 'That's not why I have kept him alive. Question me again and that fate awaits you! Do I make myself clear, sweetie?'

'Yes boss.'

Max was manhandled into my helicopter with Semyon and myself, but Vladimir was to travel with the others.

'What's he doing here?' asked Linda, a mixture of disappointment, surprise and suspicion clouding her face.

Linda Orr had been my partner in crime now for about four years. Our criminal friends saw us as a team, although I was the boss. Linda was a couple of years older than me, slim and athletic but not well endowed – muscular more than perky. Apart from our breasts, we were physically quite similar. Our physical attributes were where the similarities ended and in many ways, we were total opposites, which is why we got on so well. To anyone seeing her in the street, Linda could pass as a distinguished business woman. While she was a smart dresser when she wished it, she had little interest in the latest fashion. Although she was exceptionally bright, cunning and shrewd, she often played the blonde bimbo as a deception to our adversaries. It was Linda who planned our escape from Scotland. There was no doubt in my mind that we would outsmart our pursuers even though I had thrown a spanner in the works by bringing along Max.

I loved Linda's sense of humour and with it our verbal jousting, particularly when we found ourselves in tight situations.

'I've defected,' said Max, bringing my thoughts back into the helicopter.

'Defected! You can't defect,' said Linda, looking confused and studying me for confirmation.

'Ignore him sweetie. He's senile.'

As I spoke, the helicopter lifted into the air. It angled its nose downwards and, with its tail pointing in the air, we sped away metres from the ground, rising and falling with the terrain. Linda gazed over at me and I could tell that she wanted to ask some questions, but with the world speeding past and each of us feeling vulnerable, none of us spoke.

The pilot dropped the helicopter over the cliff edge and we plummeted towards the beach below before levelling out and tracking from the land and out to sea. The adrenaline rush was over, for the moment.

'Senile!' repeated Linda. 'Our masters won't be pleased. First, we lose the Janus Machine and now we bring Max back with us. I hope you know what you're doing.'

'Have I ever let you down, Linda?'

'I hate to spoil this love-in,' said Max. 'You don't have to worry about your "boss" at all. You do know that they will shoot us out of the sky, right? The British Government isn't going to let you simply fly out of here!'

'He's talkative for a condemned man,' said Linda, giving me a playful look.

'Remember that old mangy dog, the one we should have put down? Max is a bit like that, a bloody pain in the arse but lovable in a strange sort of way.'

'He's not going to have an accident on the carpet is he - like our dog?'

'Wouldn't surprise me, sweetie.' I said, leaning in towards Max and, in a loud and exaggerated voice continued, 'Have you got your incontinence pants on, love?'

We laughed for a second before Linda returned to her first question. 'Seriously Claudia, why did you bring him?'

Having spent most of my life lying, it was not overly taxing to dream up a fictitious but believable story. 'Remember 2008, when Max and Olivia were riding that old motorbike and sidecar around Europe?'

'A 1948 BSA A7—stunningly beautiful. Beauty - something you two wouldn't understand,' said Max, interrupting my conversation with Linda.

Before I could respond, I heard the slightest of sniggers coming from Semyon.

'Semyon,' I said. 'If Max speaks again cut his tongue out and Semyon, if you think him a comedian again, I'll cut something of yours out as well.'

'Semyon, that's a woman's name anyway,' responded Max. 'So, cutting his dick and balls out would be doing him a favour.'

With lightning speed, Semyon's hand wrapped around Max's throat and with his other hand he grabbed a concealed knife and pushed it against Max's neck.

'See how smart you are now,' he spat.

'Boys, play nicely now,' laughed Linda.

'Let him go, Semyon,' I commanded. 'And Max - no more!'

The words, intended as a threat, sounded like a reprimand of a naughty child. But he nodded his capitulation anyway.

Before returning my attention to answer Linda's question, I looked out the window to gather my thoughts, but rather than inventing more to embellish the lie that I was about to tell, a voice in my head became words from Shakespeare.

Some rise by sin, and some by virtue fall. You and I Max but which of us is which?

As unlikely as it sounds, it was as a defiant teenager that I realised that learning English would create opportunities. Without it, there was little chance of a better life. But it was not until I fled to the United Kingdom that I become fluent and discovered the joy and power of literature, poetry and the arts. I read avidly: Shakespeare, Dickens, Eliot, Hemingway, Wordsworth…, Tennyson and more. My appetite was insatiable, matched only by my ruthlessness, a paradox not lost on me. My only regret, I laughed silently to myself, was my reading of *Moby Dick* by Melville, a torture which would guarantee a confession from anyone who was forced to read it. It was so excruciating that I had come to love it.

The sound from the beating rotors as they cut their way through the air brought my focus back to the moment. We were skimming the waves heading north, flying almost parallel to the coast line, moving slowly farther out to sea. As I watched, the pilot coaxed the helicopter upwards and we gained altitude. He

35

altered course, heading out to sea. Aside from our other helicopter, we were alone in the sky. If we were being followed, they were keeping their distance.

'When they were riding that old motorbike and sidecar around Europe,' I said to Linda, 'they went to the tunnels near Walbrzch. These are the tunnels where the Nazi gold train is supposedly hidden. It's a long shot, but let's interrogate him first, just in case he knows where the train is? Then we can kill him.'

Linda didn't reply but instead gave me a half-hearted shrug of her shoulders. Even though I knew Linda well, I wasn't sure what it meant.

Was she convinced by my story, or was she keeping her reservations to herself until we were alone?

Thirty seconds later she spoke. 'Claudia, you'll have to do better than that if you don't want to end up with your throat slit.' She looked away before adding, 'We should push him out now! Before it's too late.'

'I have my reasons,' I said calmly, although I was now worried.

If I couldn't convince Linda, then I would need to invent a much more believable story by the time we reached Moscow. I shook my head.

Why did I want to save him? I owe him nothing, look what's become of my life. You should kill him now! My mind was again filling with confused thoughts.

'Are you all right?' asked Linda.

'A slight headache, that's all.'

I wasn't all right. For whatever reason, one I was yet to understand, I wanted him to live. Needed him to live, even though he abandoned me and worse, doesn't remember me.

The helicopter began to descend and a large tanker came into view.

***

Inspector Axel

'Thank you, said Peta. 'Let the AWACS know that we think Max is on board. Switch your communications with them through to the loud speaker, so that we can all hear what's happening.'

'With the Janus Machine safe and Max on board, surely they won't shoot them down?' Peta asked me.

'I don't know Peta, all we can do now is wait and see.'

The live video feed from the farm showed that the officers were safely away from the house. They were securing an exclusion zone around the area in case of an explosion. The crackle of the radio drew my attention away from the monitor. It was a broadcast from the AWACS, now on loud speaker, which occupied those in the control room as we nervously waited.

'We have two Russian TU-160 Blackjack bombers still tracking on bearing Two Two Zero and heading for a British area of interest.'

There was a slight pause before the AWACS operator continued.

'Both helicopters are now one minute from the kill zone. COBRA, we have no other assets available to intercept the bombers. Be advised that it will be thirty minutes before Yankee Five Romeo One-One and Yankee Five Romeo One-Two can be airborne. If the Russian bombers continue at their current speed and course, they will be in an area of interest in fifteen minutes. Can I confirm: the primary target is the helicopters?'

We couldn't hear the communication between COBRA and the AWACS; instead we waited for the AWACS to relay the command to the fighter jets. It didn't take long.

'Typhoons Oscar Charlie Echo 06 and 07, your targets are two bogie helicopters bearing One Two Zero, 60 miles at 500 feet.'

'Roger,' came the reply.

Turning to Peta, I said in stunned disbelief, 'They are going to take Max out!'

She didn't reply but instead stared ahead, as if she hadn't heard me. An eerie silence fell over the control room. I could visualise the two jet fighters as they swooped down on the helicopters at over 700mph. It would be over in a matter of seconds.

'Typhoons Oscar Charlie Echo 06 and 07, your bogies are bearing One Two Zero, 40 miles at 200 feet. Be warned we have shipping in the vicinity.'

'AWACS control, this is Typhoon Oscar Charlie Echo 06. I have missile lock. Please confirm that we are authorised to engage. Over.'

'AWACS control, this is Typhoon Oscar Charlie Echo 07, I also have missile lock. Confirm engagement. Over.'

'Standby Typhoons Oscar Charlie Echo 06 and 07.'

In our control room, the men and women monitoring the farmhouse stayed fixed to their screen but we knew that they were focused on the radio and what was about to happen next.

'Negative Typhoons Oscar Charlie Echo 06 and 07. The shipping is too close. Visual engagement only. Confirm?'

'Roger, visual only.'

'This is it,' I said to Peta, 'they are about to be shot down.'

Seconds later, another AWACS transmission arrived.

'Typhoons Oscar Charlie Echo 06 and 07, we have a new assignment for you. We are tracking Two Russian TU-160 bombers, 350 miles north of you. Turn north bearing Two Zero. You are to escort our friends away from British airspace. Do not engage. Repeat, you are not to engage.'

There was an audible sigh of relief from those in the control room.

'Okay everyone, back to your duties and switch off that loud speaker,' instructed Peta to the radio operator before adding, 'I want to know what's happening with those helicopters.'

Our man talking to the AWACS switched off the speaker and we waited patiently as he conversed.

'Ma'am,' said the radio operator. 'The Typhoons have been diverted to intercept and escort the Russian bombers away from territorial airspace. The AWACS is continuing to track the helicopters and has sought assistance from the Norwegian Airforce under an anti-terrorism agreement between our two countries. The Norwegians will be airborne in ten minutes.'

I still feared for Max's safety, but for a now, he was safe from 'friendly fire'. If indeed, he was on one of the helicopters.

***

Claudia

'There she is,' said Linda.

Addressing the pilot she continued, 'Right on time. Take us in.'

'Linda, your planning is impeccable as always.'

'Why thank you, Claudia.'

As we touched down on the tanker, I breathed a sigh of relief. Landing on a pitching and rolling deck is not only difficult but an ordeal for the passengers. The seaborne rendezvous, the first part of our escape plan, was complete and phase two was about to start.

***

Inspector Axel

My attention was diverted away from the helicopters and back to the farmhouse. On the live video feed, we watched as it exploded in a massive ball of flames. I knew exactly what they were doing. They were destroying any evidence, making it harder to find Max. I felt helpless and for the rest of the afternoon and late into that evening, I had to wait, watch and listen. My other disappointment was that Olivia didn't make it to the control room. The spooks arrived at Elie and took her away before we had the opportunity to intervene.

What was left of the farmhouse was secured by our officers. A forensic examination couldn't start until the site had been given the all clear by an army bomb disposal unit. As for the helicopters, not long after the Typhoons had been redeployed, the AWACS tracked the aircraft landing on a large tanker sailing in international waters. Radar monitoring, suggested that the helicopters didn't take off again, but next morning when the freighter was photographed by a surveillance plane, they were gone. Our best guess was that they had been pushed over the side.

With the site cleared by the bomb disposal team, a peripheral search of what was left of the farmhouse drew a blank. Although a thorough forensic search for evidence was yet to be completed, ground-penetrating radar revealed nothing. No hidden passages or underground bunkers that Claudia and her associates could have used to escape. We concluded that they and Max had been on the helicopters, which had now vanished.

Although we were still shadowing the tanker as it made its way to Rotterdam in Holland (where when it arrived, it would be boarded by police and security agencies), I was sure that neither Max nor our terrorists would be on board.

The only lead could have come from Jana when he was brought to the command centre, but he added nothing to what I already knew. We were dealing with a crime syndicate with links to the Russian Government. Unfortunately, before I had the chance to learn anything new, MI6 arrived and whisked him away, removing any opportunity for me to interview him. With MI6's arrival, we were politely thanked for our assistance and told that the affair was a matter of national security and that it would be handled by the secret services. Fortunately, the MI6 officer in charge, Stephen Walls, was not the cloak and dagger type. He promised, if he could be believed, to provide us with regular updates. He said, if Max was on the freighter, he would let us know immediately. When I asked about Olivia, Stephen replied that she was "helping us with our inquiries" and he expected his team to finish debriefing her by Wednesday next.

'What will happen to Olivia?' I asked.

'When we board the tanker in Rotterdam, if Max is still missing, Olivia will be deported to Australia,' he answered.

'Perhaps, in the interim, once you've debriefed her, I could assist by supervising Olivia until Max is found or a decision is made to deport her.'

Stephen contemplated my proposal for a few moments and I held my breath awaiting his reply.

'Perfect. I will make the necessary arrangements.'

CHAPTER TWO

Olivia

Olivia

The house in Elie and the surrounding streets had to be cordoned off following my rescue from the house full of gas; the plot of those wishing to capture the Janus Machine to put pressure on Max.

They underestimated my Max.

The risk of an explosion remained high until the vapours dissipated into the atmosphere. The lovely young off-duty policeman, who saved me, took me to his house while I waited for a ride back to Anstruther. The spooks, MI6 and the police arrived at the same time. A bitter argument ensued concerning who was to take me and where I was to go. An argument in which I was totally ignored. The spooks won and I was bundled into a car to be taken away. For a "debriefing" is what they told me.

"Interrogation" was more accurate and it was carried out by a most charming man, Stephen Walls. He was probably closer to sixty than fifty with a good crop of black hair, so I guessed that he dyed it. A vain gesture in my day, but not necessarily now. He was smartly dressed though not eccentric like many of his peers. He wore a plain blue tie rather than a brightly coloured bow tie and a scrunched-up handkerchief was absent from his suit's breast pocket. From the way he spoke, I could see that he was well educated; probably at Oxford or Cambridge, obviously British, but not quintessentially so. During the debriefing, he observed the mantra that I knew.

You catch more people with honey than you do with vinegar.

Although I couldn't imagine him wanting to waterboard me.

The interrogation was spread over three days and was quite civilised, more of an extended "polite chat" than a grilling. Stephen opened by sharing what he knew of Max's fate, or as much as he was willing to divulge. The information was delivered with a delightful sense of imaginary candour.

I'm telling you everything Olivia – or is that how he wanted me to see him.

But I knew exactly what he was up to,

He was trying to win my trust.

My response to Stephen's questioning was played using his methods. Games within games, though we were ostensibly on the same side. I think we each knew that the other was holding things back.

No wonder we British seem foolish to some of our adversaries. They must laugh at the "British Way." It's subtler than it appears.

'I think our colleague's lying, old chap.'

'I do hope not, that just wouldn't be cricket. Tea?'

It was clear to me, that neither Stephen nor MI6 knew who employed Max or I and if they did, they understood very little. How galling it must have been for MI6 to discover the existence of another Government secret agency, one operating since the Second World War and which had flown under their radar. Their knowledge of the Janus Machine was also tenuous. After small talk, it was Stephen's opening question, which exposed his lack of knowledge. Despite this, I remember thinking,

Don't underestimate your adversaries, particularly when they are your friends.

He might have been ignorant but he was certainly not naïve and I would have to be careful not to fall into his well-set trap.

'Olivia, the nation owes you our gratitude. Without you, the biological attack on London would have been much worse,' Stephen said. 'You know as well as I do how these debriefings work

47

and I'm sorry that some of my questions will appear pointless, shall I say. But as you know, we start from the premise that we know nothing and let you tell us the whole story.'

I acknowledged this.

'You were being held captive when Max posted the Janus Machine, but can you confirm where it was sent?'

It was then that I knew.

Well, well! MI6 doesn't know about the agency and probably doesn't know much about the Janus Machine either. And it's not up to me to tell them.

Thinking quickly, I settled on what I thought was an ingenious strategy to see me through the interrogation. I would act as if Max and I believed we were working for MI6 or MI5, and that they already knew everything. The risk was that Stephen could confess that they knew nothing, but being a pompous British man, that was never going to happen.

'Stephen, are you testing me?'

'Please Olivia, humour me. As I said, we pretend that we know nothing. You remember how this works?'

'Max would have sent it to the same post office box we always use, Stephen. The one in Exeter. The same one you sent the clue to.'

'The clue?'

'Stephen, the clue so that we knew where to search for the Janus Machine.'

Over the next three days, I answered all the questions as truthfully as I could, interspersed with the occasional, 'Surely Stephen, you already know this?' To which he inevitably replied, 'Humour me, Olivia. Tell me anyway.'

I told him how we worked for the Special Operations Executive (SOE) during WW2 and how Max had been sent to Murmansk on one of the Russian Convoys to retrieve the Janus Key.

'The Janus Key?' Stephen repeated.

'Stephen! The Janus Key. It's the thing that makes the Janus Machine work. Do you really want me to tell you the whole story?'

'It's probably wise,' Stephen said. 'Just so we are confident that we are all singing from the same song sheet, as it were.'

So, I started again, this time summarising all that I knew of the Janus Machine. Well, that's not entirely true. I gave him ninety percent of what I knew, so that it was as close to the truth as possible, but with the addition of a few well-placed lies.

'Stephen,' I recall saying, 'the Janus Machine was developed in WW2, as part of the Nazis' biological weapons program. If my memory still serves me correctly, it was invented by a scientist called Dr Von Erick Brack, at the Majdanek concentration camp in Poland. By experimenting on the prisoners, he learned how to create a biological weapon that could target specific race, age, sex, even hair colour if he so chose. The secrets of the weapon were coded into the Janus Machine. To unlock the code, you needed a cylindrical encryption key, *the Janus Key*, which must be inserted into the machine. As far as we know, there was only one machine made, but two keys, one of which was destroyed. Britain managed to capture both the Janus Machine and one of the keys. However, towards the end of the war, for safety reasons, the decision was taken to separate the key from the machine. They were hidden separately and the clues to the respective hiding places were entrusted to different people. No one person knew the final resting places. Neither Max or I were involved in hiding the key or the machine. We were however entrusted with a name, a trusted friend from the French Resistance, Pierre Gicquel. He was one of the custodians, if ever the key was to be retrieved. We were also given a code word and, if that was used, it meant the Machine was to be found.

'After the war, Max and I married and chose the guise of a doddering vicar and his nutty wife as our cover for our role as Cold War spies. As part of this deception we moved to Australia. From there we would travel around the world on Christian Missions which were in truth, spying assignments. In the 50s, 60s and even the 70s, no one knew where Australia was, let alone that it had spies. Australia and our religious ministry combined to become a perfect disguise.

'Your agency, Stephen, would initiate contact with us via an advertisement placed in one of the newspapers, hidden in the death notices section. No smart phones or iPads in those days. Over the decades, as we aged and the cold war slowly came to an end, the assignments became less frequent until finally we had no contact with anyone from the spy game. We didn't retire, as such; our old life as spies just fizzled out and along with it, memories of the Janus Machine. Initially, out of habit each morning, Max bought the newspaper to check the death notices. In later life, this became an unfortunate necessity as our friends began to depart this world. Nostalgically, Max checked to see if a message had been sent. There was nothing for over twelve years. Then, when we were eighty-four, suddenly there it was. A message to retrieve the Janus Key.'

I stopped to assess the effect of this information and then continued, 'Stephen, are you sure you want me to tell you all this? You sent the message, for God's sake.'

'Please Olivia, humour me for a little longer. That was before my time here so, hearing it from you, is much more informative than reading an old report. Please do continue.'

Pretending to be a little annoyed, even managing a slight huff, I continued. 'Okay. To celebrate our eighty-fifth birthdays, Max and I had been planning one final trip on our beloved 1948 BSA A7 motorbike with sidecar. We decided to use that adventure as our cover for this mission. The bike and sidecar were shipped from Australia to the UK, where we met up with it. Before seeking out Pierre Gicquel in France, we rode it around Britain, then we took it across to Europe. Pierre Gicquel's information led us to another contact in Antwerp.

'With both bits of the puzzle, we worked out the hiding place of the key. The tunnels near Walbrzych in the Czech Republic. Although we didn't know it at the time, because the killings were made to look like accidents and so weren't reported in the news, Pierre Gicquel and our Antwerp contact were both murdered shortly after our visits. What we also didn't know was that Claudia, we think it was Claudia, before killing our contacts, extracted clues which led them to Walbrzych. She possessed none of our WW2 experience, the context for understanding the clue, so she didn't know where to look and had to wait for us to find it.

'Our plan had been to locate the Janus Key and deliver it to an agent waiting for us in Prague. Not long after we arrived, Max suspected that we were being followed. It took us three days to locate the key. Then, before leaving Walbrzych, en route to Prague, we decided the safest option was to post the key back to the UK. To the post office box in Exeter,' I added.

This was a lie. As in Scotland, we had posted the item to our Cliff headquarters in Devon. Taking a breath, I checked Stephen for any sign that he was aware of my deception. None was apparent.

'Is that when the accident happened?' Stephen asked, breaking the temporary silence.

The events from the motorbike crash still haunted me. It was because of that accident that our children convinced us to give them

Enduring Power of Attorney, to be used in case of an emergency, they promised. Despite our misgivings, we had signed and, within months, they'd sold our house, emptied our bank accounts and shipped us off to a nursing home.

All in the name of our care, they'd said.

Remembering the accident and the events which followed no longer made me tearful. But given that this was a debriefing and I was trying to appear truthful, I considered that it may be to my advantage, if not more authentic, to give the impression that, recalling these events, could trigger a strong emotional response. It aided, in my mind, the deception. It would confirm me as an old, harmless and vulnerable woman. This was, if I had my way, the furthest thing from the truth, although I would concede the "old" part.

'Yes,' I said. There were no tears but I swallowed lightly and then allowed a slight hesitation to quiver in my voice. 'Yes, that's when the accident happened, or a better description would be, the attempt on our lives. We were never the same after that - it was a serious crash. After our release from hospital, we returned to Australia to find ourselves locked away in a nursing home and waiting for God.

'Max stopped searching the newspaper when we first moved into the home. I can't recall the exact order of events, Stephen, but I think we had been living there about twelve months when the news reported an Ebola outbreak in Africa. Max didn't say anything but I noticed that about that time, he started checking the death notices in the paper again. When Britain experienced that Ebola outbreak, closely followed by bird flu in the USA, I secretly wondered if someone had a Janus Machine. When both outbreaks vanished as mysteriously as they came, I was convinced something evil was at play.'

'Did you share your thoughts with Max?'

'No, he wasn't in a good place at that time and I didn't want to burden his mind with such dark thoughts. It was a difficult period, for both of us.'

'Go on,' said Stephen. 'I shouldn't have interrupted your flow.'

'That's okay,' I replied. 'On the 21st of March this year, which by chance was our second anniversary, two years since we had moved into that dreadful nursing home, a secret message, one agreed to years earlier, appeared in the death notices of the paper.

"DUVAL Claude of Covent Gardens. Passed away peacefully."

'It meant that we had to travel to the UK and retrieve the Janus Machine. The communication confirmed our suspicions, Stephen, about the Ebola and bird flu outbreaks. Someone had used targeted biological weapons against the UK and the USA and, maybe, the Ebola outbreak in Africa was a test run.

'We escaped from the home and flew here, to the UK. Unfortunately, initially at least, the police tried to catch us and send

54

us back to Australia. Once here, we found ourselves in an epic game of cat and mouse with the police and Claudia's people. Eventually our search for the Janus Machine took us to an old cold war bunker, under a farmhouse in Scotland. That was about the same time that the terrorists used the biological weapon against London. When we retrieved the Janus Machine from its hiding place, Claudia was waiting for us. Max escaped with the help of Jana and I was kidnapped. Do you want me to tell you about Claudia?'

'No, no, that's okay, Olivia. Jana has told us all we need to know but I do have one question that's been nagging at me. Do you know Claudia?' As he spoke he pushed a photograph of her across the table that separated us. 'I mean, have you met her before? As part of your work?'

For a moment, the question stumped me. There was something nagging in my memory.

Have I met Claudia before?

'I don't think so Stephen but there is something about her and I can't put my finger on it. Do you mind if I keep the photograph?'

'Go on, keep the picture. I ask, Olivia, because something is odd. Why would Claudia want to take Max with her?'

'I've asked myself the same question because it makes no sense. My fear is, does she want to kill him and make some grand gesture with his body? She can't want him for any other reason.'

'Olivia, is there anything, anything at all from WW2 or during the cold war, perhaps, that may be of interest to her?'

55

'Except for the Janus Machine, everything is in the past. I have racked my brain, but there's nothing of value that we know.'

And so, our chats continued over the course of the three days. Not once did I mention the headquarters in Cliff, instead telling Stephen that we would meet our contacts at the East Dart Hotel in Postbridge, Devon. A place where we stayed whilst eluding the authorities before recovering the Janus Machine.

At some stage during our conversations, Stephen told me that, when the debriefing was over, I would stay with Inspector Axel. He said that it would not be indefinitely, only until the tanker they believed Max was on had docked and been searched. I would then be returned, though deported was how I saw it, to Australia with or without Max. Stephen explained that Inspector Axel was helping Max after I was kidnapped and he'd been instrumental in my rescue from the house in Elie.

'Stephen,' I asked, with an edge of sorrow in my voice. 'How many people died from the biological attack, before we could stop them?'

'It's not over yet Olivia, but hundreds. It may even become thousands.'

***

Perhaps naively but, until the day after my debriefing and while waiting for Inspector Axel to collect me, I had a vain hope that Max was still on board the ship. That was until I read an article in the Sun newspaper which accompanied my breakfast. The headline read:

MULTIPLE nuclear-powered Russian submarines are being hunted off the UK coast, sources confirmed yesterday.

Three NATO search planes have been scouring seas off east Scotland for the last 48 hours.

A Royal Navy anti-submarine frigate HMS Sutherland has joined the hunt for the subs — armed with cruise missiles. Sources said a Royal Navy Trafalgar class hunter-killer sub is also backing the pursuit.

A Whitehall source said: "There are believed to be multiple Russian submarines off the coast of Scotland. Various assets have been deployed to identify their location and understand their intentions."

Insiders fear the submarines are fearsome Akula class boats, bristling with a deadly arsenal.

The Russian president has nine at his disposal — each with a crew of around 70.

Last May it emerged that Canadian submarine HMCS Windsor had been dispatched on a similar underwater hunt after Russia deployed five attack subs into the North Atlantic.

The new search follows a long line of inflammatory incursions as Russia flexes it muscles along its border with NATO.

A Navy spokesman said: "It's our long-standing policy that we don't comment on submarine operations. The UK has a range of assets to patrol our seas."

Putting the newspaper back on the table, I took a sip of steaming coffee, followed by a bite from my toast with marmalade, as I contemplated what I had just read. I picked the paper up again and reread the article. At that moment, I knew that if Max was still alive, he was no longer on the tanker. He, Claudia and the others would be on-board one of the submarines and long gone before the ship docked in Rotterdam. My fate was to be shipped back to Australia, discarded and forgotten. As for Max, I had no faith in the police, MI6 or anyone else caring about his predicament. Still pondering Max's predicament, I was brought back to the present by the sound of someone knocking on the door. Leaving the table, breakfast and my coffee, I meandered across and opened it to be greeted by Stephen.

'Good morning, Olivia. I just wanted to let you know that Inspector Axel is on his way. He should be here within a couple of hours. Thank you again for all your help and I'm sorry about Max. You do realise that it's unlikely that he is on the tanker, although we won't know for sure until it docks?'

He made the statement with such an exaggerated expression of sincere compassion on his face, that I thought it fake. I knew that if Max was alive, and if he was going to be rescued, I would have to do it myself. Something I couldn't do from a nursing home in Australia.

'I promise you,' continued Stephen, 'that we will do everything in our power to find him. I hope you have a safe trip back to Australia.'

'Thank you, Stephen,' I said, continuing the pretence, 'I know that you will do everything possible to find Max. I'm sorry to confess, but the fight has deserted me and I want to go home - to Australia. There is just one thing, a small favour.'

'Olivia, you know that, if I can, I will.'

'Thank you, Stephen. It's Pierre Gicquel, our lifelong friend who was murdered in Lannilis. You remember, he was killed after we visited him.'

I was worried that I might have to fake a little emotion at this point, perhaps a tear or two to help with the persuasion. But it was not necessary, for, as I spoke of Pierre, I genuinely grieved for him. No tears came but my voice crackled and croaked of its own accord.

'I want to visit his grave before going home to Australia. I don't have many years left myself and I will never come back to Europe. I would like to say goodbye. To say thank you, and I'm sorry. He died because of us.

'Stephen, I was hoping that Inspector Axel might accompany me across the channel, so that I can say my farewells. I could fly home to Australia from Paris.'

'It's a little irregular.' Stephen said, checking himself before continuing, 'but, under the circumstance, I'm sure it can be arranged.'

I started to thank him but he stopped me by continuing.

'Did you know that Inspector Axel's father, Jean Axel, also knew Pierre Gicquel?'

'We did.'

For the second time that morning my voice betrayed emotion and I needed to pause before continuing.

'Kate and Edward told us before…, you know…, before the house explosion that killed them. Like Pierre, they died because they were helping us, Max and myself.'

***

When Inspector Axel arrived later that morning, it was clear that he had spoken to Stephen about the trip to France.

'Hello Olivia,' he said, with no emotion or warmth in his voice.

'Inspector,' was my equally neutral reply.

'I'm to escort you to Lannilis and then to see you safely on a plane back to Australia.'

'Are you my chaperone or guard?'

'An escort, for your protection. We wouldn't want you becoming lost.'

'You are so kind, Inspector. Do you mind fetching my bag?' I added with an air of annoyance in my voice.

He picked up a small suitcase holding the belongings kindly purchased for me by my hosts.

'No Operation Underpants this time,' I said.

'What?'

'Nothing. Sorry, it was a private joke between Max and me. Where are we going?'

'A friend's place in Oxford. London is still on lock-down until tomorrow. We will stay in Oxford until the tanker has docked and been searched. Then it will be a train from St Pancras International Station to Paris. I'm not sure how long you will have in France before flying back to Australia.'

His reply was not abrupt, just precise, implying that there was nothing further to say.

I followed the Inspector to the car, where he opened the trunk, lifted and then placed my suitcase inside. Returning to the passenger's side, he opened the car door, took my arm and helped me inside. As he was doing this, he briefly gained my attention by staring into my eyes and, at the same time giving a subtle, almost unnoticeable, shake of his head. The message was clear: no talking. What had transpired in the house was a game. It was to continue in the car and I had no idea what was going on. He was acting as if we had a rapport, which we did not, and that I was likely to share information with him, which I would not.

He wants me to trust him by making me think that he is helping me and not MI6. I wonder if this is the beginning of an elaborate ploy devised by Stephen as a way of discovering if I'd been holding back during the debriefing.

With the Inspector assisting me into the passenger's seat, I wondered what was going through Stephen's mind. I knew he would be watching and listening. Mixed thoughts filled my mind.

'No love lost between those two. He will see her safely on to the plane.

What are they up to? MI6 will need to keep a close eye on those two. Or.

What else do you have to tell, Olivia? Share the truth with the good Inspector.'

Only time would tell whether Inspector Axel was a friend or foe but I would need to decide quickly because it would be difficult for me to escape and then find Max without help.

The drive from the country estate, where I had been an honoured guest (or was it prisoner) to Oxford, should have taken a couple of hours, but Axel insisted on going via the Police Headquarters in Exeter. The trip to Exeter was not in total silence but what little conversation there was, could only be described as courteous.

As we approached the police station the Inspector said, 'Sorry for the detour, I have to return this car to the pool. We will be taking another vehicle the rest of the way to Oxford.'

After leaving the car, the Inspector led me into the station. As we went through the front door, he handed me a note.

Say nothing. Please follow the policewoman into the bathroom. A change of clothes and new shoes are waiting for you. Leave your handbag in the bathroom. See you in five minutes.

Reading it I thought, *at least Max isn't the only one paranoid about surveillance. Maybe it's a man thing.* At any rate, this cloak and dagger stuff was becoming a little tiresome.

Saying nothing, I dutifully followed the policewoman.

Returning, sporting my new attire, I was greeted by Inspector Axel who had also changed. For the first time that day he smiled, saying, 'Hello Olivia – coffee?'

To this I replied, perhaps a little ungratefully, 'You're more suspicious than Max. Yes, coffee would be lovely.'

I was imagining a quiet chat in one of Exeter's nice little coffee houses. Instead I was ushered into one of the station's interview rooms.

'Two coffees please,' he instructed the policewoman who had accompanied me from the changing room.

'Wait,' I said as she began to depart down the corridor. 'Flat white, skim milk - and nice and hot, please.'

'Sorry Olivia, I didn't want to take the chance,' began the Inspector after the policewoman had left, 'that we were being bugged either in the car or from our clothes. Not until I know your plans, at least.'

'What do you mean, plans?' I said, trying to appear surprised by his question.

'No time for games, Olivia. I know that you don't know me but, I can tell you, Max trusted me and so must you. We both need to don our original clothes, and quickly. If they are bugged or have a tracking device hidden in them, leaving them idle will soon attract suspicion. I am going to come straight to the point. You may really want to visit the grave of Pierre Gicquel in France but, because I investigated your motorbike accident in 2008, outside the city of Walbrzych in Poland, and because I've followed you every day since you first arrived in the UK to find the Janus Machine, I understand you! I know you have no intention of returning to Australia. Not without Max.'

I said nothing, just waited. A few seconds later the Inspector spoke again.

'Did you choose France for a reason or was it because visiting Pierre Gicquel seemed like a reasonable request?

Should I trust him?

I stared mutely back at the Inspector.

'Olivia, you have to trust someone. You can't do this on your own; please let me help you.'

With a weary sigh, I finally relented. 'Inspector, you must appreciate my apprehension. You are right on three fronts, I don't know you, yet I must trust someone and, I am not going back to Australia without Max. Not willingly anyway.'

'Okay,' he said. 'We need to get you a new wardrobe before leaving here, without raising the suspicion of MI6. I have no doubt they are monitoring you. On our way to Oxford we can pull over and find a safe place to talk. Even though I'm swapping cars, it's best to play safe. We need to watch what we say to each other in the car but once we're out of the UK, things will become a little easier. You understand that the spooks will be watching you, unquestionably.

'Now, put your old things back on and meet me back here, by then the coffee should have arrived and we will just have to play it by ear. The first thing, Olivia, is to find you that new wardrobe. Keep the handbag and the phone they gave you for now. We can ditch them when we are ready to go underground.'

I went back to the bathroom where I found the shower was running. Upon my entry, a policewoman, who I hadn't seen before, switched off the shower and handed me a towel, even though I was not wet. She then slipped silently from the room leaving me alone.

Playing along, I pretended to dry myself and then changed back into my old clothes and returned to the interview room where I found Inspector Axel already waiting for me.

'Hello again, Olivia. Sorry for the detour. I hope the shower has helped freshen you up for the drive to Oxford. As you can see, I have changed myself. I ordered you a coffee,' he said, pointing to a takeaway cup sitting on the table.

'How long before we leave?' I demanded, while pulling a chair out and seating myself in front of what would be the interview desk.

'Not long. There are a few things I need to do, so it might be thirty minutes, maybe an hour.'

'These shoes are awful. My feet really hurt. I was wondering if someone could take me down the street for a little shopping. I might do a girl thing and treat myself to a new outfit at the same time. It's what we women do when the world seems a little grey.'

'I'm sorry Olivia. I'm not sure we have time for that. What about tomorrow?'

'Inspector! That will not do,' I said heatedly. 'My feet are in absolute agony.'

'In that case, I'll have someone take you right away, but we will be leaving in an hour's time.'

'Inspector,' I said indignantly. 'What are you suggesting?'

Before he could answer I rose from my chair and moved towards the door. Stopping briefly to open it, I turned back and faced him to say, as I left, 'I will be waiting for you in the foyer for that lift to Oxford. Don't be late!'

Having been shopping and abandoned my old things, we left Exeter Police Headquarters, retracing some of the route of that morning. Just short of Bristol, where we were to swing right onto the M4 and the run into Oxford, we pulled into one of those mega Motorway Service Centres.

The Inspector had been right. I had no intention of abandoning Max or being deported to Australia. Getting safely out of the UK was my number one priority, which is where the plan to visit Pierre Gicquel's grave came from. Over the next half an hour, while eating a late lunch, I shared a vaguely conceived plan of how I intended to find Max. Deliberately, I left out some of the details. I was forced to confess that, if I did find him, I had absolutely no idea what to do next. Improvise, was my best answer.

'He may be on the tanker the authorities are tracking,' suggested the Inspector, having listened to my ramblings patiently.

'Did you read the article in the Sun newspaper this morning?' It was a statement rather than a question, so I continued without waiting for his reply. 'Multiple Russian submarines are off the coast of Scotland. That's no coincidence. He's on one of those, I know it.'

'Well, for what it's worth, someone else thinks so too. I have some presents for you,' he said, reaching under the table and lifting a bag that he'd carried in from the car. 'I think that you have been speaking to someone and have a much better idea of how to find Max than the story you just gave!'

'Inspector!'

Ignoring me, he continued. 'I received a phone call yesterday. They said that I was to visit the East Dart Hotel in Postbridge, Dartmoor, and ask for Rosie, the landlady who would have something for me. I have met Rosie before, when we were chasing you and Max all over England. You stayed there with Elinor, before she was killed in Cornwall.'

He paused and then said, 'Sorry, I shouldn't have brought that up.'

'It's okay,' I said and, after a short silence gathering my thoughts, I continued. 'People around us seem to die.' The words came out before I realised what I was saying.

'Like my daughter, you mean?'

'That was insensitive of me, Inspector. I haven't forgotten Kate and Edward.'

'I know this may sound like a father speaking but I know that she isn't dead. If she was, I would feel it. I don't want to talk about it but she is not dead, I am certain.

'Sorry Olivia, where was I? Oh yes, Rosie! She gave me these.'

He opened the bag, removed two passports and two credit cards and I could see several other things partly concealed but couldn't make out what they were. However, I could see rolls of cash.

'Well that's inconvenient,' I said, before checking myself and saying no more.

'Inconvenient?' asked Inspector Axel.

I mistakenly said 'inconvenient' because I had lied to Stephen Walls throughout the debriefing. I falsely claimed that the East Dart Hotel was our contact point with our secret organisation. It was, as far as I knew, just a hotel. Is this a trap to see if I was telling the truth, one I almost fell for? Or had the Agency used the hotel as a drop point and the Inspector as its courier? Finding the truth will have to wait.

'Yes, inconvenient,' I continued, trying to cover my tracks. 'Two passports! I assume that someone wants you to come with me?'

'So, it would appear,' he said, while opening the first passport and reading the names. 'When we decide it's time to hide, I am to become Mr Jean-Marc Lemery. There's an accompanying note that says I am to be your private secretary.'

'And me?' I asked, with an air of annoyance still in my voice.

He put his passport on the table and opened the other in a manner that could have been a theatrical scene in a play.

'Lady Olivia Suzanne Elizabeth Huggins,' he said, while looking over the rim of the passport.

'Is there a note?'

'Yes. It just says, Lady.'

'And the other items?'

He put my passport back into the bag along with the credit card and pushed the package across the table before saying. 'I don't want to appear presumptuous Olivia but how did you organise this, the passports and all, when you were virtually a prisoner?'

'It was really quite easy,' I said, 'During the debriefing, I was taken into the local town near where I was being held or as Stephen would say, near the town where I was a guest and given unaccompanied free time, to wander the street, shop and have a leisurely lunch. Inspector, I believe that it was part of their strategy to lull me into a false sense of security. Conscious that I was probably being followed, I couldn't use a pay phone to call our headquarters nor the mobile phone they had given me. So, as you could imagine, I was on the lookout for another way to make contact. As chance would have it, I was able to borrow a phone from a shop assistant. He conveniently left it behind the counter while serving a customer. My call to headquarters was brief but long enough to request certain items I might need in my search for Max. Unfortunately, there wasn't enough time to work out how I was going to retrieve them. After deleting the number, I had used from the phone, I put it back in its spot behind the counter without it being missed.'

'You're quite something,' said the inspector after listening to my story.

But I was busy examining the contents of the package and ignored his compliment. I was pleased to discover that all the items

I'd requested were there, including GPS tracking bracelets. Then it dawned on me, Cliff obviously trusted the Inspector and it was time I did as well.

My attention was drawn back to the Inspector by his voice.

'It's time we were leaving.'

CHAPTER THREE

Ferrari

Olivia

It was two days later, Saturday the 16th April, when the house phone rang at our Oxford stay. Inspector Axel answered and spoke with Stephen from MI6. I hovered nearby, eavesdropping on the conversation until it was my turn to speak.

The tanker they had been tracking had docked in Antwerp and, as expected, neither Max nor Claudia was on board. Accompanying his condolences was a solemn promise to leave no stone unturned in the search for Max, an invitation to dinner that night and two tickets on the 8:19am Eurostar train, leaving London the following morning for Paris. He also took the opportunity to inform me that I had been booked on a flight from Charles de Gaulle airport, France, to Melbourne, Australia. I was shocked when he said the date: Wednesday 20th April, four days' time.

Ample time, according to Stephen, for me to visit Lannilis and the grave of Pierre Gicquel. I was, it seemed, to be trusted to fly to Australia unaccompanied. The more likely reason was their budget; it wouldn't stretch to a guard, a decision I was determined to make them regret.

I decided, during the two-day stay in Oxford, to share my plans to find Max with Inspector Axel. I told him the details that I had previously left out and we agreed to work together, as a team. However, he was concerned about one aspect, my driving. I assured him that I had once been quite handy at the wheel.

'It's like riding a bike,' I said.

***

Paris has always been one of my favourite places to stay with its rich history, architecture and little cafés peppering the streets.

What's not to love?

Well, the cigarette smoke for one thing. If only the Parisians wouldn't smoke! To be seated outside of a little café and watch the world go by is one of the great pleasures of eating and of life. Yet in France, as in many places in Europe, most people smoke. Worse, they can smoke in the outside eating areas. There you are trying to enjoy a beautiful glass of wine, nibbling some terrine or pâté, and there's cigarettes to the left of you, cigars on the right and pipes front and back. Every sight, sound and smell is tainted by putrid nicotine.

Despite this travesty, when we arrived in Paris, I was reminded why this was one of my favourite places on Earth and, after the motorcycle accident, somewhere I never dreamed that I would visit again.

From the airport, we visited one of the Inspectors contacts, to pick up some protection, as he described it. After checking into our hotel, a little before midday, Inspector Axel and I had just two and a half days before we needed to vanish from the MI6 radar. By then they would know that I had no intention of returning to Australia on their schedule.

With its view of the Eiffel Tower, our hotel was ideally positioned for the first part of the plan. By 1.00pm, having spent as little time as possible with unpacking and grabbing something to eat, the Inspector and 1 were walking near the Eiffel Tower. A security fence had been erected following recent terrorist attacks elsewhere in Paris. To gain access to the tower, visitors had to pass through check points and metal detectors, not dissimilar to catching a plane. We walked through the Eiffel Tower park towards the Champ de Mars bus stop where we caught the number 69. Riding on a bus, particularly the number 69, which drives past some of the main tourist sites in Paris is a great introduction to the city for any visitor. We had seen what we were looking for by the time the bus reached the Place de la Concorde and so changed to a number 73 for the ride up the famous Champs-Elysées, getting off at a stop near the iconic Arc de Triomphe.

'What did you observe?' asked the Inspector as if it were a test.

'The young girls with their clipboards. Romanian pickpockets working the Tuileries garden between the Louvre Museum and the Place de la Concorde.'

'Were they working on their own?'

'They were in groups of two, but never that far away from another one. Working independent but hunting in packs of about six. Three groups of two.'

'Minders?'

'I'm sure they were there - they never work without them, but I couldn't pick any. I did see them on the hill, in the Jardin des Champs-Elysées gardens. I think girls working in other areas, not just the gardens, were reporting back to them. At the very least they all seemed to be coming and going from there.'

From where we were, at the Arc de Triomphe, I could see girls on the next corner armed with their clipboards. I didn't point but gestured with my head in the direction I wished the Inspector to look.

'I wonder what their scam is today,' he said.

'The old survey one,' I replied. 'They look like they are part of the same group. At any rate, they are all dressed the same. The main activity however is in the Tuileries gardens. That's where we should do it. And Inspector, we have our Ferraris there.'

'True, Olivia, but the Ferraris are up and down the Champs-Elysées too, at most intersections. It may be best to do this in two separate places.'

'You're probably right, Inspector, but I think the Place de la Concorde will offer more options for a getaway. Did you book the restaurant?'

'Tuesday night, the 8.30 sitting for five. You have the photos and envelopes?'

Reaching into my handbag, I retrieved three unsealed envelopes. Letting two drop back into the bag, I opened one to reveal a picture of Claudia and a letter.

'Check,' he said.

Before he had a chance to ask, I reached back into my handbag and pulled out two bracelets and said, handing them to him, 'You will be wanting these.'

'Okay Mum, let's do it!'

'Am I playing your mum or gran?' I inquired, smiling.

'Mum, surely, we can't have people thinking that you're eighty-seven, can we?' he said with a chuckle.

The Inspector, playing my son, took from his pocket two tourist maps. I moved a bum bag that had been around my waist but hidden under my clothes to where it could be seen. Accepting one of the tourist maps and holding it in my right hand, I placed my left arm into his and we made our way to the bus stop and the ride to the Tuileries gardens. The trap was set.

It was a lovely spring afternoon for a walk in the gardens and we made it all the way to the Louvre Museum without being approached. Each time we came near the girls working the strip, they were already busy distracting some poor unsuspecting tourist so that they could pick their pockets. Before making the return journey, the Inspector asked if I would like to sit for a while near the pond. From there we had a wonderful view of the park, all the way back to the Paris Eye Ferris Wheel. Although I kept my own counsel, it was a welcome rest. Since the kidnapping, I had found myself struggling; it had unexpectedly triggered a little anxiety. It had become difficult sometimes to stop my mind ruminating over my health and age. Any fatigue or pain, even the normal issues associated with my years, filled me with fear. It made me unsteady on my feet and I needed to sit and rest. I knew it was all in my mind and, by God, I was going to fight it.

Dragging myself away from my worries, I looked down the avenue. Since the first time I came to Paris, I loved looking back through the park towards Place de la Concorde, but even this couldn't soothe me. It was made worse because I realised my favourite view wasn't enough to instil calm.

'*A pity. Not quite myself.*' I said it unintentionally aloud.

'Are you all right, Olivia?' asked the Inspector, with a hint of concern in his voice.

'I'm ready. Take my arm - help me up and let's go catch ourselves some pickpockets.'

Slowly, we made our way back towards the Paris Eye and, by concentrating on our targets, I felt my composure return, although I leaned heaver upon the Inspector's arm. We stopped a couple of times, pretending to consult our tourist map, before continuing our journey. Two girls approached, both aged around fourteen and dressed similarly in blue jeans and off-white tee-shirts. They looked remarkably alike with their olive complexion and black hair. All the pickpocket girls we had seen that day seemed, to us, identical. Not only did their age create law enforcement challenges but the description of the offenders would be so similar that it made it almost impossible for the police to identify a culprit. A tree hiding in a forest.

One of the two girls thrust a clipboard in front of me at chest and arm height.

'We are conducting a survey,' the girl said while smiling with disarming warmth.

With a pen that she held in her other hand, she engaged my eyes, drawing them down towards the survey.

The other girl had moved slightly to my side, the side away from the Inspector, ready to *pick a pocket or two*, as the old song goes.

'Okay,' I said, smiling back while letting my gaze be drawn downwards.

At that moment, Inspector Axel, with lightning speed, reached across, grabbed the girl's arm, and snapped one of the GPS tracking bracelets onto her wrist. Both girls recoiled angrily away from us, spitting out a tongue lashing of obscenities.

'It's a GPS tracking device,' said Inspector Axel, casually. 'You can't get it off without our help, so there is no point in running away until we are finished with you. Otherwise ladies, you may never be rid of it, not while you are alive anyway. And ladies, I have a feeling that your bosses will not welcome one of you home tonight, not while she is sporting the lovely new bracelet, as becoming as it is.'

While the Inspector spoke, my job was to scan our surroundings for a minder.

'Inspector,' I said. 'We have company.'

An athletic man, over six feet tall, was approaching fast. Inspector Axel took from his pocket his police badge and held it up for the advancing man to see, before putting it away again. The man, the girls' minder, hesitated before continuing. His angry demeanour was now replaced by an apologetic smile, his head shaking.

'What have the girls done?' he said with a Romanian accent. 'They are only fourteen, you know. I'll take them straight home and give them what for.'

He turned and faced the two girls.

'What have you been up to?'

Raising his voice, he pointed a finger at each of them in turn while saying, 'I've told you not to misbehave.'

But before he could finish his melodramatics, Inspector Axel interrupted.

'Cut the rubbish and listen closely. One of your darlings is wearing a GPS tracking device. It's impossible for you to remove, but we can do it, for information. We are looking for someone and, before you say anything, we don't expect you to know her, but someone connected with your syndicate will. In exchange, we will remove the device. My colleagues from Interpol are diligently photographing you for posterity as we speak and have been taking pictures up on the hill.'

Inspector Axel paused and pointed towards the area, the one where we had seen the girls and their minders meeting earlier.

'My colleagues are concerned that nothing should happen to the young lady wearing the bracelet; we wouldn't want her to lose a hand or worse. If something were to happen to her, we will have you, all of you,' he said, pointing towards the hill, 'listed as terrorists right across Europe.'

'We are not terrorists,' said the minder, interrupting angrily.

Ignoring the interjection, Inspector Axel continued speaking.

'When you and your friends are picked up on terrorism charges, we can hold you almost indefinitely, as you must know. We will probably have to release you, eventually. When we do let you go, we will let it be known how helpful you were, giving us information about the Russian Mafia. We will arrest some of them shortly after your release.'

Turning to face me, he said, 'How long will any of them live, once the word is on the street that they are informers?'

'Hard to say,' I replied, 'a couple of weeks, but it's what happens to their families that I would fear. The Russian Mafia likes to ensure its message is clear.'

'You don't frighten me,' the man said calmly. 'You threaten us with being known as informers, but, at the same time, you want us to be informers. You're mad!'

'The irony is not lost on us, but we aren't mad, just persuasive,' I said.

'You don't know what you are getting yourself into,' complained the minder.

'That's exactly what we are hoping for,' answered the Inspector. 'The envelope please,' he said, looking to me.

I handed him the envelope and watched as he passed it to the minder, saying, 'The instructions are inside. You will find them very clear. I'm afraid, although we do enjoy your company, it's time for us to bid you a good day.'

Confidently, arm in arm, the Inspector and I walked away and on towards the Place de la Concorde and the waiting Ferrari. In the excitement of the moment, I had forgotten my worries and hoped that my anxiety was over.

***

That afternoon there were six '*Drive a Ferrari*' signs near their accompanying cars that we had seen while travelling on the bus. They started at the Place de la Concorde and one could be found at almost every intersection leading up the Champs-Elysées, towards the Arc de Triomphe. Although the sign said "Drive", that was a marketing ploy; a ride in a Ferrari was what they were selling.

Our choice of car was based on its location, a place offering me the best chance of escape, once I had stolen it. Since its release, I had wanted to take a Ferrari F40 for a spin but luck wasn't with me that day. A Ferrari California was parked on the Place de la Concorde, our preferred spot. It was attended by two men, one a dapper and handsome young man, in his late twenties. The other was a little older and larger and undoubtedly the minder.

'There you are, Mother!' said Inspector Axel, still holding my arm. 'This is the California convertible. I told you we would find one here.'

He turned towards the dapper man who stood next to the sign advertising a Ferrari drive for fifty euros.

'Do you mind if we take some photographs, with my mother standing next to the Ferrari?'

The young man glanced quickly towards the minder before saying, in a delightful French accent, 'No not at all, you are most welcome.'

'My mother has always had a fascination with Ferraris. My father wasn't interested in cars at all.

'She lives in Australia and I think at eighty-seven years of age, this will be her last visit to Paris. I thought I might treat her to a ride. She loves the open top California.'

'I would be happy to take her for a spin. It's a perfect day for a ride,' said the dapper-looking man, now smiling, realising that he was about to make a sale.

'That would be wonderful,' I said, interrupting the Inspector and the salesman's conversation. 'Oh, would you mind? Could I sit in the driver's seat?'

Then looking at the Inspector, I added, 'You could take a photograph of me, perhaps even a little video, with the sound of the engine. Maybe, if you paid just a little more, you could film me revving the motor.'

'Mother!' the Inspector said, with humour and a touch of exasperation in his voice.

He turned away from me and faced our dapper driver and his minder. I could just overhear the conversation. 'Please accept my apologies for my mother. Since I last saw her, she seems to have lost any inhibitions. Embarrassingly, she will even talk about people when they are standing right next to us. She can say the most outrageous things. She's also becoming obsessive over certain things, like these Ferraris. She becomes both as excited and egocentric as a three-year-old. That's on one of her good days.'

'That's okay and it's wonderful that she still has such a strong passion for life. Your mother is not French, yet you are?' responded the dapper man.

'She's English. My father was French. They met during the war and I was brought up between England and France. After my father died, Olivia, my mother, went to live in Australia with her sister. I stayed here, in France.

'Would 250 Euros give her a good ride with a bit of noise?' I heard Inspector Axel ask.

As he continued the conversation with the men, I opened the door and slid into the driver's seat of the Ferrari while placing my handbag on the passenger's seat.

After making myself comfortable behind the wheel I yelled out, 'Come and take a photograph!'

As I said it, I could imagine the Inspector rolling his eyes and giving a sigh before saying something like, 'Do you mind?'

On cue, the Inspector was standing next to me, camera in hand.

'Not this side. Take the photograph from the passenger's side,' I nagged.

'Yes, Mother.'

'Ask that handsome young man to sit next to me, the one who's going to take me for a drive.'

'Do you mind?' I heard Inspector Axel say.

The passenger side door opened and, after putting my handbag on the floor, the dapper man got in and slammed the door behind him.

'If you will excuse me, Olivia, I will reach over and start the engine. You can give her a little rev while your son takes a quick video. Then I will take you for a nice drive around Paris.'

'Ask that other nice man to take the photograph,' I called to Inspector Axel from across the car. 'So that you can be in the shot as well.'

I watched as the Inspector turned and moved, with the camera held out in front of him, towards the minder. The moment he stepped away from the Ferrari, I revved its motor to 5,000 rpm, discreetly pushed the clutch and, while smiling at my passenger, pulled back on the flappy paddle gear box which engaged a gear. Still grinning, I dropped the clutch. The traction control must have been on because the Ferrari launched itself backwards down the road with such a force that we were both thrown forward in the seats. I slammed my foot on the brake with all the strength I could muster. The car stopped as violently as we had taken off, coming to a halt just before slamming into the car behind us. Simultaneously, I had thrown my other foot onto the clutch, so that, when we came to a halt, the engine continued to run.

'Whoops,' I said, pulling the paddle shift the right way to engage first gear. For a second time, I revved the motor and dropped the clutch.

The Ferrari engine, with its deep-throated roar, forced us back into the seats and catapulted the car forward. Without any wheel spin, we hurtled up the road. I changed into second gear and we were gone.

'What are you doing?' yelled my passenger, regaining some of his composure and realising that I was stealing the car, with him in it!

Swinging the Ferrari left, we sped toward the Fountain des Mer.

'What do you think?' I said casually. 'Should I go all the way around the Fountain and then up the Champs-Elysées or should I go the wrong way up the road? It's much quicker but then again we might hit an oncoming car!'

It was a rhetorical question for I wasn't expecting an answer. At any rate, it was a decision that had to be made before I had a chance to complete the sentence. As traffic was light, I decided to go the wrong way around, weaving in and out to miss oncoming cars, on an excessively large oblong roundabout around monument square and the fountain.

The wheels squealed and the engine roared as I flung the Ferrari off the roundabout and turned left onto the Champs-Elysées, then accelerated to 6,500 rpm before popping the next gear.

'They will kill you for stealing the car. It's not mine,' said the passenger.

'What's happened to that lovely French accent of yours?' I said coolly as we approached the first intersection.

To my relief, the lights were green and, with some quick manoeuvring, we easily avoided the slower vehicles and accelerated aggressively up the road. We were now out of the parkland and entering the built-up area where the sound of the Ferrari's engine, echoing off the buildings, became pure magic.

'That's a nice sound,' I said to my guest, but he didn't reply.

Ahead I could just see the nose of another Ferrari poking out into the road. I guessed that the message was out and they were ready to give chase, once we went through the intersection. The minder must have raised the alarm. For a brief moment, my thoughts wandered to the Inspector but I knew that he could take care of himself and I should concentrate on my driving.

'You're a real nutter, lady.'

'I think you'll find, young man, that the word you're seeking is "courageous". Now, my friend, there's something in my handbag,' I said, turning and pointing to it on the floor, next to his feet.

'Watch out!' he screamed.

I had taken my eyes off the road for only a second but, when I looked up, I could see that we were centimetres from the back of a little Fiat. Slamming on the brakes while swerving hard to the right at the same time, I managed to avoid the car by passing it on the inside, but the manoeuvre caused the back of the Ferrari to slide out. Casually I corrected the steering to counter the drift. The car responded so I hit the accelerator again and continued racing up the road. Although my heart was in my mouth after the close call, I hid any sign of fear and continued the conversation in a calm and controlled manner.

'In my handbag, on the floor, you will find an envelope. Take it out and open it.'

The lights at the next intersection, the one where the other Ferrari was waiting, were turning amber as we raced through. A slight bump in the road lifted us out of our seats as the Ferrari left the road before crashing back down with a crunch. Glancing in the mirror I saw that we were being chased. I must have looked away for a fraction of a second too long because my attention was drawn back to the road with another yell of panic coming from the passenger's seat.

Slamming on the brakes and dropping back two gears, I swerved onto the wrong side of the road, narrowly missing a lumbering delivery truck that had merged into the left-hand lane. Once past, I flung the car back onto the correct side of the road, much to the relief of the oncoming vehicles. This manoeuvre slowed our escape and the pursuing Ferrari came up onto our tail. Hitting the accelerator, four seconds later we are travelling at 130kph, rocketing towards the notorious Arc de Triomphe roundabout.

'We are looking for that woman,' I said noticing that he had opened the envelope and was holding the photograph of Claudia.

'Keep your eyes on the road,' yelled my passenger, distress in his voice, having seen me glancing towards him again. 'Look, lady, I don't know her. You are going to get us both killed. Please lady, watch the road!'

We were now two intersections short of the Arc de Triomphe and, for the first time since I stole the car, the traffic lights in front turned red as we approached.

Do I brake and try to nudge my way across the intersection, against the traffic, or accelerate and pray that luck is with me?

'I've lived a good life,' I sung aloud. 'Hold on!'

'No!' pleaded my passenger.

'Here we go,' I shrieked, pushing my foot flat to the floor.

The intersection was over in a blur, accompanied by the sound of honking horns and screeching brakes. The infamous Arc de Triomphe roundabout lay directly ahead.

In a calm lady-like voice, hiding the sheer terror that was swirling inside, I spoke once more to my passenger.

'Along with the photograph you will find an invitation to dinner on Tuesday night at the number 58 Tour Eiffel Restaurant, in the Eiffel Tower itself. Tell your boss to bring whatever we need to find the lady in the picture.'

'And in return?'

90

'We tell them where to find this wonderful machine. Security at the Tower is tight, everybody passes through X-ray machines. None of us will be armed, your boss and ourselves will be quite safe.' Then in a jovial voice I added, 'if I don't get us both killed beforehand that is.'

After my poor attempt at humour, we arrived, mildly out of control, at one of the world's most chaotic roundabouts.

To outrun our pursuers, I needed to traverse the roundabout at speed, but in all the traffic that was impossible. Even so, we were thrown from side to side in our seats, as I swung the steering wheel around trying to push my way through while avoiding the other vehicles. I hit the accelerator, leaping the car forward, only to slam my foot on the brake a second later. Amid the chaos, I stole a momentary glance in the mirror. We'd lost the pursuing Ferrari but had been joined by the Gendarmes, the police.

The sight of a Ferrari being pursued by police around the Arc attracted the other roundabout users to us like bees to a honey pot.

I would have thought the French, with their disrespect for authority might have shielded us from the police. No such luck. Instead, we became the target for their dented and beaten up old cars masquerading as Exocet missiles. They launched themselves in our direction, intent on inflicting damage. Maybe the French like Italians less than the police or was it their chance to play Demolition Derby with a $300,000 sports car that was exciting their senses?

One crazed Parisian, a lady with jet black hair and bright red lipstick, positioned her car in front of us for a head-on assault. We came close enough to see her satisfied smile. Just before the collision, I wrenched the Ferrari to the left and accelerated aggressively. In the mirror, I watched as she collided head-on with a pursuing police car.

My planned exit off the roundabout was to take the Avenue Victor Hugo but, in all the excitement, I missed the road. We would have to go around again!

This gave the police the opportunity to start blocking the twelve exits. When we reached the Champs-Elysées, our original entry onto the roundabout, another Ferrari was waiting to join the chase. Too intent on driving, I kept my eyes forward and didn't notice if the car was in pursuit. We were now back at where the lady with bright red lipstick and Citroen was embedded into the front of a police car, I gave a little toot of the horn and friendly but mocking wave. Our antics had triggered more crashes and our second lap of the Arc was akin to picking a way through a minefield. We avoided broken glass and stationary cars, some on top of another, and made it back to the Avenue Victor Hugo but, by then, it was sealed off by the police.

It was a split-second decision that sent me hurtling towards the Avenue Kléber, the next exit after my target. Luckily, the police had not yet finished blocking the road and they were forced to jump for their lives as we sped off the roundabout and rocketed onto the avenue. I put my foot to the floor and madly accelerated past them, down the road at an ever-increasing speed.

'Shall we do that again?' I said, while lifting both hands off the steering wheel and throwing them in the air above my head and yelling – 'Yessssssss!

'Please lady, the steering wheel!' came a hoarse whisper from my passenger.

Having returned my hands to the wheel, a glance in the mirror told me that the other Ferrari was giving chase. Unlike when we were going around the Arc, this time I had a chance to get a good look at the car. It was an F40 and worth a cool $1.8 million US dollars. This made me smile, because I knew that they wouldn't dare chase us in that for long.

'A Ferrari F40,' I said to my passenger. 'It's following us. I don't want to appear ungrateful, but I think I should have gone shopping a little farther up the road. Your California is nice, but it's not an F40, and riding in an F40 is on my bucket list and through the streets of Paris! Can you imagine it?'

My humour again failed to meet its mark. My passenger stared mutely ahead until he noticed that I glanced across at him.

'The road! Watch the road!'

Having left the roundabout and safely negotiated the first intersection and a pedestrian crossing by blasting the horn continuously as we approached, there was now a long straight before we reached the next major obstacle, an intersection of five roads. Traffic was everywhere but the bus lane on the far side of the road was clear for as far as I could see. Veering onto the wrong side of the road, I left the Ferrari in second gear, using its screaming engine as a warning for unsuspecting people who we were approaching. On we raced, through all the intersections, swerving often and leaving a trail of chaos and confusion in our wake.

Keeping up the guise of an eccentric old lady, I decided to give a guided tour of our journey.

'My friend, you have not been the best of company. In fact, you have not been much fun at all. Let me share with you where we are heading because that's the type of person I am – caring! I'll remain on this avenue until we reach the Trocadéro Gardens, near the museum. I think it's called the Cité de l'architecture et du patrimoine. You're from Paris. Is that what it is called?'

I didn't expect him to reply but, to my surprise, he did and spat, 'Who cares!'

'Oh, that's right, your French accent was a con. You probably don't know what it's called anyway!' I said with a taunting smile before continuing. 'I hope to turn left at the gardens onto Avenue du Président-Wilson, heading up to the Pont de l'Alma bridge. I think that would be a lovely spot to cross the river.'

Maintaining my steady, composed voice, but now removing any air of sarcasm from it, I issued an ultimatum. 'When we reach the gardens, I will give you the briefest of chances to escape. Don't lose the photograph or the invitation.'

'They will kill you,' he said. 'You're a mad, raving old lady.'

That was the response I expected from my passenger to my generous offer of freedom.

'You prefer to stay?'

'No!'

The museum and the gardens were now rapidly approaching. I would need to slow and then dispose of my passenger, while avoiding my latest police pursuers. At the last moment, I chose the risky move of going the wrong way around the park. Watching me swing onto the wrong side of the road, the police yielded and did not follow. Seconds later, I came to an abrupt halt facing an oncoming bus, which luckily also stopped.

'Get out,' I commanded.

My guest, in his haste to escape, fell from the car and onto the road. He was still lying prostrate when I switched off the traction control and, with the door hanging half open, lit up the tyres, sliding sidewards around the bus and accelerating away, towards the bridge, in a plume of rubber-burning smoke. The door gently closed itself, unphased by my driving.

How I made it across the bridge, along the Quai, past the Eiffel Tower and into the underground car park of our hotel, the Novotel Tour Eiffel, without being seen, I don't know. My escape had been achieved without a single scratch on the car.

The day was not yet over, for we had one more guest to invite before our list would be complete. For that, we needed to wait until dark.

CHAPTER FOUR

Submarine

Max

My transfer from the tanker to the Russian Akula-class submarine had been a most undignified but speedy affair. According to Claudia, the submarine was being hunted by NATO and UK forces. Surfacing next to the tanker was not dangerous because it was in international waters and could not be fired upon. Nevertheless, military submarines are a weapon of stealth and being discovered would have been embarrassing and dented national pride. The Russian Navy's ability to operate undetected with impunity close to the shores of its foes was important to them. *If we were discovered*, said the submarine captain to me later, *NATO would shadow us all the way back to Russia and I would be reprimanded or face some other disciplinary action. I might even lose my command!*

Claudia understood the risk the submarine was taking. She knew that if my presence, and particularly my age, caused the submariners to be discovered, our trip on their vessel would be an uncomfortable one and would anger the Kremlin and her Mafia boss. Before the transfer began, the captain offered me, through Claudia, a deal, one that could be made only by someone who respected the age-old traditions of a British gentleman. In return for not being incarcerated in the submarine's brig, I promised to cooperate with my *loading* onto the submarine and agreed that I would *not attempt an escape, make unnecessary noise, or cause any trouble* until we were off the submarine. I also promised to wear the rubber shoes that I would be given once on board. Having given my word, to Claudia's disgust, the Captain was convinced that I would honour it. Of course, I would.

It was long past midnight, in the early hours of the morning, when the transfer began. Because of my, let's say, less than nimble capacity, I was strapped to a stretcher, craned over the side, and manhandled down into the hatch. Exhausted, I have almost no recollection of my undignified conveyance, drifting in and out of sleep during the process.

Once on board, Claudia and I were given a cabin to share. She patiently, almost tenderly, helped me into the room and onto my bunk where I fell into a deep sleep. When eventually I opened my eyes, the clock on the wall was showing 10.30 hours. I noticed that the bed next to me was empty with no signs that anyone had slept in it. Claudia was seated at a small table to the right of the bed and was staring warmly back at me.

Did she hear me stir and turn to see me or had she been watching me sleep, acting as my protector during the night?

'Good morning Max,' said Claudia kindly. 'Captain Andrey Yegorov is waiting for us. You must keep the promise you made to him and stay as silent as a mouse.'

Silent as a mouse, I thought, confused*? Claudia doesn't speak like that!*

With the words still running uneasily around my head, I listened intently, trying to understand what was behind the way she was speaking.

'Sonar is bouncing all over the place; someone really wants to find us. Now get dressed, I'll be back in five minutes.'

She's treating me like a bloody child, I contemplated angrily. *It's our daughter Jane in disguise.*

The door opened and then closed again as Claudia left me alone.

Am I being patronised, respected, or conned? Or are cracks showing in her harsh exterior?

I wasn't sure what to think but my training had taught me not to respond to my emotions. Only time would tell but I resigned myself to watching her actions and ignoring her words.

I'll look for a weakness that I can exploit.

Having dressed, I found that I was a little unsteady on my feet. Claudia noticed and without comment, discreetly helped me walk to the control room where Captain Andrey Yegorov was waiting. To my surprise, the room looked just like it did in the movies. Someone was talking to the helmsmen, who were seated behind what looked like a half steering wheel. In front of them were large computer screens. Banks of electronic instruments, covered in lights and gauges, lined the walls. Each was being monitored intently by the men on duty.

'Good morning Comrade Max,' said Captain Andrey Yegorov, raising one finger to his lips, as he continued talking. 'Once more, we play our dangerous game, a game of chess against our old adversary.'

Even at the best of times, my ability to recall one liners from movies was terrible. In fact, I was the last person you ever wanted on your trivia table. But I immediately recognised the line from the film, *The Hunt for Red October*, and retorted with the only other line I knew. A line I recalled because it sounded more of a statement from a British sea captain than a Russian. Not the sentence, but its tag line.

'You're afraid of our fleet,' I replied trying to copy Sean Connery's accent, but doing it poorly. 'Well, you should be. Personally, I'd give us one chance in three. More *tea* anyone?' emphasising the word *tea*.

'I like this man,' laughed Captain Andrey Yegorov, giving me a gentle slap on the shoulder as he spoke. 'My attempt at humour aside, NATO, the Norwegians and the British are all looking for us. After picking you up, we slipped into the noisy coastal waters to give them the slip. It's full of ships, marine life and everything that makes detecting us near impossible. What's better, is that Europeans are environmentalists and won't use their sonar close to shore. We must be getting a little too predictable. They have guessed that we would head for the coast and we have a contact above and are hiding in the shadow zone, watching. When we can, we will sprint and drift away from them. Next, we must avoid the undersea surveillance systems - underwater listening posts. We do that all of the time, it's not difficult. All going well, by tomorrow we will be with the whales where there will be no sonar to worry about. After that, we'll track out into the Arctic. The ships and planes will have lost interest in us by then but, we know that a British Trafalgar class submarine is about so we must be on our game and make sure we are not shadowed.'

'Crazy Ivan,' I said.

'You watch too many movies, Max, but sometimes they get it right. It was nicknamed that during the Cold War. We call it clearing the baffles. For the moment, we need to be very quiet and wait.

'I believe you to be a gentleman, Max and that you will honour our agreement. How do you English say? Will be on your best behaviour.'

'I am a man of my word, Captain.'

'As am I. There are, I'm afraid,' he said solemnly, 'not too many of us left.' Then brightening his tone, added, 'How do you like my ship, Max?'

'It's my first time on a submarine,' I replied.

'Ah, a virgin. She's recently been overhauled, but enough of that. You would have been enjoying our hospitality for about five more days but, with this unwanted attention, we won't dock in Russia until Wednesday - next week, if all goes well.'

'Where?' I asked.

'Severomorsk,' came his reply.

'Severomorsk, Murmansk. I haven't been to Murmansk since the war. It's a place I have a desire, perhaps need, to see again.

'You served on the Convoys to Russia during the second world war?' asked the captain, with a genuine tone of interest reflected in his voice.

'A long time ago, but you don't forget. The touch of war influences you in ways unimaginable at the time. Not always for the worst, Captain, but you, yourself, must be aware of the insidious nature of the past. It can chip away at our humanity, poison our capacity for goodness. Its potential for making a good man can be lost. I've often wondered,' I said, looking towards Claudia, although not intentionally, 'why traumatic experiences affect people differently? For some the past dominates and they repeat it, doing the very things they hated, becoming what they swore never to be. Others can break free and choose their own life, be the person they want to be. They don't forget, but instead, forgive and become free.'

'That is true,' said the Captain. 'Those of you who remain, the men who sailed on the Convoys to Russia, are considered heroes in our country today. My father was one but with the Russian Navy, of course. I am honoured to have you on board my submarine, Max, regardless of the interest that our friends have in you. Now, I would ask that you return to your room while we try to avoid detection. Once we are free of the vessels searching for us, you will be able to move about the submarine quite freely, with Claudia as your guardian that is. Do stay away from the missiles and the nuclear reactor,' he added with a chuckle. 'And, if all goes to plan, I hope that you will both be my guests at dinner this evening.'

The captain turned to one of his officers, saying something in Russian which Claudia interpreted for me. The soft, patronising tone of her voice earlier, in our sleeping quarters, was gone, to be replaced by bitterness, underlined by exaggerated politeness.

'Sweetie, the captain has asked the officer to escort us back to our room.'

The man gestured to us and we followed him out of the control centre.

Life on a large submarine reminded me of the two things I loathed the most. One was a long haul international flight where there is no sensation of movement – then without warning, the frightening feeling of leaping into the air or dropping like a stone.

The second is sleeping in the inside cabin of a cruise ship where there are no windows to the outside world. With no natural light, time ceases to have meaning and the internal body clock goes awry. On a cruise ship, once you leave your cell, the real world is not far away.

Both of my dislikes were evident on the submarine. Without warning it would aggressively dive, tipping everything off the table. All I could do was to hold on as it continued forever downwards. The hull would creak and groan in protest at the depth but still we headed deeper. Our feeling of control deeply affects how we act. Here ignorant, with no control or understanding of the events going on around me, I felt helpless.

In the absence of natural light, the seconds, minutes, hours and days are relevant only in the context of a sailor's routine. The schedule of activities and meals gives structure and creates an artificial day and night. Sleep time is set by a clock hanging on the walls and waking is via an alarm that you have set.

With no work, schedule or routine, other than eating and sleeping, the ten days dragged. Claudia showed open disdain for my presence and, while I wondered what had brought about this change, I let myself slip into the old routine from the nursing home, sleeping much of the time. It was a little over four weeks since Olivia and I escaped our prison in Australia and I was a transformed man. As I dozed for another nap, I was acutely aware how quickly my routine could revert. Without Olivia to prod, hassle and cajole me, fatigue became my companion and sleep a blissful mistress.

I discovered that Linda, Semyon and the other reprobates who were on the helicopters with us were not on board the submarine. I overheard that they had been put ashore in Europe for other business. With luck that would be the last I saw of them, but something told me I would meet Linda again.

***

On Wednesday, over a week since I was bundled onto the submarine, natural light awoke me from my lazy slumber and chased the sickly sleep from my old eyes. Again, I was unceremoniously hauled from the submarine like a sack of potatoes. I wanted to visit Murmansk, to remember and pay my respect to the Arctic convoy sailors and all those who perished during the war. I asked Claudia but she dismissed my request with a disdainful snort, before regaining her composure and saying, with a belittling smile.

'Sweetie, a chartered flight is waiting to take us to Moscow. There will be no time today, perhaps another occasion.'

My gentlemen's agreement with the Captain was now behind me and Claudia had seemed to want me to live.

Why would I be here otherwise?

The Captain's promise had shackled me but Claudia had disarmed me too; I had failed in my *duty* to escape.

Now, that she was back to her frosty self, my apprehension grew.

Maybe she would decide that bringing me along was an abysmal mistake? What's to stop her killing me, a ritualistic penance to the sordid underworld in which she lives?

Escape while we remained in Russia seemed unimaginable. For the time being, my fate rested with the Gods and the meeting with Claudia's Mafia boss.

Over twenty years ago, when we were spies, Olivia and I had dealings with the Russian Mafia. I still remember it as if it were yesterday. We were gathering intelligence on their involvement in illegal arms sales to the Middle East, when quite unexpectedly, the trail led us to the seedy world of child sex slavery, and human trafficking. For two years we searched to find a girl, about twelve years old when we first saw her picture. When I overheard that we were meeting 'Pakham,', I knew that this was Russian for *Mafia boss*. I also heard Claudia say that his name was Monya Mogilevick.

The name was unfamiliar, not surprising as our last involvement was just prior to our retirement. I still wondered what became of that beautiful but sad girl. She was called Lucia Da-dic, from old Yugoslavia, as it was called then. We'd broken into the

Mafia compound and entered the house. We found her there, waiting in a bedroom. She'd ran towards us, her arms outstretched, telling us that she knew that we would come. That memory still haunts me. The Yugoslavian police told us that she would be reunited with her family. For the first two years, we'd written to her family but our letters were unanswered.

Time moves on, but I never forgot beautiful Lucia running toward me, her arms stretched out - reaching for me, saying, '*I knew you would come*. But we left. We'd betrayed her.

The trip from the submarine base to the airport had taken half an hour. A luxury private jet was waiting for us and, other than the unseen pilots, we were alone on the flight. Once in the air, Claudia left me to freshen up, returning tastefully dressed in a skimpy black number. With the change of clothes, her demeanour mellowed, becoming friendlier, offering me a drink of spirits which I declined. She chose the seat opposite me for the flight, but when she didn't engage in conversation, I put my head back and pretended to sleep. Occasionally, I would steal a look at her through half-closed eyes. She seemed intent on studying me, like on the submarine but her stare was irritated.

She hasn't softened, she's angry I thought.

I took another peek.

That's not anger, it's displeasure. No...., perhaps disappointment even regret? Regret that she would have to kill me? Regret for having brought me along? I can't decide.

A new Rolls-Royce Phantom was waiting for us at the private runway when we disembarked from the plane. The chauffeur opened the door so that I could climb into the back before doing the same for Claudia. The car whisked us away and Claudia again offered me a drink of spirits, which I refused.

'You should,' she said, 'It may be your last.'

She consumed two stiff drinks of Scotch between the airport and the house. As on the plane, we didn't speak and my apprehension grew.

We arrived at a heavily fenced and well-guarded mansion. Leaving the car, as we made our way into the house to meet Monya Mogilevick, the Pakham, I noticed that the guards and the staff accorded Claudia profound respect. Likely she held a senior position within the syndicate or was she Monya's mistress? Perhaps his lover? I trailed behind Claudia, feeling invisible to the people we passed.

We stopped in front of large wooden double doors. Claudia brushed her hands down the black dress as if straightening the material.

'Are you ready?'

Except for the offer of alcohol, these were the first words she had spoken to me since leaving the plane, but I knew the question was not for me.

She knocked on one of the doors twice gently, and a few seconds later they swung open.

Monya was seated at the head of a long elegant table in a palatial dining room. He was eating alone but was expecting company because the table had been set for two additional guests, one to his right and the other to the left. The man who opened the door greeted Claudia in a cultured English voice before leading us across the dining room to Monya.

'Claudia my dear, it's so good to have you home,' said Monya, indicating the vacant chair and place setting on the left side of the table. 'Come, my dear, join me.'

He turned and looked towards the man who had escorted us into the room and said, with a smile, 'You may leave us.'

When the man left the room and the doors had closed, a waiter dressed in a white shirt, black bow tie and black trousers, appeared from the side of the room and escorted Claudia to her seat. Monya waved his hand and another waiter appeared. He led me to the place setting on the opposite side of the table to Claudia. If she had been fearful of meeting with Monya, I couldn't tell because she moved gracefully, glowing with confidence.

She is an enigma. Now, far from the cold-blooded killer I know her to be.

'Our friends in government,' Monya said, 'are pleased with the way things turned out in Britain. You had NATO and the British scurrying around. As for us, we made billions from the venture, all thanks to you.'

He raised his wine glass towards Claudia before noticing her glass was empty. He stared towards one of the waiters who appeared with a bottle and filled Claudia's glass. The theatre then resumed. Monya raised his glass and clinked it with Claudia's. They each took a sip, followed by silence as they studied the wine. The waiter filled my glass. I considered the hypocrisy of drinking to their success but raised the glass to my lips and drank anyway.

'I can imagine it now,' Monya said, praising himself. 'The British, Americans, the other countries we extorted, congratulating themselves. They believe that they have won. But as we know the Janus Machine was a diversion, I did tell you that, yes?'

When Monya spoke, Claudia smiled warmly. The conversation was temporarily halted as a waiter put a meal in front of Claudia and the other waiter did the same for me.

'My dear, things are going well but I do need you to go to Dubrovnik a little earlier than we were planning, just to ensure it stays that way. We've been monitoring Professor Akihiko, the head of our cyber team. There are some anomalies in his profile. Nothing significant on its own. Recently he twice walked to work using a different route and stopped for coffee at a new café. The following day he reverted to his usual pattern. He occasionally forgets his mobile phone and he did so on both of these days. You see, Claudia, on the first anomalous day he ordered the wrong coffee. A mistake with his order possibly, or was he was nervous, on edge? He knows that we watch him and it would be inconvenient if he betrayed us.

Have one of your chats with him, let him know that I am concerned and tell him that we will be watching him closely.

'I want to know what risk he poses and if any of our cyber operations have been compromised. No one must know of the blockchain project and how we feed the IT community, to our advantage, of course. Our source code must form the foundation for the new technology, especially when the banks start "chunking" their transactions. If he has been disloyal I will kill him myself but, if he is being blackmailed, well that may be to our advantage. I will meet the other Brotherhood members soon and they will wish to know that their investment is progressing nicely. Your visit to Dubrovnik will be a health check. Examine all of our cyber-operations, not just the blockchain project, understood?'

'Yes, Monya,' answered Claudia, lowering her head slightly.

'Good. After Dubrovnik, I have another opportunity for you.'

I ceased eating and observed the conversation. No attempt had been made to hide their secrets and I was being ignored, as if I didn't exist, which did not bode well for my future.

'An opportunity,' Claudia repeated, 'by which, you mean a problem.'.

'At our house in Macinec.'

Macinec. That's the town where Olivia and I found and freed Lucia. This is the same syndicate, operational after twenty years and using the same house.

I felt angry.

111

How could this be? We shut that place down. *Stay calm!* I whispered to myself.

I took a slow, purposeful sip of wine and let the liquid swirl around my month to savour its flavours before swallowing gently. My composure returned using this simple performance, which went unnoticed. I focused my attention on the interaction between Claudia and Monya. Something was different. I wondered if Monya sensed it.

'Some of the girls aren't being well prepared. There have been complaints from some of our important customers. I would like you to stay there for a while to help Anna and make sure she understands what we expect. I would like you there before the next shipment arrives at the end of next month. Visit Dubrovnik and then have a little holiday before you go. You will have time. Stay on the yacht when you finish your work at Dubrovnik, yes? You have earned it and I know how much you love sailing around the Greek Islands, up and down the Adriatic coast. One of our favourite things, after all. I won't be able to join you this time, my dear, although I will still fly down on Saturday for the reception. Linda will also be joining you at Dubrovnik, I want her to take over from Anna at Macinec, eventually.'

'Anna?' asked Claudia.

'She can stay at Macinec, for now. If you think she can't work with Linda, you know what to do.

'Now my dear, what about Max! Perhaps you can enlighten me as to why he is here, enjoying my hospitality?'

This is it.

I was not afraid. I desperately missed Olivia.

I want to be with her when I die.

'It was a split-second decision.'

'So I have heard, out of character, don't you think?' replied Monya coolly.

'His, and Olivia's, fame grew as we hunted them across Britain. When the media realised that they were the eighty-five-year-olds who rode a motorbike and sidecar around Europe, the interest in them was insatiable. I had a dread that I would create a martyr if I shot him. A rallying point for the people of Britain and perhaps other parts of the world against us - organised crime. I thought it wiser to take him with me and let time fade their memories. We can dispose of him when we are ready or let him die of old age: *Max passed away peacefully of old age* the headline would read. For us, he is forgotten, as are we.'

It took me a few seconds to comprehend what Claudia had said, it was not what I was expecting.

Why the change? Once again, she is rallying to my aid.

I wasn't out of danger. Monya was revealing little as he placed his knife and fork on his plate, picked up his glass of red wine and took a long sip.

'Martyrdom can be inconvenient, even dangerous. You are my favourite, Claudia, but this is not to go wrong. We are not in the business of running a nursing home. Take him with you, he can stay at Macinec for the time being. He looks harmless enough but don't let him out of your sight until you reach Macinec.'

'Come Claudia,' said Monya, standing and reaching out his hand, 'I've missed you.'

Claudia responded by taking Monya's hand and raising herself from her place at the dining table. For the first time since arriving, she stole a sidewards glance at me. The same look as the one that I awoke to that first morning on the submarine. With it, something stirred deep within me, a nagging feeling.

I know this woman. Who is she?

Monya's gaze followed Claudia's and came to rest on me.

'The staff will take care of you,' he said. 'Make yourself at home but don't do anything silly.'

'I thought you didn't want me to let him out of my sight,' said Claudia with a giggle.

'Starting tomorrow,' he replied, while touching her lightly on the bottom.

CHAPTER FIVE

Eiffel Tower

Olivia

The sun was setting and twilight shrouding Paris as we left our hotel to entrap our final guest for Tuesday night's dinner. From the Eiffel Tower, following the tree-lined footpath along the Quai Baraly in the direction of the Australian Embassy, stalls line the street. It's a pretty, park-like area, with the street stalls nestled between the trees on the right and the Emile Antoine Sports Stadium on the left. If you reach the Bir-Hakeim bridge, then you've gone too far. The covered stalls sell tourist wares, food and cheap art. The retailers face a footpath which runs alongside the sports stadium and back onto a bike path that runs parallel to the main road. Street sellers add to the market stalls, trying to offload their counterfeit tourist wares like cast Eiffel Towers of all sizes, hats and an assortment of trinkets, all neatly laid out on cloth. When a warning is given of police approaching, the street sellers pull cords attached to the cloth creating a bundle that is thrown over the shoulder to be set up again once the danger has passed. The Eiffel Tower precinct is notorious for its pickpockets but not at this street market. This is the home of a much more lucrative criminal con: The Shell Game. This is one where the victims need to feel safe enough to have their money-filled wallets out on display.

The shell, or three cups and ball game, is probably one of the oldest swindles of all time. Some believe it dates to the Ancient Greeks, or earlier. The fleece requires an operator and confederates and it's impossible to win. Yet, every night, naïve tourists walking through the market, part easily with their hard-earned cash to the tricksters.

There are many variations to the game but tonight it was the traditional three cups and ball. The ball is placed under one of the cups so that it can't be seen. The cups are shuffled in plain view of the spectators. The players are invited to bet by choosing the cup that they think holds the ball. The confidence trickster rigs the game by sleight of hand and the ball is moved during play and replaced as required. To entrap the unsuspecting player and to convince potential players of the game's legitimacy, accomplices, posing as participants, win a few games while intended targets look on. On some occasions, if the confidence trickster believes that a player has deep pockets, they'll allow the player to win before beginning the scam.

Tonight, we were in for a treat as the full con was on display.

Many of the onlookers watching the game were part of the scam and our operator was using the multiple player version of the trick where a confederate and victim play the swindle together. Traditionally the confederate is female as men don't like being beaten by women. The game is rigged for the woman to succeed, encouraging the man to continue playing and betting. Psychologically he wants to beat the dealer and the woman who is beating him. Watching the foolish man play, forking out money in pursuit of his chauvinist pigheadedness, I wonder if Max feels ashamed of his gender sometimes? Even knowing how the scam works, I marvelled at the operator's sleight of hand. Aware that I must not watch the cups being moved, because that's the distraction, and that I must keep my eyes fixed to the centre for the swap, I still didn't see when it occurred.

Once, when Max and I were in Westminster in London, England, I thought I would con the trickster. This was the first and only time I played the game. Having, from a safe distance, scrutinised the scam being played out, I moved closer and watched an accomplice win two straight games before leaving, saying she wanted to go before losing her winnings.

'Anyone else want to play?' called the charlatan.

I allowed my gaze to meet his.

'Come on Madam, see if you can take my money too. I'm having a difficult day. You women are fleecing me dry; much better eyes than the men.'

I came forward and he placed the ball under the centre cup and then started his shuffle. From what I had seen, he was not allowing a first win to a real victim to entice them into a higher bet. The trap was being sprung on the first try. On every occasion that I'd watched, it appeared to the victim that the ball was under the middle cup, but it had always been the one on the operator's right. The shuffling stopped and the three cups were in a straight line in front of me.

I moved my finger towards the middle one, then hesitated, pointing to the cup to his right, saying, 'What the heck.'

'Oh, hesitation!' said the operator loudly, teasing the crowds, 'should she have gone with her instincts or is she right and it's under this one?'

He pointed to the cup I had chosen.

'Will she win the cash?'

Holding up the money, he waved it about, for all to see. Then as quick as a flash he lifted my chosen cup to reveal no ball. And in a continuous motion he turned over the middle cup and there it was.

Once he held up the cash, I knew that I was in trouble because that was the distraction for his sleight of hand. My £50 lesson – it's impossible to win. But, I don't mind being conned when I know I'm being conned – and I was well and truly done.

The Inspector and I left the spot from where, at a safe distance, we'd been watching the game and walked back towards the Eiffel Tower. We then doubled back, this time taking the cycle path that ran behind the market stalls. Having already walked along this path on the way to observe the game, we knew that a minder was standing behind the operator, out of sight. He'd concealed himself between two of the market tents and was in a perfect position to watch the game. He, like other minders we'd met, was a tall man. This one was heavily set and intimidating, a figure more at home guarding a brothel than a shell game. He looked out of place, at odds with the environment he was guarding. Our earlier reconnaissance hadn't uncovered other minders which was reassuring considering his size.

We now knew seven people were part of the game and they were the ones we could identify. The warning signs were clear and we knew it was going to be a risky exercise. Attaching a tracking bracelet to this minder might prove to be the most dangerous part of our venture, so far. The Inspector expected no trouble from the minder once he produced his police badge but we decided not to approach him together. I'd remain a tactful few paces behind the Inspector, out of sight and hidden between the trees. At any sign of trouble, I would be able to rally to his assistance and brandish the pistol which was hidden in my handbag.

From the safety of my vantage point, I watched as the Inspector moved towards the man. He spoke and the man turned and faced the Inspector as he approached. I saw the police badge being held up and the minder, on cue, put his arms out in front of him. The Inspector snapped the tracking bracelet onto his left wrist without encountering any resistance. With no warning, the minder swivelled to his right and grabbed the Inspector by the throat, lifting him off the ground. Startled, I broke cover and headed to his aid.

Advancing, I heard the minder growling, 'You thought I was on my own. That was very stupid of you.'

From nowhere, two burly, flat-headed minders appeared and moved to the assistance of their companion. Inspector Axel struggled to break free. Both of his hands gripped the arms of the man who was trying to strangle him.

'Gentlemen,' I said, speaking to the strangler and his fast-approaching friends, 'I suggest that you let the Inspector go.'

The thug holding Inspector Axel turned his head, peering in the direction of my voice, and saw my pistol, which had been hidden in my handbag, pointing in his direction.

'Now please,' I added.

He let go of the Inspector who, when his feet touched the ground, took a step backwards, drawing his pistol as he moved.

'I wondered where the old hag was. I thought it was past your bedtime, or that you'd run out of incontinence pads and couldn't come out.' The minder laughed as he spoke. 'We were waiting for you, but I should have guessed the Inspector couldn't come without his granny for protection.'

As the man talked, he was joined by his colleagues and I moved in to stand next to the Inspector. In the background, I saw other people, those who had been part of the scam, leaving the game and moving in our direction. This was turning nasty. We had to leave, and fast.

'Well that's most pleasing and we are glad that you were expecting us,' said Inspector Axel calmly, holding up the envelope containing the picture of Claudia and the invitation for dinner on Tuesday night at the Eiffel Tower restaurant, 'Then you will know what this is. As much as we enjoy your company, I think it's time we were moving on. Before we go, I will just leave this here for you.'

He placed the envelope on the ground.

'Now we bid you a fond goodnight.'

The minder laughed at the Inspector's comments and then looked towards his colleagues who looked as equally bemused.

With our pistols pointed in their direction, we walked along the bike track towards the Bir-Hakeim bridge. I couldn't sustain walking forwards while simultaneously pointing my gun backwards so had to leave covering our rear to the Inspector. On our left two of the men who had been following were shadowing us using the footpath which ran in parallel to the cycle track. Even taking the Inspector's arm for assistance, I knew that I couldn't walk fast enough to outrun our pursuers. When we reached Rue Jean Rey, the bike path would merge with the footpath and I knew that we would be caught in a pincer movement. Luckily, as we arrived, a throng of around a hundred people were pushing past and around each other. We concealed our weapons as we reached the crowd and plunged headlong into the crush.

The mob was a blessing and a curse. The crime gang could use it to their advantage by knifing us and walking on, anonymous amongst the pack. Shooting us was an impossible proposition for our hunters. A small benefit, given our predicament. Stealing a quick glance back, I caught a glimpse of the men as they mingled with the crowd.

'What are we going to do?' I said, struggling to catch my breath but, before the Inspector could answer, I continued, 'We could pull our guns and face them; that would bring the police!'

'What about finding Max? You would be deported,' replied the Inspector. 'We still have the upper hand. With the tracking beacons and stealing the Ferrari, they can't be certain we're operating alone. They seem content to follow us while we are in this crowd or maybe they're checking we are on our own. But they will try to take us out when the opportunity arises.'

As we approached the next intersection, near the Bir-Hakeim metro station, the number of people on the footpath increased. The area was a hive of activity, a busy tourist spot with eating places, restaurants, fast-food stores and cafés spilling onto the side walk stretching around the corner, all filled with people.

'Let's wait them out here,' I suggested to the Inspector, pointing to a vacant table in a busy outside café.

He nodded his agreement and we took a seat. Seeing us, two of our chasers drifted past and settled on a table at the other end of the café, with a clear view of where we were seated.

'Now what?' asked the Inspector. It was more of a question to himself than to me.

'Red wine?'

My answer must have taken him by surprise because he laughed and shook his head.

'Why not? Red wine seems as good a plan as any.'

As he spoke we noticed two police officers patrolling the street accompanied by two army personnel. They were crossing the road, moving in our direction.

'Wait here,' instructed the Inspector, before striding toward the patrol. I looked to our assailants who guessed that we were seeking assistance. One, realising I was peering at them, lifted his hand, held two fingers in the shape of a gun, moved it towards his head, pointed it at his temple and mouthed *Bang*. Glancing away, I found Inspector Axel, and watched as he produced his Police ID and then pointed towards our pursuers. They'd left and were heading back towards the Eiffel Tower but not before kicking a chair at my table as they passed.

'Come on,' called the Inspector, beckoning me to join him with the patrol.

By the time I reached him, Inspector Axel was thanking them for their assistance, intending to go on without their protection.

'Let's go,' he said, and we left their sanctuary, eager to return to our hotel, preferably safe and unseen.

Sometimes, I am amazed at how much it's possible to cram into one day. I'm not sure what time we finally made it back to our hotel, but I remember that it was still Sunday. With all the excitement of the day, the moment my head touched the pillow, I fell into a deep sleep.

***

Monday passed without incident and we kept a low profile. We stayed in the hotel, eating all of our meals in their dining room. Other than essentials, I rested and was content to let myself doze for much of the day, recharging my batteries for the adventure ahead.

Nothing whatsoever to do with my age.

We concluded that our guests would try and capture us before we reached the restaurant however if we made it into the Eiffel Tower precinct with its enhanced security, we should be safe. Having reviewed our plan to get to the Tower we were confident that it would work. But privately I wondered.

Would they all turn up and would our plot to escape work?

Sunday night had been a close call. It was clear that the Romanian gang running the cup scam had been tipped off and were expecting us. This could mean only one thing. The clan leaders were talking to each other. This raised our confidence that a representative from each syndicate would accept our dinner invitation, as a precaution.

Our successful departure from the dinner relied upon us convincing our guests that we were working with the intelligence community. We needed to maintain the upper hand, make the clan leaders realise that it was in their best interests to co-operate with us if they wanted the bracelets removed and the Ferrari returned. If they suspected that we were working alone, we would be at risk unless we involved the police but then I would lose any chance of rescuing Max.

Finding a company that ran an evening bus tour to the Eiffel Tower had not been difficult. Swamped with choice, we settled on *"Ever Young—tours for the discerning traveller over seventy."* What made this group stand out was the priority access to the Tower mentioned in their advertising brochure. No standing about and waiting in long queues for the security checks. Their advertising guaranteed access after screening and they even offered a hotel pick up and drop off service. A perfect choice, we thought, as our plan required for us to be in a large group. One we could hide within.

'It's not unusual for a son or grandson to accompany an elderly parent, aunt or uncle,' said the man when Inspector Axel, posing as my son, rang to enquire about the booking. 'In fact,' continued the receptionist. 'We have a few younger people with the group tonight.'

'Well, that's a relief. How many are in the group?' asked the Inspector.

'We are almost full. If you make a booking it will take us to - let me check - sixty.'

'That's excellent. I would like to make a booking for two, with a hotel pick-up please.'

Our plan for reaching the Eiffel Tower restaurant was set.

***

The bus arrived at our hotel just before 6.00pm. As had been promised, the Inspector was not the youngest in the group and the tour was almost full. Our disguise for the first part of the night's plan consisted of hats and jackets. The jackets hid our dining clothes and concealed padded cushions - these would give us the appearance of added body weight. I chose to carry a walking stick instead of my handbag. In the plan, I was to be accompanied into the Eiffel Tower by another woman as we suspected that the Romanian crime gangs would be on the lookout for an older lady and younger man.

Once on the bus, I spotted a woman sitting on her own and asked if I could join her. The Inspector found another seat behind me. My instincts had been correct. The lady I chose was travelling on her own and welcomed my company. Our hotel was near the

Eiffel Tower, so we were the last ones to board. Within ten minutes the bus had joined the host of other tourist buses at the Eiffel Tower.

'Would you mind helping me off the bus?' I asked the lady sitting next to me.

'Not at all, dear,' she replied.

Once at the bottom of the stairs, I expanded my request to include aiding me through the security check point.

'My son,' I said to her, 'is coming. He is at the back of the bus and will meet me inside the security fencing.'

With the stick in my left hand and the lady on my right arm, I kept my head bowed as we shuffled towards the check point. I stole a glance and saw one of the men we encountered on Sunday night standing next to our entrance. He was scanning the crowd. We joined the queue of the seventy and overs to pass through the metal detectors. Unluckily, we were going to pass right in front of him.

'Oh, my dear,' I said to my escort. 'I forgot to ask you your name!'

'Sally,' she replied. 'Did you say that your name was… Faye?'

'Yes, Faye, my dear. Can you tell me where you're from? I don't travel much anymore and I do love hearing about where people live.'

That was all Sally needed and she chatted profusely, providing a detailed description of her home, life, family and all manner of things. The line moved quickly and we became closer to the man seeking me. I hoped that my chatty friend would aid in my disguise.

To my horror, the line stopped as we reached him. Sally was still chirping away but I heard none of what she was saying because my ears were filled with the thumping of my heart. I lifted my eyes. Luckily, he was scanning the crowd off into the distance. For a moment, I thought that my elementary mistake of looking up had been unnoticed but then his eyes dropped and he saw me.

'Hello,' he said, with a snigger. 'Nice disguise!'

As quick as a flash, I hit him with my walking stick.

'Help!' I yelled. 'This man tried to touch me. Pervert,' I called, giving him another whack.

All the old ladies in the line and those from others rallied to my aid. Armed with whatever they were carrying, handbags, walking sticks, tourist maps, they lashed harmlessly out at him with their beatings. The sheer number of the shouting and rampaging pensioners that formed the attack forced him into retreat. The line moved forward and we entered the metal detector within the security hut.

Inside, Sally and I joined the Inspector who had gained entry without incident.

We stayed with the tour until it was almost over. As everybody else was preparing to leave, we told our tour leader that we had decided to stay and would find our own way back to the hotel.

We walked to the first level where we discreetly removed our overcoats, ready for dinner. We hung the discarded coats in the lavatories and hoped that they would not trigger a bomb scare.

It was 8.40pm when I looked at my watch.

'Are you ready?' I asked the Inspector.

He nodded as he said, 'As ready as I will ever be, Olivia. Let's go and find Max.'

Dressed for dinner, we entered the restaurant for our 9.00pm sitting. A waiter escorted us to a table for five where our three guests were waiting for us. The server pulled the chair out from the table and guided me into my place before doing the same for the Inspector. Returning, he took the white napkin from the setting in front, opened it and placed in neatly across my lap, repeating the same ritual for Inspector Axel. Another waiter then joined him and introduced herself as our wine waiter while handing a wine list to both of us.

Our guests, two men in their mid to late fifties and a woman, perhaps ten years younger, watched the theatre in silence.

'Gentlemen and Lady,' Inspector Axel said, looking to each of our company in turn. 'Can I suggest a bottle of champagne.'

He looked towards the wine waiter. 'Perhaps your Perrier-Jouët Belle Epoque,' I knew that the Inspector was establishing the tone, the unwritten rules, for the way in which tonight's negotiations were to be conducted.

'Thank you, Monsieur,' said the waiter while collecting the wine lists.

The other waiter produced the menus, telling us that our dinner guests had already ordered. We made our selection and the waiters withdrew. Finally, we all sat at the table alone.

'Thank you for joining us this evening,' said the Inspector. 'As you know our agencies are looking for Claudia, the lady in the photograph we gave each of you.'

'As you would know,' said the woman guest, sarcastically, 'it would be unwise for us to be informers. Our reputations rely on trust and any assistance we give will trigger a reprisal. Such things can easily escalate into gang war, a situation we all prefer to avoid.'

The men, who were seated on either side of her, remained expressionless as she spoke. When she finished, there was again silence.

I let the silence linger for a few seconds before joining the conversation.

'This is a little different. Claudia and her syndicate are terrorists. They have used a biological weapon against Britain and blackmailed the United States and many other countries for billions of Euros. If you refuse to cooperate, the governments of those countries will seek retribution against those they see as hindering our investigation. They may even think that you are assisting these terrorists.'

I paused briefly to let the magnitude of what I had just said sink in.

'Organised crime is one thing – but terrorism, I assure you, is something entirely different.'

As I finished speaking and before they had an opportunity to respond, the wine waiter appeared holding the bottle of champagne we had ordered. She poured a taste into the Inspector's glass for sampling.

'That will be fine,' he said.

Glasses filled, the other waiter appeared and entrees were served.

'Are you saying,' said the man sitting on the woman's right, looking at Inspector Axel and not at me, 'that by withholding our co-operation, we will be seen as helping terrorists?'

Inspector Axel seemed totally engrossed in his food and ignored the question until he had finished chewing.

'That's precisely what we are telling you and I don't need to spell out what this will mean,' I said.

The man's eyes shifted from the Inspector and he met my gaze. We each ate in silence.

The entrées were swiftly cleared away and replaced by the main courses. Inspector Axel dutifully ordered a bottle of red and a white wine for the table.

The woman broke the silence, saying, 'My acquaintances here don't believe that you are working for the "agencies" you cite.

I have a more open mind, which is why I agreed to meet, rather than dispose of you.'

'The GPS tracking bracelets,' interrupted Inspector Axel, 'and ones that can't be removed, aren't regular issue of the police or Interpol.'

'A gimmick,' said the man speaking for the first time on the woman's left. 'My contacts at Interpol know nothing of this operation.'

'That's true,' replied the Inspector calmly. 'We are working with the British and MI6.'

'We will see,' retorted the man before focusing back on his meal and then adding, 'Not a bad steak. Enjoy it for it may be your last meal.'

'We have designed a little test for you, to see if you are telling the truth,' said the woman in a flamboyant, almost jovial, voice. 'But first finish your dinner and enjoy the wine. We wouldn't want you dying on an empty stomach.'

I struggled to fight an overwhelming desire to steal a glance at the Inspector. The tables were being turned and control of the evening was slipping away from us. It took a lifetime of training to hide the panic I was feeling and to stop myself asking, 'What test?'

The main course was finished and cleared away with the same efficiency as the entrée before anyone spoke again. It was the woman who again took the lead.

'Believe us or not, we don't know where Claudia is. We do know who she is and for whom she works. Claudia is commander for a Russian billionaire property developer and Mafia boss called Monya Mogilevick. She is also his lover. He is part of what they call the Brotherhood, made up of twelve syndicates, each with its own boss. They all report to Monya. This makes him a dangerous and powerful man. My cousin Sandor, in Rome, will know how to find her.'

From her pocket, she retrieved a card, but hid it as the waiter approached and proceeded to set our desserts in front of us on the table. Mine was a cheese platter.

With the waiter gone, she again removed the card from her pocket, this time holding it up so that the Inspector and I could see it.

'His girls work the number 64 bus route from the Termini to the Vatican. Write your phone number on the card and give it to one of the girls. They will recognise our symbol, as will my cousin. He is expecting you and, for his own reasons, is willing to help. Before I give this to you, you must pass our little test.'

She looked expectantly to the man on her left, one with a small scar above his right eye.

'Hello, Inspector Jacques Axel of Interpol,' he said, and just like the other man, he seemed quite content to ignore me. 'You see, we know exactly who you are. Perhaps you would like to tell us our names.'

He paused as if waiting for a reply. After a few seconds of silence, he continued, 'Surely Inspector, if you were working with MI6, you would know who we are?'

We could do nothing except stare blankly back at him because we had no idea who they were.

What the hell are we going to do now? This is not going to end well.

'No, I thought not,' he continued, now turning his interest to me. 'And you Olivia.'

Before he could say my surname, he was interrupted by a vaguely familiar male voice coming from directly behind me. Accompanying the voice came the light touch of a hand as it gently settled upon my shoulder in a reassuring way.

'What do we have here?' said the voice. 'A genuine collection of nasties. Ivan Conners, Brida Sztojka and Nilola Raffael, not the kind of people you would ordinarily expect to see together. This must be a very special occasion.'

Our dinner guests' attention was drawn to the man speaking from behind me and I resisted the urge to turn to put a name to the voice I recognised.

'And who are you?' said the woman that I now knew as Brida Sztojka, in a most unfriendly tone.

'You're not telling me that you don't know who I am! I think you have failed your own test,' he said in a teasing tone.

He waited a second or two before continuing, this time in a more serious manner. 'My name is Stephen Walls and I am the head of MI6. We take a very dim view of our agents being threatened. You didn't for one moment think we would let Inspector Axel and Olivia meet you unaccompanied?

'I'm here with my counterpart from Israel – Mossad,' said Stephen, pointing to a table a few settings away from ours. 'Claudia is a mutual friend, who managed to upset the Israelis and the United States as well as the British. We Brits would much prefer to gain the information we need over a civilised dinner.

'My counterparts in the CIA and Mossad have less pleasant ways of encouraging cooperation. Perhaps you would prefer that I leave and Yossi Pardo,' he said, pointing towards his table and at a man seated there, 'comes to join you?'

'What we told Olivia and the Inspector is true,' said Brida Sztojka, now more conciliatory, 'My cousin in Rome will know how to find Claudia. Now what about my Ferrari and the bracelets?'

Reaching into his pocket, Stephen took out the set of keys belonging to the Ferrari. They were the same keys that I had put into the safe in my hotel room earlier. He dropped them onto the table.

Thank goodness, we had taken the precaution of leaving our false passports and credit cards with a friend of the Inspector.

'You will find the car downstairs,' he continued. 'A couple of my people are chaperoning it until you arrive.'

'And the bracelets,' said Nilola Raffael, the man with the scar.

Stephen again reached into his pocket, this time dropping what looked like two small magnets onto the table. 'These will remove them. Now gentlemen and lady, dinner is over and I think it's time you were leaving us. You won't be seeing me again. If we have the need to talk with you again, that pleasure will fall to my associates at Mossad. It is in your interest to ensure that we don't need to chat further.'

Who gave MI6 a copy of the bracelet keys? I have the originals in my pocket. Cliff?

Our dinner guests remained mute, gathered the keys and magnets from the table, stood, and without looking back, started to leave the restaurant. As they moved towards the door, I saw two other men withdraw from another table and follow them out. I didn't ask, but wondered if those men were ours or theirs.

'May I join you?' asked Stephen politely and, without waiting for us to respond, took a seat at the table. 'The consensus from the agency is that I should have you both arrested. Give me one good reason why I shouldn't? Both of you.'

Stephen stared at the Inspector, speaking directly to him in a stern voice, 'Your duty was to see her safely on a fight back to Australia – tomorrow. You have betrayed our trust.'

'I'm entertaining,' I said, interrupting his reprimand.

'Entertaining! God give me strength, Olivia. Entertaining! A secret agent is meant to be a grey man, invisible, blending in. We didn't need you to carry your mobile phone, or even wear the shoes we gave you, the ones with tracking devices hidden in them. No Olivia, all we had to do was watch the nightly news. News Headlines – eighty-seven-year-old grandmother steals a Ferrari and is last seen driving at a hundred miles-an-hour down the Champs-Elysées with the police in hot pursuit. Do you have any idea how many favours we had to call in? The French police wanted to throw the book at you. Don't look so surprised Olivia! You don't really think you out-drove the police and avoided all the road blocks to make a clean getaway on your own? You know the French will want something in return? I don't like being in debt to anyone. But the French, Olivia? The bloody French!'

'Grey person,' I said.

'A what?' replied Stephen, with a look of surprise on his face.

'You meant a Grey Person, not a Grey Man. I'm a woman, Stephen, not a man.'

Stephen looked first to me and, in total disbelief, slowly turned to look at Inspector Axel who smiled and then shrugged.

'All right,' he continued, this time in a less exasperated tone. 'Since you left London there has been another development. A cyber-attack by ransom-ware worm called WannaCry has caused widespread chaos to the British Health System as it struggles to cope with the aftermath of the biological attack. There is speculation from GCHQ that Russian hackers with links to the government are behind the attack. The worm shares segments of code known to have been used in the past by the Russians. We think that your Claudia could be involved and so we are going to let you go, to see what you can find out. As far as we are concerned, you're not working for MI6 and we will deny any knowledge of you. Understand that you are on your own.

'She's your responsibility, Inspector. I assume that you have a plan of how you are going to skip the flight to Australia and escape from France undetected. I don't want to know what it is. Go to Rome and see what you can discover. Inspector, if your plan for leaving France is to hijack a plane, I will be most disappointed.'

'Stephen,' I said indignantly, 'I would never do anything so rash as to hijack a plane.'

He ignored me totally and continued speaking to the Inspector. 'She is your responsibility Axel! Do we understand one another?'

'Yes,' replied the Inspector.

'I'm not some chattel to be talked over,' I said.

'Indeed, you're not,' said Stephen kindly. 'You're a wonderful but exasperating lady and one that I can't help but admire. I wonder how you do it sometimes. You're not as young as you once were!'

I thought for a second before responding proudly, 'Intensity of desire, Stephen, that's the secret.'

Stephen smiled softly and said, 'Indeed it is, Olivia, *intensity of desire*, yes I like that. I like that very much. If we can help you, we will, but next time you might not be so lucky. Take your cell phone with you, the one we gave you, so we can track you and be careful!'

CHAPTER SIX

Russia

Claudia

The morning light that shimmered off the window woke me before the alarm, set for 6.00 am on my watch, had a chance to go off. He was still sleeping and, for a fifty-year-old, man some fifteen years my senior, Monya was not unattractive. Unlike many of the Mafia bosses I'd met, Monya kept himself in shape. He was not obsessed with physical fitness as I was, but looked after himself.

Trying not to disturb Monya, I arose and slipped into my sports gear before heading out for a 14km run, followed by a thirty-minute workout in the gym, a hot shower and breakfast. With luck, Monya would be gone by the time I returned and I could leave for Dubrovnik without having to saying goodbye.

There was no frost on the ground when I left the gates of our fortress to pound the roads for the next hour. Jogging gave me the opportunity to enjoy the solitude.

I'd discovered the magic of exercise after running away from my parents who lived in a little village called Kula Grad, near Zvornik, in Bosnia Herzegovina. I was seventeen at the time and it was at the height of the Balkan War. I left to be with my boyfriend Ratimir, a commander in one of General Ratko Mladic's paramilitary militia. He let me train with him and his troops, a militia called the Yellow Wasps. I discovered that extreme workouts could distract me, helping me shelve the worries of daily life and ease the mental stress that I carried from childhood. I came to realise that a strong body needed a strong mind too. Through military training, I learned to focus and control my anger. What started as Ratimir's girlfriend joining him, changed and I became a supreme, cold and calculating killing machine as part of the militia.

During the training, they sent me on 10km cross country runs with a sniper rifle strapped to my back. While still breathless, I would have to drop to the ground and take a shot. I was taught to smother all distractions by visualising a tunnel to shoot down. It hid the rest of the world, leaving only the target to focus on. I learned to control my breathing and regulate my heartbeat. I would command my heart to stop and my breathing to cease, pulling the trigger in that moment when there was no movement from my body. The bullet would run true. The instant the shot was taken, I would rise again and run once more, only to drop to the ground for another shot. On occasions, my training would force me to hide, lying or sitting still for hours, waiting for that perfect shot.

Normally when I jogged I freed my mind from its clutter. Not today - thoughts circulated and I felt the anger, one long ago suppressed, bubbling to the surface.

Is it seeing Max again after all these years that has awoken my past and reminded me that I despise who I have become? Is it his fault?

I ran, pounding harder.

Is it that I must go back to the house in Macinec, the place where, as a child, that I was held prisoner, that is making me so angry? Monya knows how much I hate going there, although I don't think he knows why.

I increased my running pace but still my mind swirled.

I remember seeing Max from my bedroom window. He looked up at me. Me, fourteen-year-old Lucia. When our eyes met, for the first time in my life, I felt safe. Then he came to my bedroom door and I ran into his arms. Then he left me! Max and Olivia stayed for a few days but then the police took me to my parents in the village of Kula Grad. It was Max who abandoned me to people I no longer knew, a family who expected me to be the eight-year-old child they lost six years earlier, little Lucia Da-dic, the girl of their dreams but a fantasy. I was no longer that girl. Max promised me that he would stay in contact, that he would write and visit but he didn't.

143

Like everyone else, he deserted me. I hated this life almost as much as I hated living with Tamara.

Ahead, our fortress, Monya's mansion, came into view. On my watch, not even an hour had passed and, despite running as fast and as hard as I could, I was still angry. Uncontrolled rage made me vulnerable so I went straight to the gym. I filled the bench press machine with the heaviest weights I'd ever lifted and pushed up.

If Max had not abandoned me, I would never have joined the Yellow Wasps.

The thought enraged me and I pumped the weights as hard as I could up and down until my arms, chest and heart were about to burst.

If I had never joined the Yellow Wasps, I wouldn't be here! But this is my life, a life I love. Thankyou Max.

Straining, I tried to push the weights up for one final time, but was overcome by the resistance and had to give in to the machine. Exhausted, I felt at peace. Panting, flat on my back, calm and control had returned.

I am Claudia.

It had been my boyfriend Ratimir's suggestion.

'If you are going to join the Yellow Wasps, you should be known by another name,' he had said. 'A name that will strike fear in the hearts of those who hear it.'

I invented it by rearranging the letters in my first name and using the first two letters of my family name. I went from Lucia Da-dic to *Claudia*. It was also his idea that, before I was introduced to General Karlovic to demonstrate my talents, I should make up a tag line: a word or phrase I would say to someone, just before I killed them.

The night I met General Karlovic, we were waiting in an old disused factory in the town of Zvornic. Ratimir had told me that this was to be a test of my loyalty, to see if I could be trusted to carry out a special mission, one that would make me revered and feared across the Republic. I remember seeing General Karlovic walking towards us. He was prominent, even in the dim light, and I could hear his boots crisply striking the concrete floor, splashing through the pools of water that gathered there from the rain seeping in through the leaking roof.

His soldiers, dressed in their military fatigues, dragged three prisoners tied and blindfolded behind him. He halted a few feet in front of us and Ratimir saluted before taking a couple of steps closer and they embraced warmly. I watched in silence as they talked together, paying no attention to me. I still remember gazing out of the cracked windows, seeing nothing but the bleakness of the night and hearing the howling wind rattling the loose iron that clad the building. Finally, after ten minutes, I was introduced.

'Ah, Claudia,' he said, looking me up and down, 'I've heard so much about you.' He looked me up and down again, slower this time, before continuing. 'These scum,' pointing to the three men, 'are traitors to the Republic.

'On your knees,' General Karlovic said as he waved to the soldiers accompanying the prisoners, who pushed them to the ground. 'Claudia, remove their blindfolds, so they can see us'

I walked over to where they were kneeling and, one by one I ripped the blindfolds from their heads. Watching them, I took two steps backwards.

The General came and stood beside me.

'They have been giving information to the United Nations,' continued Karlovic, 'and we must make an example of them. This one here,' he added, pointing to a person who was around eighteen years of age, 'was helping his father by spying on us.'

'Please don't hurt my son,' begged the man kneeling next to the boy.

'Which one shall we kill first, Claudia?'

It was not a question to me but to himself.

'That one,' said General Karlovic, pointing to the man who was neither the father or the son.

'I want you to shoot him, Claudia, over there, where it won't make such a mess.'

He pointed to a spot on the concrete floor a few metres from where we were standing.

General Karlovic then nodded to two of his soldiers, the ones accompanying the prisoners. Standing either side of the condemned man, they put an arm under each shoulder and hauled him unceremoniously to his feet. The prisoner let his legs hang limply below him as he was dragged across the floor with his feet scraping behind. When they reached the execution spot, he was pushed onto his knees again.

I walked slowly, but without hesitation, to where the man was waiting to die.

The soldiers stepped away and he remained motionless on his knees watching me approach. Withdrawing my pistol, I made sure that our eyes met and, when they did I, gave him a half-smile.

Lifting the automatic gun, I levelled it in front of me. Taking my other hand, exaggerating my movements to increase the theatre of his death, I put a round into the chamber by pulling back and releasing the slide mechanism. It made that distinctive metallic noise, the sound of imminent death. Letting the pistol drop to my side, I continued straight to him and then shifted, finally standing next to him.

'Hello, sweetie,' I said in a calm, sexy and alluring tone.

I raised the pistol to his head, making sure that he felt the cold of its steel resting against his temple. Without faltering, I squeezed the trigger, discharging the round.

Bang!

A single shot rang out and he fell to the ground.

Stepping away, I lifted the muzzle of the pistol to my lips, and gently blew as if blowing away any residual smoke.

The two remaining prisoners, the son and the father, now sobbed in fear.

'Who's next?' I asked General Karlovic.

'You can choose, Claudia. I am going to let one of them live, to tell the others what happens to those who betray us. You decide which one it will be.'

'Please, please, take me,' wept the father.

'You speak again, either of you, and I will find and kill all your family, your wife, daughter, mother. All of them!' snapped General Karlovic.

I made my way back to where the remaining prisoners were kneeling on the floor.

Standing in between but in front of them I said coolly, 'Look at me, both of you.'

They obeyed and lifted their teary eyes.

'Do I have the father or the son!' I said while lifting the pistol to my lips.

I licked its barrel, and then rubbed it up and down the son's face.

'Sweetie, I think I want you. I'm getting excited just thinking about killing you. Oh, so young. Delicious.'

His sobbing became an uncontrolled howling and a puddle of urine formed around his knees.

'He's pissed himself,' I said with an air of disgust in my voice. 'Goodnight sweetie.'

Without bothering to drag him to the execution spot.

Bang, he was gone.

I rose from the bench press machine, annoyed that memories had again invaded my thoughts, and made my way to the shower room. Inside, I turned the water pressure up as high as it would go and the temperature to as hot as I could bear. The flow and heat pounded my body. Taking the soap in what had become a daily ritual, I scrubbed my body repeatedly, pushing harder as I rubbed. Still I felt dirty - unclean. Holding the soap, I rolled it around and around between my hands and found myself reciting Shakespeare aloud:

'What is it she does now? Look how she rubs her hands.

It is an accustom'd action with her, to seem thus
washing her hands. I have known her continue in this a
quarter of
an hour.
Yet here's a spot.
Hark, she speaks. I will set down what comes from her, to
satisfy my remembrance the more strongly.
Out, damn'd spot! Out, I say! – One; two: why, then
'tis time to do't. – Hell is murky. – Fie, my lord, fie, a soldier,
and
afeard? What need we fear who knows it, when none can call
our
pow'r to accompt? – Yet who would have thought the old
man to
have had so much blood in him?

149

Letting the soap fall to the ground, I lifted my head towards the shower head and felt the cleansing water washing across my face.

I am Claudia. I AM CLAUDIA.

After fifteen minutes or longer, I turned off the water, took a large white towel, and gently dried myself. After dressing, I felt refreshed, renewed and ready to face another day.

Max was in the dining room drinking a cup of tea when I joined him.

'Good morning Max, I trust you slept well.'

'Claudia. I see you're still with us.'

'I saved your life, so perhaps you should show me a little gratitude.'

'You have a perverse way of looking at the world, Claudia. Where's your boyfriend, Monya?'

'He had some other business to attend to this morning, otherwise I am sure he would have seen you off personally. An important man like yourself.'

Why do I find Max so infuriating?

Outwardly, I maintained my calm appearance but, having just seated myself at the table, I stood and said, 'Let's go, we are leaving for Dubrovnik.'

'I haven't had my breakfast yet,' he replied in a grumpy old man way.

That will teach you for pissing me off.

'I apologise Max but the plane is waiting for us. We can arrange for some breakfast on board, caviar perhaps! I wouldn't want you going hungry.' Without giving him the opportunity to reply, continued, 'Now, wait here until I return.'

'Do you mind if I wait outside? I would like to have some fresh air before the flight.'

Before I could say no. Max had left the table and was heading towards the door. All I could do was watch him leave.

Unbelievable.

A few moments later, whilst gazing out of the window, I saw him appear at the front door and walk down the steps onto the gravel driveway. He stopped next to one of our guards who was watching a fellow of his on a scooter doing donuts in the gravel. Max and the guard appeared to talk, then they laughed.

Can he speak Russian? No that would be impossible.

The guard gave him a slap on the back before waving to his companion who rode over.

'No!' I yelled, as loudly as I could, but the guards couldn't hear me through the window.

Both guards were hysterical as they steadied the scooter and helped the eighty-seven-year-old Max onto the seat. Zoom! He was off and the scooter wobbled from side to side. For a moment, it seemed as if he would fall. Then the scooter steadied and I saw Max turn, raising his hand to wave, then grabbing the handlebars again before he tumbled. This brought more laughter from the guards and it reminded me of a clown I had once seen riding a motorbike at the circus. Then the scooter was upright and accelerating away, down the driveway and out the gates. He was gone before the guards knew what was happening.

Here we go again.

I had just spent the last few weeks chasing him and Olivia all over the UK and now I was in Russia and about to do it again.

'Sweeties, what were you thinking?' I demanded of the guards as I walked outside.

They were laughing and refusing to take his escape seriously.

'Well?' I repeated, 'Sweeties, what were you thinking?'

'It's all right Claudia,' said Ivan, one of the guards. 'It's has no petrol. He will be waiting for you a hundred metres down the road, tops.'

'You'd better be right,' I snapped. 'Send for the Rolls, I have a plane to catch.'

CHAPTER SEVEN

Rome

Olivia

Having pissed off the Romanians, we believed that it was only a matter of time before they told the Russians we were searching for Claudia. The Russians would then come looking for us. The Inspector and I agreed that it would be safest if we vanished, using the new identities, passports and credit cards given to us by Cliff. I became Lady Olivia Suzanne Elizabeth Huggins and the Inspector my private secretary, Mr Jean-Marc Lemery. With MI6's tacit blessing, we no longer had to flee France by the next day, to return to Australia. Instead, I used my new credit card and spent Wednesday shopping for a wardrobe and luggage suitable for *Lady Olivia*.

The Inspector hadn't wanted me wandering the streets but I argued that, with the protection of MI6 and the threat of Mossad, the Romanian crime gangs wouldn't dare touch me.

'What about the Russians?'

'Too soon,' I replied.

My first task on Wednesday was to hire a driver for the day, Sebastian, who arrived at our hotel promptly at 9.30am. The instruction to his company was clear, the itinerary was dream shopping for the day. We started on the left bank of the river, at the Boulevard Saint Germain, taking Rue du Bac, which runs through the elegant 7th arrondissement. The neighbourhood streets were exquisite and Sebastian recommended we follow Rue d'Assas past the Luxembourg gardens before doubling back and navigating the Boulevard Saint Germain for morning tea and then some luxury shopping around St-Germain des Prés. Before returning to the Boulevard Saint Germain, I asked that we visit a small speciality store, Au Service de la Liturgie (Liturgical Vestments), at 8 Rue Madame.

Despite my confidence concerning the Romanians, I didn't want to chance my luck by waltzing around the Champs-Elysées. But Lady Olivia Suzanne Elizabeth Huggins couldn't leave Paris without visiting the 'Triangle d'Or, the Golden Triangle, the most luxurious place on the right bank. It's the area made up of the Champs-Elysées, Avenue Montaigne, Ave George V and Rue Francois 1er. The shopping possibilities were overwhelming and poor Sebastian was run off his feet. Louis Vuitton, Dior, Chanel, Gucci, Pucci, Ferré, Givenchy, and Celine were some of the places we visited.

With the car now brimming with boxes and bags, the final item I needed was luggage, to transport it all.

'Sebastian, darling,' I said, 'your taste has been impeccable. One more thing before you take me home.'

'Madame?'

'Luggage.'

'Certainly Madame, you would be wanting gorgeous luggage?'

'Absolutely, Sebastian.'

'Can I suggest Luis Vuitton on the Champs-Elysées. I'm sorry Madame, I do know you asked to stay away from the Champs-Elysées, as much as possible.'

'That's quite all right Sebastian, Luis Vuitton sounds perfect.'

Fifteen minutes later, Sebastian was dropping me outside.

'I'll call you when I'm ready to be picked up. I won't be long so try and park somewhere nearby.'

'Certainly Madame.'

As he had promised there was a good selection of *gorgeous luggage*. I chose three suitcases - poor Inspector Axel, or Jean-Marc as he would be tomorrow, would find it difficult to carry any more. In addition, I purchased an elegant cane in case I needed the aid of a walking stick. The luxury sales associate arranged for my purchases to be taken to the front entrance ready to be collected by Sebastian whom I had called.

To my horror, when Sebastian arrived, he was escorted by the young man I kidnapped in the Ferrari. He was smiling as he approached.

'Hello again Olivia,' he said. 'I see you have met my good friend Sebastian.'

'Madame, I assure you,' said Sebastian, 'I have never met this man before in my life. He is carrying a gun.'

'That's quite all right, Sebastian.'

I turned to the Ferrari man and gave him a look of contempt.

'What is it that you want?'

'Brida Sztojka, with whom you had dinner on Tuesday night, sends her warm regards and wishes you well on the next part of your journey. I told her of your desire to ride in a Ferrari F40 and, provided you promise to stay in the passenger's seat, it would be my pleasure to give you a ride back to your hotel, with a few detours, so you can take in the sights on your last day in Paris.'

'Last day?' I said, inquisitively.

'Of course, Olivia. We both know that the Russians will be looking for you by tomorrow. So, this will be your last day in Paris. Please let me make it a memorable one for you.'

'You promise to keep both hands on the steering wheel,' I teased.

'Goodness no, Olivia,' he said, smiling. 'That wouldn't be memorable and I'm sure that's not what you would want.'

In for a cent, in for a Euro. Why not?

It was dusk when the F40 dropped me at my hotel. It had been a wonderful ride and my driver had been delightful company. I had called the Inspector so that he knew I was off galivanting around the city and wouldn't be worried. I told him to expect Sebastian, who would be delivering the days' purchases. It took me the rest of the evening to transfer the shopping into the suitcases, ready for our trip to Rome. Our flight was booked for 10.00 in the morning.

'What shall I call you tomorrow?' Inspector Axel asked before bidding me goodnight, 'Would you prefer Lady Olivia, Ma'am or Madame? Perhaps even Mademoiselle,' he added with a teasing smile.

'Mademoiselle.' I sighed. 'If only I could turn back time. No Inspector, it's m'lady.'

'Me lady,' he repeated in a confused tone.

'No, no Inspector, m'lady. It's an old joke that Max and I share. It comes from a 1960s television series called *Thunderbirds* and a character called Lady Penelope Creighton-Ward.'

'Of course! I know it. Olivia, you forget that it was my father, Jean Axel, who was French and he escaped to Britain in 1940. Perhaps, I should have been called Parker on my new passports and not Jean-Marc Lemery.'

'Touché, Inspector. From tomorrow, once we leave the hotel it's m'lady. You may introduce me, when the need arises, as Lady Olivia, reserving my full title, Lady Olivia Suzanne Elizabeth Huggins for those more formal of moments.'

'As you wish m'lady.'

***

The next morning a taxi arrived and drove us to Charles de Gaulle airport which was as busy as usual. We were booked on an Air France plane to Rome, flying business class for the two-hour, five-minute flight. Security at the air terminal was tight but nobody questioned our new identities or passports and, if I must say so myself, I looked very distinguished in my new outfit and carrying my elegant cane which upset the metal detectors.

By 9.40am we were seated aboard the plane and waiting to take off. In business class, a dedicated cabin crew member attends to you, offering pre-flight drinks while waiting for the other passengers to board.

'Excuse me, Madame and Monsieur, would you like a drink before we take off? Champagne perhaps?' asked the cabin crew member politely.

'Water, I think,' said Jean-Marc, now pretending to be my private secretary.

'Yes, thank you, I will have the same,' I added in the most aristocratic manner I could muster.

'Sparkling?'

'Indeed, yes, we will both have sparkling,' I concluded.

A minute or so later, a member of the cabin crew, a man in his early thirties, returned.

'Madame,' he said, which attracted my attention and caused me to look in his direction. As I did so he held out the bottle of sparkling water for me to take.

Looking as annoyed as possible and in my most indignant voice, I chastised him. 'Do I look like the kind of woman who would drink out of a bottle!'

He withdrew his hand immediately, adding, before scurrying away, scolded, 'Certainly, not Madame,'

'Why do I have a sneaking suspicion you are going to enjoy this,' whispered Jean-Marc.

'Me?' I said, in a nonchalant manner.

The flight to Rome was uneventful until we started to land. The change in air pressure, as we descended, made my ears ache. I was in agony and the pain did not abate until we prepared to leave the plane. I felt disorientated, slightly deaf and my balance was unstable. Embarrassingly, it was the cabin crew member whom I had belittled, that organised a wheel chair and then insisted, with grace, on pushing me into the terminal.

'Is there anything else I can do for Madame?' he said as he prepared to leave me.

The wittiest and humblest answer I could muster was, 'A bottle of water would be nice.'

He smiled and gave me a peck on the cheek before saying, 'Au revoir.'

Jean-Marc and I remained in the terminal for an hour before I felt ready to stand. The pressure had still not equalised in my ears and I was unsteady. With his assistance and my trusty cane, I could walk. We had planned on catching a train into the city but now settled on a taxi. My excess baggage, which started as fun was proving to be an inconvenience. I could see some charitable donations coming up.

Our choice of hotel was based on its proximity to the Termini, which was where we would catch the number 64 bus, once I had recovered. We had taken two adjoining suites at the Metropole hotel on Via Principe Amedo and Jean-Marc had helped me into my room.

'Inspector.'

'It's Jean-Marc, m'lady,' he replied.

'Jean-Marc,' I said, contritely. 'I won't be able to fly. Wherever they send us in search of Max, I can't fly. I'm so sorry.'

It was close to 4.30pm by the time I felt well enough to walk to the Termini and catch the bus. I had slung an inviting handbag over my shoulder with a plump enticing purse hiding inside. Although we didn't hide the fact that we were travelling companions, we kept a discreet distance from each other as we waited for the bus to arrive. From the corner of my eye I saw a girl, sixteen or seventeen years old, hovering nearby. I felt sure that she was a pickpocket. Strangely, she appeared to be on her own. The bus arrived and Jean-Marc and I boarded using the middle door. I found a seat next to the door while Jean-Marc pressed himself into the space between the door and my seat. Within three stops the bus was almost full and people were pushed against one another. A scruffy man with his big belly sticking out, stood directly in front of me looking leeringly down at my handbag resting on my lap. Another man, standing next to the girl we'd seen at the Termini, had a shopping bag and was pushing against Jean-Marc. From where I was seated, I could see, as his bag brushed against Jean-Marc's leg as a distraction, while the girl was attempting to put her hands in his pockets. Jean-Marc knew what was happening and stuffed his hand into the exposed space, sealing off her access. Smiling, he leaned over and spoke to me.

'If this wasn't so serious it would be funny. They don't care that we know that they are trying to steal from us. I push her away and she comes back again for another go. It's like chasing flies away at a picnic. That man,' he said, while looking to the person leering over me, 'he's making no secret that he wants your handbag. I feel sorry for the locals who must endure this every day. The three of them are working together, I think it's time we produced the card Brida Sztojka gave us at the Eiffel Tower.'

I opened the catch on my handbag, reached in and removed the card with the emblem emblazoned on it. I held it up so that the leering man could see. From the expression on his face, I could tell that he immediately recognised it.

He reached down and took it gently from my hand, saying, 'Have you put your phone number on the back?'

I didn't speak but instead nodded affirmation. At the next stop, all three got off. Through the bus window, we watched them huddle together in conversation, except that now they were four. One of them had escaped our notice - the three stooges had been the real diversion.

Never underestimate your opponent.

We had both done just that.

Ordinarily I would have alighted the bus near Vatican City, walked leisurely back to our hotel and enjoyed the famous sights along the way. But today, with my balance not fully recovered, we returned to the hotel to rest and await the phone call. It was exactly 6.30pm when my mobile phone rang.

'Olivia?' the voice asked.

'Yes.'

'You had dinner with my cousin Rita?'

The phone whet silent while he waited for my reply.

'No, her name was Brida! We had dinner on the Champs-Elysées.'

The man at the other end of the phone laughed.

'We are testing each other, Olivia. My name is Sandor and it wasn't the Champs-Elysées, it was the Eiffel Tower. Enough of this silliness. I will send my driver for you and the Inspector. Don't worry, you are in no danger. Not from me, at least.'

'Do you have the news we seek?' I asked.

'Enough to make it worthwhile coming to dinner,' he said, chuckled and added, 'other than my great company that is. I must apologise in advance but I'm sure you will understand; please bring no weapons. A car is waiting for you downstairs and, again, another apology for having you followed to your hotel. Don't worry, we are not going to blindfold you or anything silly like that. You will find it's a most pleasant drive to my humble home.'

We were driven into the stunning countryside of Lazion and the village of Sutri some 50km north of Rome, to a secluded villa. It was still daylight when we arrived at Sandor's humble abode which was surrounded by a magnificent garden, dotted with olive trees and roses. According to the driver the grounds covered over two hectares.

Sandor proved as charming a host as he had been on the phone. He told us that Claudia was known for her passion for cruising the Adriatic coast and the Greek Islands on the super yacht of her lover, the Mafia boss. An associate of his, who lived on the Island of Corfu, had told Sandor that the yacht was being prepared for use. He was trying to find out when the yacht was to sail, its destination and who the passengers would be. He told us that snooping on the Russians was a dangerous game but that his friend would be at the New Corfu Fortress at 9.30am on Sunday 24th April and then again on Monday 25th. If we wanted to talk to him we would find him there. Sandor was firm in telling us that he could give no guarantees that Claudia would be on board.

This was the only lead we have. What choice - take it or leave it!

The challenge that now faced us was reaching Corfu without flying and the solution was obvious: a cruise ship leaving Venice on Saturday, in two days' time, for an eight-day voyage taking in Corfu, Santorini, Mykonos, Dubrovnik, Split and then back to Venice. The only remaining berths were inside cabins on E deck, not quite how Lady Olivia Suzanne Elizabeth Huggins had envisaged traveling.

At the same time as securing our sea passage, Jean-Marc booked first class tickets on a high-speed train leaving Rome on Saturday morning for Venice. We had hoped to travel on Friday but decided on an additional day's rest for me. This meant that we had little room for error.

***

The hotel concierge organised for our luggage to be taken to the railway station and we made our way across an hour before the train was due to leave. Standing in the middle of the station, I waited and looking up at the arrival and departures board, the platform number for our train finally appeared.

'At last,' I said to Jean-Marc, relieved.

Our next task was to find the platform and the man with our bags but, as I turned to leave, I spotted, in the middle of the station, an abandoned suitcase.

'Oh no,' I said worriedly to Jean-Marc pointing. 'They will close the railway station. An abandoned suitcase. They will think it's a bomb, even though it's obvious that it's not. Well we can't let that happen!'

While I was complaining, two policemen joined by two army offices appeared and were now standing, looking at the bag.

'At any second, they will radio in and the evacuations would start,' I said. 'Come on.' Grabbing Jean-Marc by the arm, I marched him across to the police and soldiers.

'Sorry, sorry,' I started calling as we approached and, pointed my walking cane towards the suitcase while saying, 'It's mine.'

Standing with the police and soldiers, I continued talking without taking a breath. 'Go on Jean-Marc, open the bag and show them it's mine!'

I tapped him with my cane as I spoke.

Before they had a chance to object or even comprehend what was happening, Jean-Marc was kneeling and popping open the catches on the case. I held my breath, but luckily it didn't explode. He, with some trepidation, lifted the lid.

'Go on,' I persisted, 'find something with my name on it.'

Speaking with an elevated voice, while giving him another light tap with my cane, I said loudly, 'Lady Olivia from England.'

He cautiously began sifting through the luggage: boxer shorts, men's shirts, and ties. From its contents, it was obviously a man's case and not a woman's.

'I'm sorry Lady Olivia,' apologised Jean-Marc, 'but it would appear, m'lady, that this is not your case after all. Standing, he turned towards me. 'I did caution m'lady, that although this looked like one of your pieces of luggage, I had organised the hotel concierge to have your things waiting for you on the platform.'

'Yes, indeed, that's clearly not my luggage,' I responded indignantly. 'What are you waiting for Jean-Marc, we will miss our train. Don't dilly dally, young man.'

I prodded him again with my cane and we left the police and soldiers with the both open mouths and suitcase and headed for the platform.

'Take my arm, Jean-Marc,' I ranted as we disappeared into the distance, 'you know I'm a little unsteady on my feet this morning.'

'Yes, m'lady!'

The high-speed trains in Europe are wonderful and first class is a delight. We had comfortable leather chairs and were separated by a writing table. Even better, we had the carriage to ourselves. As in the plane, a steward offered us a glass of champagne but we settled on juice. A TV monitor displayed the news; it had no sound but showed English subtitles. Below it was a digital readout of our current speed. This was going to be a relaxing three hour and forty-five minutes' ride to Venice and I settled back into my chair for the trip.

I dozed off and on and in between would steal a look at the TV.

We were perhaps forty minutes into the journey when I noticed, with a shock, the news headline.

Bomb Explosion at Rome Railway Station.

'Inspector, Inspector!' I called urgently.

'Lady Olivia, you must practise. I am Jean-Marc,' he replied with a yawn, having been woken from a slumber by my calling his name.

'Yes, from now on I promise but, Jean-Marc,' I said unhurriedly, 'turn around and look at the TV headlines. A bomb has exploded at the Rome railway station. Do you think it was that suitcase?'

Before he had a chance to answer, our photographs, taken from CCTV footage, were being blasted all over the screen and with it a caption reading.

Nationwide search for suspected train station bombers.

CHAPTER EIGHT
Dubrovnik

Claudia

The guard had been spot-on and, not long after pulling out of the gate, there was Max, on the scooter, marooned by the side of the road. Seeing the approaching Rolls Royce, he stuck out his thumb and pretended to be hitchhiking.

'Get in,' I ordered, after we had pulled over. 'How on Earth did you outfox me in the UK? You're a bumbling buffoon. It was Olivia, for sure. Behind every good man is a better woman.'

I immediately regretting saying *Good Man*, knowing I was inviting a retort. 'Don't say anything,' I commanded, pointing a finger towards him. Then it struck me, this was the game I loved to play with Linda, bantering back and forth.

Is he really a buffoon or is he very clever and am I falling for his tricks?

Monya's private jet that had flown us to Moscow was fuelled and waiting to take us to Dubrovnik. This time we weren't alone and were welcomed aboard by a smartly dressed hostess.

'Good morning Claudia and sir. My name is Nikola and Monya has asked me to look after your needs on the flight. Can I get you anything?'

'Breakfast,' Max said before I had a chance to decline the offer.

What the hell, I thought, why not and said, 'That sounds good and so does coffee.'

'I'll just fetch the pilot and co-pilot their coffees,' said Nikola, 'and, the moment we are in the air, I will organise your breakfast.'

We had been on board for ten minutes when the plane started taxiing down the runway followed by a sprint into the sky. Outside, not a cloud could be seen and I gazed out the window, entranced by the endless blue and the green of the countryside. Soon, Nikola was back, holding a tray, on which were positioned our coffees.

'Milk?' she asked.

'That would be nice,' said Max.

I nodded, still admiring the beautiful scenery from my window.

Nikola placed the coffees on a table that separated Max from myself. Two minutes passed before I focused my attention inside

170

the plane and moved my hand to the coffee cup ready to take a sip. I noticed that Max hadn't touched his drink and was gazing at me.

'What's wrong?'

'Have you met Nikola before?'

'No.'

'It's probably nothing. Olivia tells me all the time that I'm paranoid but something doesn't feel right. Nikola is too nice - you don't know her and she was ignorant of my name. If Monya had asked her to look after you, he would have told her who was flying with you. But, maybe he wouldn't? I don't know, Claudia, but I would feel a whole lot better if you went up front and checked on our pilots, before I take a sip – you know, to make sure the coffee has agreed with them!'

'It's not unusual for a hostess to be on a flight but, you're right, I haven't met Nikola and Monya would generally tell me if someone new was on the scene.'

I too was now feeling uneasy.

He would always tell me.

Before rising from my seat, I checked for Nikola and, seeing nothing, I assumed that she was busy in the galley.

'Wait here,' I said, 'and yell out if she returns and starts towards the cockpit while I'm in there.'

I made my way to the pilots and tapped lightly on the door. There was no reply so I turned the door handle, pushed the door open and poked my head inside. Max was right, the pilot and co-pilot were slumped at the controls. The plane must have been on auto-pilot as we were flying level and steady. Quietly, I pulled the door closed and made my way back to my seat, unseen by Nikola.

'Your right,' I whispered. 'The coffee must be drugged, but I couldn't tell if the pilots were unconscious or dead. We're on autopilot.'

'What's the plan?' asked Max quietly.

'Let's play dead and, when she gets close enough, we take her out. Wait for my move.'

Max didn't reply but closed his eyes, sank back into his chair and let his arm fall over the armrest and into the aisle. I took a similar pose but with head resting back against the seat and my mouth slightly ajar. I held my eyes lightly closed so that I could just make out the shapes in front of me.

We didn't have to wait long and I sensed her before I saw her. Then she spoke.

'Well, well, well, the great Claudia. Not so impressive now, are we and they said you would be difficult to kill.'

Lunging with the ferocity and speed of a cobra, I struck, gripping her around the throat. The motion sent her crashing to the ground and her head thudded and then cracked when it slammed into the floor. She went limp as I fell on top of her.

'How is she?' I heard Max ask.

'Dead!' I replied coldly, while standing.

'Well that's taken a nasty turn. I hope you can fly this thing?' he added sarcastically before continuing. 'Do you know why she would want to kill you?'

'I have no idea,' I confessed. 'Any number of people would be pleased to see the end of me.'

'What a wonderful life you must live, Claudia but back to my serious question. Can you fly the plane?'

'No.' I said and paused before taking a deep breath. 'Let's hope the pilots are alive.'

Grabbing Nikola, I pulled her out of the way so that Max could leave his seat without tripping over the body.

'Come on,' I said. 'Let's go up front and find out what we are dealing with. I have no intention of dying up here!'

We made our way to the cockpit and, as before, the pilots were slumped at the controls. Firstly, I checked the co-pilot.

'He's dead.' I said to Max.

'And the pilot?' he asked.

Turning, I placed two fingers on her neck and felt for a pulse.

'She's alive! Can you hear me?' I said loudly, but she didn't respond.

I put both hands on her shoulders and repeatedly shook her gently while saying again, 'Can you hear me?'

Her eyes opened and stared blankly back at me before closing again.

'Come on, wake up, wake up,' I said loudly while shaking her more vigorously.

This time, when her eyes opened, they showed some signs of life, awareness like a candle fighting to stay alight in a breeze.

'Will you be able to land the plane?' I demanded with no regard for her wellbeing.

She shook her head.

'Can we get you anything?' I heard Max ask kindly.

'Water,' she rasped in a voice reminiscent of a person dying of thirst after two weeks lost in a desert.

'I'll get it,' Max answered before leaving the cockpit.

Why didn't I ask if she needed anything?

I dismissed the thought as weak and stared out of the windscreen into the expanse of blue.

'What the hell are you doing?' yelled Max angrily when he returned. 'Keep her awake, keep her talking or she will die and we with her.'

I knew that he was right so began shaking her again. 'Max is here with your water. Come on, wake up! We have your water.'

She roused and Max pushed past me holding the glass. He took her head and cradled it with a wrinkled hand, lifted it and pressed the glass tenderly against her lips, helping her to take a sip of water.

'We think you were poisoned. We are sorry but your co-pilot didn't make it. Now listen to me, you have to stay with us.'

He looked directly into her eyes and in a firm but caring voice said, 'Do you understand me. You can't go back to sleep.'

Before she had a chance to respond, he continued, 'I want you to tell us how to land this plane.' Turning to me he directed, 'Claudia, get the co-pilot out of that seat. You're going to fly this thing.'

He returned his attention to the pilot. 'What's your name?'

'Melanie-Jane.'

'I knew a Melanie-Jane once, a wonderful artist – she had this mad dog but kind of cute. Can you paint?'

'No,' she replied, 'but I do have a crazy dog, a golden retriever called Basil.'

'That's it, Melanie-Jane,' continued Max. 'I want you to keep talking to us and I want to hear all about Basil but can you walk us through a landing first? You will do the chit-chat and we'll do the flying.'

'I don't have to because we have ILS, an Instrument Landing System on board. All you must do is put out a MAYDAY call. We change course towards a major airport and traffic control will do the rest. They will tell you how to program the computer and the plane will land itself.'

'Sweetie, that's not going to happen,' I interrupted. 'If we do that the authorities will be all over us when we land. They will use it as an excuse to raid Monya's house and our government

175

connections won't be able to stop them. We either land at our private airstrip or crash into the sea where nobody can find us.'

'I'm sorry, Claudia,' said Melanie-Jane, 'I'm not thinking straight. There is another way. We have parachutes onboard. I will tell you how to lose altitude until we are at a safe height to open the doors. You two bail out while I hold the plane steady and level, I'll then use the auto-pilot to get me over the sea before ditching her nose first into the water. Nobody will ever find it.'

'What about you?' asked Max.

'Someone has to fly it into the water, assuming I can. Unfortunately, my arms seem to be numb but some feeling is returning.'

'That's not going to happen either,' I interjected harshly, staring at Melanie-Jane. 'You won't be capable of flying it into the sea.'

'For a second, I thought you cared,' said Max mockingly.

'I care about a lot of things and not dying is one of them,' I snapped back. 'Okay Melanie-Jane, let's land.'

She didn't respond.

'Max, wake her up.'

Looking over I saw her head had slumped as if unconscious. It took a couple of attempts before Max could again rouse her.

'What do I do?' I asked.

In a groggy but coherent voice, Melanie-Jane started her landing instructions.

'Look out of the window. We are flying level because the autopilot is on. When you want to descend, push gently on the stick, the steering wheel in front of you, and pull back when we are ready to level out, just like a video game. Because you can see the ground out of the window and the sky at the same time, you will know when we are flying level again. Look to your right. See a button glowing blue and displaying the letters AP? That's the autopilot. I want you to look directly in front of you. Can you see the compass? It has an image of an airplane inside of it.'

'Yes,' I answered.

'Good, underneath, there's a digital readout from the compass giving us our bearing. It's showing SW 225. That means we are flying South West on bearing 225, and you need to stay on that course. Now take a deep breath and hold the wheel. Max, I want you to push the blue button and switch off the autopilot because I want Claudia to take us down a few thousand feet.'

'This one?' Max asked, pointing toward the blue button, but Melanie-Jane didn't respond. He gave her another gentle shake before repeating the question.

'That's it, now push it in and remove your finger.'

The moment the autopilot light went out I could feel the plane through my hands.

'I've got it,' I said.

'Good, Claudia, now push gently forward on the stick.'

I followed her instructions. The nose of the plane tipped downwards and we began descending. Through the window the ground that was once a blur took form and I saw that we were flying over a mountain range which was becoming closer.

'When do you want me to level out?' I asked, but Melanie-Jane didn't respond.

'Melanie-Jane!' I repeated loudly. 'When do I level out?'

She didn't answer.

'Max!'

'You're doing well,' Max replied calmly, 'but I think you should level out now, because we have some towering mountains in front of us.'

I pulled gently back on the stick until we were flying level.

'Is she dead?' I asked.

When he didn't reply, I looked across and saw him checking her breathing.

'Unconscious again,' he said finally.

Holding the plane level, I could see that, within five or ten minutes, I would either have go up and over or around a looming mountain.

'See if you can wake her,' I said and then listened.

Max called out, 'Melanie-Jane, wake up, Melanie-Jane.'

After a few unsuccessful attempts, he fell silent before asking a question that I was not expecting, not here and not now.

'Why didn't you kill me back in Scotland?'

Before I had a chance to answer, the plane suddenly started dropping, free falling towards the ground. It was not a dive, more a falling brick. The force knocked Max off his feet and I managed to stay at the controls only because I had the wheel to hold onto. We were out of control and losing altitude. If we didn't stop the descent we would smash into the mountain side.

I pulled hard back on the wheel, trying to regain some height, but still we fell, heading closer to the ground. I pulled back even more. The control panel in front of me lit up like a Christmas tree with flashing lights and warning buzzers simultaneous echoing throughout the cockpit.

'Push down!' Max yelled. 'Push down or we'll stall.'

Contrary to my intuition which was telling me to pull back, because we were still heading downwards, I did as he instructed and pushed forward.

'More power,' he commanded next. 'The throttles are in the middle and on your right. Push them forward, gently.'

With the stick pushed forward the nose slowly began to respond and faced towards the ground. Following Max's instructions, I added more power and the ground raced towards us. Looking to my right and then to the left, I saw that we were diving between the mountains and into a valley.

'That's it,' I heard Max's voice say as our plane screamed ever downward. 'Now ease back on the stick. I'm going to reduce the power for you and, when she points upwards, I will give her a gut full.'

A what?

'More power,' Max said.

Gradually our decent began to slow, but the ground kept racing towards us.

'Come on,' I said. 'Pull up, pull up.'

We were now so close to the earth that I could make out individual rocks below; then, as if the plane heard my command, the nose began to lift. Still the land was rushing closer until finally we began to level out and fly around forty feet above the ground with mountains surrounding us on either side. The plane slowly lifted skyward and, at the same time, shook violently as Max pushed the throttles forward and the jet engines roared with maximum power.

With the immediate threat of crashing into the ground over, the next obstacle, a solid wall of rock, now confronted us as the valley came to an end.

'Climb, come on climb,' repeated Max, and I pulled back harder on the stick. The engines bellowed.

As the mountain loomed in front and slamming into it seemed inevitable, sweat started trickling down my face. I recalled my military training and focused. Evermore we pointed skywards until the plane felt as if it was climbing vertically, scaling the mountain only feet away which filled the front window.

When everything seemed lost, the mountain peak fell away and we cleared the top. Breathing out in relief, I heard Max's voice and glanced over. I saw him hanging onto the pilot's chair, trying to stop himself from being sent flying to the rear of the cockpit.

'Ease the nose down, Claudia,' he said coolly, 'and reduce the throttle. I can't reach it for you. Then let her climb gently. We still need to get over that big one in front.'

With the crisis over, the cockpit gradually returned to normal. The alarms ceased flashing and buzzing, engines gave a more comfortable hum and Max stood without clinging on.

'I think we hit an air pocket, or air turbulence – anyway, well done, Claudia.'

'Thank you, Max,' I said, wiping the perspiration from my face with one hand and levelling the plane with the other. 'Once we clear that big one, we will be free of the mountain range, then we will have to think of putting her down. How's Melanie-Jane?'

'Melanie-Jane,' I heard him call before saying, 'I almost managed to rouse her, but then she drifted off again.' After a short pause, he said. 'Claudia, you didn't answer my question from before. Why didn't you kill me in Scotland?'

He's still asking me, after all we've just been through and what is to come. What is it about this man?

In truth, I had been thinking about this question since Scotland. I always knew at some point he was going to ask but hadn't settled on an answer. Sometimes I rehearsed punishing him for not knowing who I was and blaming him for everything I hated about my life. At other times, I heard myself speaking warmly and saying, *you don't remember me? I was the little girl you saved*, and thanking him for all I loved about my life. I'm unsure how long I was lost in my own thoughts before I heard Max's voice breaking the silence.

'I know you, don't I?'

'What makes you say that?'

'I saw it written in your eyes the first morning on the submarine and then again when we were having dinner with Monya. You gazed at me with warmth but I sensed disappointment too, perhaps because I hadn't recognised you. Mostly, when you look at me, you can't hide the loathing and I fear that must be an awful burden for you to bear. Your feelings are contrary but together they tell me that I should know you.'

There was an awkward moment of silence before Max continued, 'You're wrong, Claudia, because I have never forgotten you. I still see you in my dreams and you are forever etched into my heart as that little girl and not the woman you are. I see you now.'

He paused again, trying to entice me into filling the void.

I wasn't going to say anything but, despite the lump in my throat and my lonesome emptiness I had to know, I found myself saying. 'When did you know?'

'I was reminded of you when Monya mentioned Macinec. Then slowly it seemed to make sense. I wasn't sure until now, when you asked me, *when*.'

I felt tricked but relieved at the same time and, unsure of what to say, chose silence. Max wasn't going to let up.

'Is this the life for which you hoped?'

'It's the life I know,' I replied.

'That wasn't my question.'

'Sweetie, you don't know me,' I retorted angrily, before regaining my composure and continuing. 'You have no idea of the kind of person I am.'

'I was there when you shot Elinor and Detective Wells in Mawnan cemetery and it was most likely you who caused the crash in Poland that almost killed Olivia and me. Yet, I have seen you show mercy. We are all complex, Claudia, people made and formed from our experiences, which is why I want to ask for your forgiveness. Forgiveness for the hurt that Olivia and I have caused you.'

'Don't preach at me,' I snapped, before once again quelling my anger. 'I'm not one of your Sunday parishioners.' Then in scornful laugher I added, 'Sweetie, were you really a priest or was that just your cover as a spy?'

'I'm not talking about religion. If you can't forgive you will forever be the victim, blaming everyone but yourself for whatever wrong befalls you. Seeking revenge because of what someone did, or didn't do. Forgiveness isn't about forgetting or excusing but, by forgiving, you are accepting the reality of what happened, rather than being bound by it. You become the master of your own destiny, as someone once said.'

'Pathetic,' I mocked. 'If you are going to throw around other people's quotes, you should at least know where they come from. Sweetie, it's from Napoleon Hill and, if you really trying to pull at my heart strings, why not try Nelson Mandela, *I am the master of my fate: I am the captain of my soul.* I'm no longer that little girl. I am Claudia. So, stop this now and it's time you woke Melanie-Jane again.'

'You're well-read but you still haven't answered my question. Why didn't you shoot me?'

'If you must know, I was about to pull the trigger when I recognised you, from Macinec. It was unexpected, I was unsettled and I couldn't go through with it. Whatever the reason, it doesn't really matter, because here you are.'

'Yes, here *we* are! Do you know, Claudia, you're not angry at me because of Macinec. You're angry because you cared.'

Max turned away from me, placed his hands around the pilot and shook her gently.

'Melanie – Melanie-Jane, you need to wake up.'

We had flown clear of the last mountain and I felt my hands relax on the wheel. Glancing at the compass, I saw that we were tracking 225 south west, our intended course. The terrain below had become a little less rugged but seemed an impossible landscape on which to land. Off into the distance, the Mediterranean was coming into view. My heart started to race as I deliberated on what I was about to suggest.

'I'm going to fly out over the sea, look for a spot where we won't be seen and ditch the plane into the water. We'll not survive but our secrets will go down with us.'

I eased forward on the wheel, frightened of crashing prematurely, but wanting to lose altitude.

'See,' said Max, calmly considering the situation. 'You do care, a misguided loyalty I grant you, but loyalty nonetheless.'

'You make me laugh, Max. Don't you ever give up? Crashing into the Mediterranean isn't my road to Damascus. I'm not going to have an epiphany, or dramatic conversion just before I die—*please God forgive me for all my sins and by the way I'm sorry about all those people I killed, oh and the stealing. Don't forget the tax evasion and being a despicable person – Amen! Can I have eternal life now*? Sweetie, what a load of rubbish! I'll leave that kind of hypocrisy to people like you.'

I glanced at the compass then eased back on the wheel, levelling out ready to fly over the sea. When Max did not reply, I peered across at him, disappointed that our argument had come to an end. Then, our eyes met and he smiled.

'Can you promise me one thing Claudia, if we walk away from this? Your knowledge of Shakespeare, poetry, the classics and religion, it's not what one expects. Not just because of what you do, but where you are from. I would love to know the story, so promise me that you will tell me.'

I laughed again, but before I could respond to Max, I heard a groan coming from Melanie-Jane. She was coming around.

'Is she awake?' I asked.

He didn't answer me but instead started chatting to our pilot.

'Welcome back, we were becoming worried. You still have to tell me all about Basil, your crazy dog.'

I saw Melanie-Jane smile when he mentioned her dog.

'We have cleared the mountain range and the Mediterranean is in front. It's time we thought about putting this baby down. Do you think you can do that?'

'I can't use my arms and legs,' replied Melanie-Jane. 'I have some movement but they are weak. I can't hold the stick or use the rudders. I can try and talk you down.'

She turned her head towards me but she was looking at the compass and other instruments and not me.

'Excellent, we are on the right heading. The altitude is too low because we need to make a turn, and we are carrying a little too much airspeed. Considering everything, we are in excellent shape. Claudia, you see the compass in front of you?'

'Yes,' I answered.

'Good,' continued Melanie-Jane. 'We are going to make a gentle right turn in two stages because we don't want to bank. I want you to ease the plane to the right by turning the wheel until the compass reads 270. Slowly, now.'

Cautiously, I turned right.

'That's it,' I heard the pilot say encouragingly. 'Ease up a bit – very good – now a little more, okay that's perfect, we are coming up on 270 so level off. Very good, our airspeed is still good and we didn't lose much altitude. Now for the next part. Again, I want you to ease her to the right until the heading reads 310.'

I took another deep breath, focused and felt a feeling of control wash over my body.

'Here we go.'

As we approached the heading 310, I straightened the wheel.

'Okay,' said Melanie-Jane. 'Max, I want you to pull back on the throttles, those levers in the middle, very gently until I say stop.'

I could see Max from the corner of my eye following Melanie-Jane's instructions. As he pulled back on the throttles, the engines changed tune and I felt the aeroplane slow.

'Now Claudia,' continued Melanie-Jane, 'ease the nose down. We are beginning our landing.'

'Where?' I inquired.

'Soon you will be able to see our runway but, before we can land, you need to attend to our landing sequence. On your right, you will see some levers, next to the throttles. They are the slats and flaps. In a minute, I am going to get Max to give them a couple of clicks, which will allow us to fly at a lower speed without stalling, the speed we need for landing. In front of you is an airspeed indicator. With help from Max, I will keep that in the green for you, so that you don't have to worry about the plane's speed. When I put on the flaps, I want you to push forward just a fraction more on the stick, but not yet.'

From the window, the runway came into view. The terrain below was now rugged and was moving closer as we descended.

'Okay Claudia,' Melanie-Jane instructed, 'here we go.'

Max applied the flap, causing the plane to slow and continue its descent towards the runway.

I loosened and then tightened my grip on the wheel, flexing my fingers as I did. Unexpectedly, the plane rolled, dipping to the left and then to the right and then back to the left. At the same time, it dropped and I could tell that we were not going to make it to the runway. In front, a red light started flashing and a cockpit alarm sounded. With the plane pitching one way and then the next, I moved the wheel to the right to correct the wings when they dipped to the left and then to the left when they dipped to the right.

'Hold the stick still!' commanded Melanie-Jane in a loud rasping voice, still affected by the drugs. 'Power Max, give me power!'

Like a waking giant, the engines roared to life, causing the plane to shake as it rolled.

'More power,' she demanded. The side to side rolling eased but the ground raced to greet us. 'Pull back on the stick.'

I instantly obeyed and with millimetres to spare we scraped over the trees.

'Landing gear, Max,' was her next command. 'There on your right.'

The plane shuddered again as the landing gear descended and locked into place. We were straying too far to the left and would miss the runway.

'Claudia,' ordered the pilot calmly, 'correct the drift. I want you to steer to the right and Max will power down.'

The tone from the engines changed once again, the roar becoming a hum.

'Stick forward. Claudia, bring your feet together, there are two pedals in the middle. They are the brakes. Wait for my command.'

I did as she had instructed.

'Bring the stick back,' she said next as we cleared the trees and were now over the runway. 'A bit more, that's it. Max, power down, power down. More please.'

THUD and then a screech as the wheels under the wings hit the ground.

'Nose down, all the way. Power off. Brakes, squeeze the brakes.'

The change in the sensation of speed was immediate the moment we hit the tarmac. The plane now raced along the bitumen like a car out of control. The end of the runway was fast approaching.

'We're not going to stop!' I cried.

'Be buggered if we are going to die after all of this,' swore Melanie-Jane. 'Max, pull the throttles all the way back and put her into reverse.'

The engines came to life again but this time they were almost deafening in their roar. I joined the chorus by pushing harder against the pedals and saying.

'Come on, come on, slow down.'

The end of the runway was seconds way and we would be sent hurtling into the trees if we did not halt the forward motion. At the last moment, the plane's front wheel smashed into a hole and we came to a rest.

'Power off, Max,' came Melanie-Jane's voice.

She then gave a deep sigh and said, 'We are down. Well done everyone and welcome to Dubrovnik.'

CHAPTER NINE

Venice

Jean-Marc

'Inspector, Inspector!' Olivia called urgently.

'Lady Olivia, you must really try and practise. I am Jean-Marc, your private secretary,' I replied with a yawn, having been woken from a slumber.

'Yes, yes, from now on I promise. But Jean-Marc,' she said unhurriedly yet with a touch of exasperation showing in her voice. 'Turn around and look at the TV headlines. A bomb has exploded at the Rome railway station. Do you think it was that suitcase, the one I encouraged you to open?'

"Encourage" is not how I recall it.

Before I had a chance to answer, I watched as our photographs, from CCTV footage taken at the station, were being displayed on the screen accompanied with the caption: *Nationwide search underway for suspected train station bombers.*

'Well, that's taken a nasty turn,' I said. A statement that caused Lady Oliva to smile and for me to look back inquisitively.

'That's exactly what Max would have said,' she replied and I could tell that she was thinking of him, missing him as we faced another apparently insurmountable obstacle to his rescue, being wanted by the Italian Police.

At the mention of Max, I hesitated for a second before taking the opportunity to ask the question that had been on my mind for a while.

'Have you thought about why Claudia would take Max with her? I wondered if you had met her before?'

Olivia wasn't surprised by my question - she may have asked herself the same thing.

'You're not the first person to ask me that,' she said. 'Stephen did during my debriefing. At the time I said that I didn't know but I have a nagging in the back of my mind that won't leave me. The more I examine her photo, the more I feel that I'm missing something important. Claudia killed without mercy when we were in Cornwall, so she must have had a reason for taking him. We know nothing that would be of interest to her. There must be a link between us and the answers on the tip of my tongue but it won't come. I'm sure it's important but, in the meantime, my good secretary, we should concentrate on how we're going to get ourselves out of the Venice railway station. The police will be everywhere at Venice and they have our images.'

'I've been thinking about the same thing but, other than leaving on the wrong side of the train and making a break for it, I am at a loss. No disrespect intended, that option would be difficult at your age.'

'As Max would say, Jean-Marc, I have a cunning plan.'

'Why am I not surprised.' I said, smiling as I shifted my weight to the back of the seat, ready to listen to what I imagined was going to be something unexpected.

I had chased Max and Olivia across Britain and they were ingenious in the ways they avoided capture. My favourite was when they concealed themselves as pillion passengers on the back of Harley-Davidson motorcycles with burly bikers as their drivers. It didn't occur to our police at the road blocks to look for two eighty-seven-year old's wearing black leathers and riding astride thumping machines, they simply rode right on past and it was rumoured that they even waved.

'Can you reach the small travelling case?' asked Lady Olivia, pointing to a piece of her luggage stored overhead. 'When I went shopping in Paris, I took the opportunity to purchase a few things, just in case we needed to blend in,' she said smiling, which I immediately knew meant, "Stick-Out".

I rose, took down the case and placed it on the table in between us. 'Where, may I ask, did you go in Paris?'

'Do you require an address or the name of the shop?'

'Let's start with the address; consider it a test of my shopping knowledge.' I said and, in a teasing voice, added. 'Places of note for the discerning Paris shopper, m'lady.'

'Number 8 Rue Madame.'

'Lady Olivia, that one is not ringing any bells, I must confess.'

'Well done, Jean-Marc you're right on two accounts,' she said, giving me a wry smile.

Her statement took me by surprise and I stared back blankly trying to make sense of the clue that had been thrown my way.

She nodded towards the case and I opened the lid, revealing liturgical vestments. A black priest's cassock, a wide-brimmed hat and white collar. Searching underneath, I found clothing for a nun, but not the full black habit. Instead it was a blue tunic, white shirt and a modest blue veil. In addition, there were two pairs of black shoes. I looked up in astonishment.

'You can't get the good old-fashioned nun's habit by walking in off the street. They are made to order, or so the man behind the counter told me. I could have gone to a fancy-dress shop but an astute observer would have been able to tell the difference. Anyway, the church is modernising, so I am a contemporary nun, which is bit of a hoot at my age.'

'Don't you think a nun and priest going on a cruise together may seem a little odd?'

'Odd? Not in the least,' replied Lady Olivia. 'They will think you are my carer or my doctor. I would be a real cougar if it were lover. But anyway, by the time we board the ship we will be Lady Olivia and her private secretary again.' Olivia continued, her manner becoming serious, 'There's no time for idle gossip, we will arrive in Venice Santa Lucia station in ten minutes. I suggest we change and take ourselves and our luggage to where the economy meets the business class carriages. With good fortune, people will be milling around the door, when the train stops, we can slip off with them, hidden amongst the crowd.'

I wanted to remind Olivia of what Stephen from MI6 had said, about being a grey person, going unnoticed. Her strategy of being obviously different had worked before and it was too late to argue with her. Before we changed, I couldn't resist asking about her pun.

'Your little joke, Lady Olivia, or should I say, Sister Olivia. That the shop address was not ringing any bells and you replied that I was right on two counts?'

'Was it that bad, Jean-Marc? Perhaps because Max was a priest, I think everyone will understand a little religious joke. You confessed that "it was not ringing any bells". When you said, *I must confess* – confessions - and then, *not ring any bells* – the bells rung during the Catholic Mass, before the consecration and the showing of both the Eucharistic Bread and chalice. You see, both are references to religion, priests and nuns.'

I sighed, and shaking my head said. 'Lady Olivia.'

***

We both changed and I was surprised by how well the new disguises hid our identities.

Sister Olivia, as she now was, looked unrecognisable and I faded from view in my religious orders.

It's strange how priests are both visible and invisible simultaneously.

Our bags were now fewer in number because, following the flight from Paris to Rome, we had each ditched all but one suitcase and Olivia's travel bag and elegant cane. We made our way through the carriage to congregate with the other passengers disembarking at the final stop: Venice Santa Lucia.

The train slowed and finally came to a stop. Rather than the pushing and shoving we had expected, the button on the train exit was pushed for us and the horde of passengers waited as two other travellers lifted our luggage from the train and placed it on the platform before returning to help us down.

When I booked the cruise, the website had said that ten cruise ships were due in Venice on this day. It recommended pre-book of a taxi to the cruise port because of the expected high demand. It was no surprise that the train station was like an ants' nest with countless people scurrying around. We stood still for a few minutes,

196

surveying the scene. The police were manning all the exits but did not appear to be checking documents, but as people walked past in single file, they examined them intently. Along the platform, I saw luggage trolleys with the names of the cruise ships attached to them.

'Come on,' I said to Sister Olivia.

I dragged both of our cases, leaving Olivia to manage her travel bag, and went over to the porter standing next to the trolley with our ship's name on it, enquiring as to what the signs meant.

'Twenty Euros each, Father and we will take your bags to the cruise ship for you. When you get on board they will be waiting outside your stateroom door. All I need is to see your boarding ticket. If you have printed the luggage tags, that would be fantastic, otherwise we can make them for you.'

'Sister,' I said, looking at Olivia, 'I think it will be far easier than trying to lug them there ourselves.' Then looking back to the porter, I continued, 'They're all yours.'

Cassocks are designed so trousers underneath can be reached. From my pockets, I took our cruise tickets and luggage tags. Handing the tags to the porter, I swiftly flashed the boarding pass which I hoped would satisfy his requirements. Immediately, he looked uncertain.

'Father,' he said with an air of embarrassment, 'the sister's ticket said Lady Olivia.'

'Ah, you have a keen eye, my son. Indeed, it does. Once we are free of the railway station and before we board the ship, the sister and I will be changing our clothes, to travel incognito as it were. People can feel uncomfortable around us. That's why we are keeping our little travel bag with us. It has our civilian clothes in it. I'm sure you understand.

'Indeed I do, Father. My brother is a policeman and, when he's away on holiday, he invents another occupation if someone asks what he does for a living. Father, your secret is safe with me.'

'Saying you're a nun,' added Olivia, 'can be a real show stopper. People flee.'

The porter laughed and said, 'I can imagine they would Sister—' but stopped himself, before saying, 'Sorry Sister, I meant no offence.'

With our heads slightly bowed, as if in silent contemplation and without looking overly suspicious, we joined the line to file past the police and out of the exit. Slowly, we moved forward, with me dragging the hand luggage and Olivia tapping away with her cane. As we drew closer, I could see that the police officers were holding photographs.

As each person approached, they studied the photograph and then the face of the person next in line. Even if it was a child, a person obviously not the bomber, they repeated the process.

Slightly behind the police was a group of other people who had been pulled aside for a thorough security check. Police, accompanied by army personnel, were searching their suitcases and checking their identification. Alarmingly, most of those being stopped were elderly women. Despite our disguises, Olivia's age would categorically have her pulled aside.

This is not going to work, we must come up with an alternative plan, before it's too late.

I tapped Olivia gently on the shoulder and called, 'Sister.'

She turned, unable to hide the fear she was feeling as we approached the security check. I indicated, by turning my head, that we should step out of the line, which we did only metres away from the exit and the awaiting police. Ordinarily, this would have aroused the suspicion of the police but, today, we were two more of many people milling around, even this close to the exit.

'Sorry Sister, I need to powder my nose before we leave.'

Olivia gave me a— *what on earth are you talking about?* look.

'Use the gentlemen's, a toilet stop,' I continued.

Without waiting for a response and, dragging her travel case behind me, I left Olivia alone to watch the crowed.

The men's privy was busy but not overly crowded. Within a minute a cubicle had become vacant. After entering, I waited a brief time before opening the door again but this time stepping out backwards.

To the first person I saw, while feigning distress, I said, 'It's a bomb. Look! Someone has left a case in there— just like Rome.'

Olivia's travel case, with items removed that could identify, was on top of the toilet seat. To any onlooker, it was clear that it had been deliberately placed there and not left behind accidently.

Walking as quickly as I could to re-join Olivia, I said to many passers-by, 'There's a bomb in the men's toilet.'

We pushed back into the queue, before the panic had a chance to reach where we were. Turning to the person behind and the person behind her, I repeated my story, 'There's a bomb in the men's toilet!'

I could feel the line begin to surge. The panic which I'd set in motion when leaving the toilet was spreading and was now being fuelled by people in the line.

'Hold onto me,' I said, grabbing Olivia tightly, as we were pushed forward.

'There's a bomb,' I heard someone else scream.

The line surged again and I tightened my grip on Olivia. There were now three people in front of us and then the police. Those in front pushed past without waiting to be checked. The police were distracted from their duty, looking about and assessing the alarm rippling through the station. Comprehension swept across their faces. If they did nothing, in a matter of seconds, the crowd would be a stampede and people would be crushed to death. They flung open the gate and we were pushed through by the force of those behind us.

Once out of the station, I immediately stepped to one side and pulled Olivia over to me, heading off at right angles to the others, trying to reduce our chances of being trampled. After twenty paces, we made our way down the steps in front of the railway station and out onto the edge of the grand canal with its water bus stops.

The area in front of the canal was a hive of activity with people milling around, seemingly unaffected by the chaos unfolding in the railway station behind.

'I think we should move away from here as quickly as we can and catch a water taxi from one of the quieter canals to the cruise port,' I said to Olivia.

With her arm still linked through mine, we turned left, intending to walk to the Ponte delle Gugle, a historic canal bridge famous for its gargoyles, where I thought that we would be able to secure transport. As we began to leave, I became aware of two men, and while it was impossible to be certain, they appeared to be Russian thugs.

'Olivia,' I whispered, 'I think we are being followed – Russian Mafia.'

'How can that be?' she replied. 'They surely weren't expecting a priest and nun.'

It was then that it occurred to me, why we stood out as the Inspector and Olivia.

'Your elegant cane, Olivia, you're still using it. Maybe that's how they identified us. As soon as we lose them, we'll remove these costumes and dump the cane. Perhaps a nice umbrella will do instead? Then we'll get ourselves onto that ship.'

We pushed into the crowd and weaved through the flood of people, trying to lose the men watching us. A narrow lane, the Calle de la Misericordia, appeared on our left and we stepped in, hoping they did not see us turn. It was deserted and wouldn't offer any protection if we were followed.

'Where are we going?' asked Olivia.

'See up there, in front of us?' I said, pointing to a large green sign, which looked deservedly out of place, hanging from the side of a building. 'That's the hotel Santa Lucia and it backs on to a park, the Parco Savorgnan. I thought we could slip through the hotel, into the park and come out near the gargoyle bridge. Hopefully, that will give the Russians the slip.'

'Jean-Marc,' quivered Olivia's voice and I looked at her, concerned. 'It's like someone has just walked on my grave, a disturbance in the force as *Star Wars* watchers would say. Something is not right but I can't quite put my finger on it. It's something about that name – Santa Lucia.'

Checking behind and, although concerned for Olivia, I was relieved as we were the only people in the lane and had not been followed.

Looking back towards the sign, I said, 'It's been a difficult start to our day. I can understand why you may be feeling a little unsettled. Let's grab a coffee and a bite to eat before we take the water taxi, be tourists, if just for half-an-hour.' After a short pause, I added, 'Lucia is also the name of the Venice railway station. That's probably where you've seen it. Not one of our best experiences, was it?'

'That maybe it,' replied Olivia, sounding a little more assured.

We entered the hotel, walked through their outdoor eating area, and into beautiful gardens. Feeling safer, we didn't rush but instead savoured the greenery as we seated ourselves on one of the garden benches in this secret oasis of Venice. Later, we left the gardens through another building and came out on to a canal.

To my dismay, we'd not lost our Russian friends and they were waiting for us, twenty metres away from where we stepped out. The foot traffic was light running alongside of this waterway, the Fondamenta Venier Sebastiano. There were no bustling cafés and a place that had tables and chairs outside was empty. The Mafia could easily take us out here, slipping away unnoticed, through the same gardens through which we had just walked.

'Olivia, we're in trouble,' I said, indicating with my eyes towards the thugs.

I quickly scanned the area for possible ways of escape. Spotting a water taxi expectantly waiting for its next fare, its motor idling, I guided Olivia hurriedly across to it. Before we reached it, I whispered into her ear, 'Let me get in first.'

'Buongiorno – good morning, my son,' I started, with a reassuring smile to the boat master, trying to be as charming as possible while hiding my sense of urgency. From the corner of my eye, I could see our pursuers closing in, now alerted to our intended means of escape. 'The good sister and I would like to go the Cruise Port.'

'Si Padre,' he said and extended his hand towards Sister Olivia, who rather than accepting it, took a step back in hesitation.

'Perhaps my son, you could help me aboard first, then we can both assist the good sister. She's a little hesitant of stepping onto a rocking boat, seeing she needs a walking stick for balance.'

Olivia briefly waved her cane in his direction for added effect.

He extended his hand again, this time to me and I took it, stepping off the dock and on to the vessel. Our hunters had now broken into a sprint, trying to close the gap before we fled. The taxi man, being unaware of their approach, turned leisurely and put one leg up on to the edge of the boat, then paused to ensure his footage was solid by moving it back and forth a couple of times. After what seemed an age, he leant forward and reached out towards Olivia. As he did so, I gave him a great big, heave-ho-push, shoving him over the edge and into the water. Olivia slipped the boat's tether from its bollard and leapt into the taxi. It all happened with such speed and agility that I was stunned.

'At eighty-seven!' I said aloud, before regaining my sense of urgency and racing to the front of the water taxi and its controls.

I pushed the engines to full throttle and the bow lifted clean out of the water by the sudden acceleration, which forced me to hang on tightly to the steering wheel so as not to fall. I glanced over my shoulder, frightened that I may have sent Olivia cartwheeling over the stern of the boat and into the water. I needn't have been concerned because she gave me a grin and a friendly wave with one hand, while holding onto her nun's veil so it wouldn't blow off in the wind, with the other. Seeing her seated on the red leather, I noted that she looked elegant, almost regal. With a flag flapping behind her hair, it reminded me of a scene from some famous black and white movie. One whose title I couldn't remember. My thoughts didn't wander for long because, in our wake, I could see the Russians, who had stolen a boat and were now in hot pursuit.

Passing under the gargoyle bridge I opened the taxi up to full throttle. I didn't hear it, because of the noise of the motor echoing off the buildings and sound of the boat cutting through the water, but a bullet shattered the windscreen in front of me. I should not have been surprised, but I was momentarily taken aback with the realisation that they were now trying to kill us. I glanced over my shoulder. Olivia must have heard the shot and was ducking for cover by lying across the back seat.

'Hang on,' I yelled, weaving the boat first to the left and then back to the right as another bullet embedded itself into the wood next to me.

Bang, bang, bang!

Now I could hear guns being fired in quick succession but was forced to straighten the boat ready for a turn. Another five or six rounds rang out and two large splinters of wood flew into the air near me. Peering behind, I saw that the Russians were now metres away from us. We launched out into the Grand Canal, narrowly missing a water bus that was making its way up the passage along with a string of other sea craft. I yanked the wheel hard left and we sped off in the direction of St Mark's Square.

Behind, I saw that our pursuers were temporarily delayed when they sideswiped a small craft. We were moving away too quickly to be certain but I think they sank the vessel. I turned my eyes and attention back to the front, in time to almost avoid a collision with a jet ski. I swerved to the right but it still wasn't enough to miss it.

CRUNCH!

Our boat was tossed to one side as we caught the back of the ski, knocking the rider, a police officer, into the water. There was no time to stop and check if the rider was injured because, once more, shots echoed around us. They were gaining on us fast.

The Grand Canal is the main route through the middle of Venice. Water vehicles of all shapes and sizes traverse its passage in an order that seems chaos to a casual observer, akin to driving down a busy eight lane freeway. I weaved, trying to overtake or dodge other vessels. Sweeping at high speed around a bend, another smaller canal, hidden by a floating pontoon, probably a bus stop, appeared on our left. At the last moment, tying to outmanoeuvre the Mafia, I attempted the turn. It was wider at the entrance than most of the canals which allowed me to maintain our momentum. But then, as if out of nowhere, we were confronted by a gondola, making its way leisurely from one side to the other, carrying honeymooners or lovers. There was little chance of avoiding it and we crashed through the middle, cutting it in half. We didn't stop, but dressed as a priest I felt compelled to offer a prayer for their safety and that they could swim.

The small canals criss-crossing Venice were remarkably similar, narrow waterways surrounded on either side by tightly-packed buildings, hundreds of years old, towering three and four storeys above with the elegance expected from one of the most beautiful and romantic cities in the world. Crossing the canals at regular intervals, ancient stone foot bridges connected a maze of narrow lanes.

The sound of gunshots from behind forced a refocus on the escape! In front of us, another canal was entering from the left. We took it and sped off in a new direction. A wail of police sirens joined our symphony of commotion, disrupting the serenity of this ancient place.

Our waterway joined a T-intersection and I turned left, which was a mistake. We entered a long straight canal with nowhere to hide. A smaller waterway, branching off to the right, appeared but was gone before I could consider attempting a turn. There was no option but to keep going, speeding towards another T-junction. More gunshots rang out and I glanced behind. The Mafia were shooting at the police giving us the opportunity to increase our lead. At the intersection, I veered right and, to my horror, we left the protection of the narrow waterways, finding ourselves in the harbour, a huge space of open water.

Ching!

A splinter of wood shattered next to me, then another and another. Bits of the boat were now flying off around me. If this continued, we would be killed or sunk. The open water was too dangerous, so I moved close to the buildings before heading left and then left again, hoping to re-enter the narrow waterways. Unfortunately, another wider canal appeared, but this time with boats moored on either side, there was only just enough room to pass other water users without crashing. It proved difficult for the Mafia to gain on us. In my desperation to outrun our pursuers, I side-swiped a couple of other craft on the way past, causing more damage to our boat.

Sweeping around a bend in the waterway, I recognised the gargoyle bridge. We were back where we started, about to re-enter the Grand Canal.

At full throttle, we raced out into the canal. Glancing to my right, I could see water police rapidly approaching with their lights and sirens blaring. Once more, we turned left, retracing the route we had taken minutes before, including following the smaller canal, the one concealed by the bus stop. This time, before I reached the T-junction, I went right.

SMASH!

The Mafia rammed the back of our taxi. Looking back, I saw the bow of their boat above Olivia's head, before slipping back into the water, taking more of our bodywork with it.

Our latest direction was a narrow waterway which became narrower as we progressed, to the point where it was difficult to navigate at speed. Although I heard more gunshots, I think we were each concentrating, the police, Mafia and us, on not crashing rather than the pursuit or the escape. We maintained our distance from each other and no bullets found their mark. Walkways or little bridges passed overhead with people watching the action, attracted by the sounds of the police and the commotion. The waterway widened and I opened the throttles but, rounding the next corner, my heart jumped into my mouth. A water taxi was leaving its mooring and we scraped its nose right down the side of our boat as we sped past. There was an explosion of sound behind us as our pursuers smashed into the taxi. I throttled back, turning hard left into another canal and then right into another before allowing us to drift to a silent halt.

'Are you all right?' I asked Olivia, while glancing back to see how she had fared during the chase.

Olivia was seated in the middle of the back seat and staring at her feet, where I saw water beginning to pool.

'I think we're sinking,' she reflected. 'Inspector – Oh, you know what I mean, Jean-Marc. How is it that I manage to race around the streets of Paris in a stolen Ferrari and not put so much as a scratch on it but when you are at the wheel ...'

She paused to look at the wreck that was the boat and I took my chance to interrupt.

'I take it that you're fine,' I said, managing a smile.

I searched for somewhere to hide and noticed some of the buildings had underground boat houses. Quietly, we slipped underneath one of the buildings, leaving daylight behind. While it was not pitch black, we had to be careful guiding our sinking taxi, in search of a place to tie up. Olivia joined me at the front of the boat as the water was entering rapidly at the rear.

If we sink now, Olivia may find it difficult to swim.

'Perhaps a life jacket may be in order,' I suggested.

Olivia declined but instead encouraged me to find dry land.

'Before my stockings get wet,' she said.

After a couple of minutes of exploring the under-building maze, with the back of the boat about to sink under the water line, a dock came into view. We pulled up and I helped Olivia off the boat.

'It's time we got out of these costumes and went back to being Lady Olivia and her secretary,' I said, 'but I'm afraid your cane has to go.'

'You mean, the *elegant cane*, has to go,' Olivia teased. 'Perhaps an umbrella, as you suggested?'

'An elegant umbrella, m'lady.'

A powerful light cut through the darkness and halted our banter in its tracks. It was coming from the direction of the canal and flitted from side to side, as if someone was searching. We could hear a boat, its motor gently burbling, as it wove between the stumps of the building. Olivia and I could hide, but our moored water taxi would give us away.

I wondered if we would be able to escape before they seal off the building but there was no time.

Concealed behind large wooden pillars at the end of the dock, we waited as the searchlight grew brighter and the sound of the boat louder. The dock was lit up as if it were daylight and we huddled behind our screen as the light swept back and forth. Darkness descended again and the sound of the boat became more distant.

'They're gone,' I said. 'It's time we were out of here.'

Except for the *elegant* cane which went over the side of the dock to join our sunken boat in the murky water below, we bundled up our religious attire and disposed of it in a dark alcove. We found our way up from underneath the building and out onto the street.

On most corners in Venice are signs pointing to San Marco, St Mark's Square. Although we had no idea where we were it was a simple matter of following the signs and, within minutes we were hidden amongst the hundreds of visitors in the square. Stopping only to purchase the umbrella, deciding against the intended coffee and cake, we took a water taxi to the cruise port.

***

The sight and size of the cruise liners took us by surprise. They were astonishing, but we were not sure whether this was in a good or bad way.

'They're enormous,' said Lady Olivia.

It took a moment to find our bearings before we joined the stream of people following the signs to their ships.

The cruise terminal was as busy as any airport and it was overwhelming and chaotic with people wandering about searching for information about what to do next. Soon after arriving, we were greeted, given information with forms to complete, taken a numbered ticket and told to wait for our number to be called. Once summoned we entered another queue for the check-in windows. Time seemed to be passing slowly because Lady Olivia and I were keen to be aboard and underway before the authorities tracked us to the ship. As we knew they would.

'Welcome, Lady Olivia,' I heard the check-in attendant say, having taken her passport. 'This is your boarding pass and you will be staying with us on deck five in one of our lovely inside cabins. Have you travelled with us before?'

'No,' replied Lady Olivia, sounding most offended. 'I'm afraid this was a last-minute decision. My private secretary assures me that none of your better suites were available but I would be

212

most grateful if you could check again. We will pay for an upgrade, of course.'

Having failed in her bid for a better cabin, we passed through the metal detectors, had our photos taken by security and a photographer working for the ship who hoped to sell the result to us during the cruise at some ridiculous inflated price, and found ourselves on deck five, where outside the cabin doors, our luggage was waiting.

'At least something has gone right,' I said to Olivia upon seeing our bags.

Ignoring my observation and giving me a kindly smile, she replied, 'You promised me a coffee and cake, before you took me for the joy ride. Give me ten minutes to freshen up and then let's have something to eat. I've something to tell you.'

Deck 12, at the stern of the ship, had a lovely outside eating area. I found Olivia a shady spot while I went and selected an assortment for lunch, deciding upon a wine instead of the coffee.

'We deserve this,' I said, giving Olivia the wine glass, 'even though it is before five.'

'Max would say it's after five somewhere in the world,' she said and, lifting her glass, she clinked it with mine. 'Cheers. Welcome aboard Jean-Marc, at least we made it this far.'

We ate quietly and were mesmerised by the people as they visited the eatery. Most had plates of food filled to overflowing and scoffed it down as if it were their last meal on Earth. Not able to finish their culinary selection, they'd slip away returning with deserts stacked one on top of the other.

'People come on cruises for the food,' I said, raising one eyebrow as I spoke.

'Indeed, they do,' replied Olivia, 'and there is plenty of it. I have something I've been wanting to tell you!' She paused and waited for my full attention. 'I *have* met Claudia before, I'm certain of it, and believe her real name is Lucia. The last time I saw her, she was only fourteen and a prisoner in Yugoslavia. That must be twenty years ago and she has changed such a lot. The more I study the photograph of her, the more certain I become. It was the hotel sign, the one saying, Santa Lucia, that made the connection for me - although it took me some time to realise it. It makes some sense, why she didn't kill Max. She must have recognised him but why she would take him with her, I can't fathom. If she didn't want him dead, why not let him go?'

Olivia stopped speaking and peered around, as if contemplating what to say next.

'There's no wisdom in taking him,' she said, 'because she can't tell the Mafia bosses the truth. They will want him dead. I wonder, does she have a plan or are things unfolding as they develop? Maybe she doesn't know herself? Max is the chink in her armour, if we find her, and if Max is still alive, we may have a slim chance.'

I listened to Olivia as she told the story of Lucia, the girl in a picture and how they spent two years searching for her before the rescue. They freed her from the Russian Mafia and returned her to her family just as the Balkans war was breaking out. So, the promises they made to stay in contact were unfulfilled and when the war was over, she had vanished.

Throughout our lives we encounter many people but every now and then we are touched by someone. Listening to Olivia, as she recalled the story, I knew that Lucia had left her mark on Olivia and, from what she told me, more so on Max. Whether she could reconcile Claudia being Lucia, I didn't ask and it didn't matter. For over an hour, I was spellbound listening to this grand old lady recounting the many adventures she shared with Max. When she had finished, I was aware that I was part of a wonderful love story and not merely the rescue of Max.

The thought overwhelmed me and I felt alone. She had shared a lifetime with Max and, even in these twilight years, I knew that she must love him - why else risk everything to find him. What touched me was how she showed that love. It was simply the way she spoke, with admiration, respect and caring, as deep as that. I was moved by her but also felt empty. My wife had died and my daughter was probably murdered. I had no one who deeply cared for me and I doubted, having now met Olivia and Max, that I had truly loved anyone.

'The ship's leaving,' said Olivia excitedly, which made me smile.

Despite the difficulties of our day and the challenges that awaited us, she was still able to find joy.

And so must I, I said privately to myself.

From our seats, we had a magnificent view. Our ship towered above Venice, dwarfing it in its shadow, and we looked down upon the City in all of its majestic beauty and history. It was a wonderful experience but what a travesty it must be for those on shore and for those who call Venice home. To see these huge ships dominating the skyline as they slip from their moorings! But today we were on board and marvelled from our vantage point. Venice was truly a sight to behold.

CHAPTER TEN

Kupari

Claudia

'Yes, well done everyone,' I repeated and, for the briefest of moments, I wondered if Max had saved me again.

I dismissed the thought as pure folly as I reached over from the co-pilot's seat and lightly touched Melanie-Jane on the shoulder in recognition of what she'd achieved during the landing.

'You too, Max,' I added.

He responded by stretching one of his hands towards me and, before I knew what I was doing, I had taken it and given it an affectionate squeeze.

Stop it!

I castigated myself irritably, then realised that both of my feet were firmly pushing down onto the brakes. With the easing of my leg muscles, the pressure came off the pedals and, in unison, the rest of my body relaxed and let out an audible sigh while involuntarily repeating the words. 'Well done everyone.'

'What now?' Max asked.

'You stay here with Melanie-Jane while I make some calls from the cabin. We will be needing a clean-up team, to dispose of the bodies.'

'And medical help for the pilot?'

'Sweetie, of course,' I replied, not meaning for the vexation I felt from his question to have crept into my voice.

Pulling myself out from behind the controls, I stepped over the co-pilot's body which I'd unceremoniously dragged from the seat and dumped on the floor. I paused and opened my mouth, as if wanting to say something but the moment passed and I hurriedly left the cockpit.

Nikola's body was where we left it and I had to step around it. As no one was watching, I turned and stared at the lifeless corpse. As with the co-pilot, I felt nothing, no sadness, remorse, guilt, victory or pride.

Nothing!

Lifting my hands, I studied them, turning them over a couple of times. *Would this death stay and haunt me later?*

Hanging on the wall, next to the table where Max and I had been sitting, was a secure phone line. Like any large and well organised criminal group, we ran a twenty-four-hour crisis response room. All I had to do was dial, provide an authorisation code, and wheels would be put into motion. Depending on where in the world the call originated, assistance was not always available from our criminal group. In those instances, help could be provided by other Brotherhood members who had a presence in that country, but only in extreme cases, and provided that Monya approved the request. Dubrovnik, being one of our own areas of operation, meant that medical and clean-up crews were on hand. Having placed the call, we could wait for the emergency team or I could leave using the car, kept in the shed at the runway, for our use during visits.

My next phone call was to Monya and he listened as I recounted the flight and expressed my concern that Nikola had managed to breach our security. He shared my disquiet and told me to lift our alert level to orange, the second highest. 'It would stay there,' he said for the duration of the cyber-attack on London and until we understood how Nikola came to be on board our plane and whether it impacted our operations.

Monya was planning to join me on Saturday and host the reception we were holding on board the yacht for key government officials, whose approvals we'd need to purchase the old resort at Kupari, near Dubrovnik.

'It's possible,' I said to Monya, 'that the plane's landing gear has been damaged. It was quite a landing. We won't know for certain until the engineers have examined it. I wouldn't count on it being available for Saturday.'

We debated whether a private plane should be chartered for him to fly but, with the security breach, he decided that he'd skip the trip. I would handle the purchase negotiations in his absence and he spent the rest of the call explaining what he wanted from the deal.

'Nevertheless,' he said, as his parting shot on the subject, 'I want that land and its buildings.'

To that end, I was to ensure our guests were exquisitely wined, dined and entertained. It was to be a formal, husbands and partner, affair - bribery was acceptable and expected but prostitutes were not to be at the party.

Towards the end of the lengthy conversation, as the rescue crew arrived outside the plane, Monya told me about Olivia and Inspector Axel. They'd been in France searching for information about me and were heading for Rome. As a precaution, a price had been put on their heads.

'Nevertheless,' he said, 'given their previous tenacity, it would be unwise to underestimate their ability to find you. I would be disappointed if I found myself playing host to both Max and Olivia. That would be intolerable. Do I make myself clear?' Monya said.

'That won't happen,' I promised Monya.

Having hung up the phone, I was struck by the uncomfortable realisation that I may encounter Olivia. Yet again, my decision to bring Max was looking shaky. Pushing Olivia to the back of my mind, I opened the door, allowing the clean-up crew to board the plane.

'Don't touch Nikola, the steward,' I commanded, pointing to the body on the floor. 'Not until I've had a chance to thoroughly search her and go through her belongings. The pilot is this way.'

I led them towards the cockpit saying, 'We think they were poisoned and the co-pilot is dead. Concentrate on the pilot.'

When we arrived, Max was caring for Melanie-Jane, trying to keep her talking.

Seeing us, he said to her in a gentle and reassuring voice, while stroking her cheek softly, 'Help's here.'

The scene made me angry and I wasn't sure why.

'Sweetie,' I said coldly while reaching out towards him. 'Come on, we need to keep out of the way of the medical crew.'

It was the right thing to say for the occasion but it was not what I was thinking.

Back in the cabin I searched Nikola, to no avail. Her ID was likely to be false, unless Nikola Tesla was her real name - which I doubted. I kept the identity document, nonetheless. She wore no jewellery and her handbag that was in the galley was empty, except for lipstick, sunglasses and tissues. There were no keys, coins, till receipts; nothing to tell us who she was.

I gave the bag to one of the clean-up crew saying, 'Destroy everything, sweetie, and no photographs. I don't want any records that links her to us.'

'Boss,' said one of the clean-up crew members. 'Don't you want to try and find out who sent her?'

'Sweetie, I don't care who she is, where she's from or who sent her. More importantly,' I repeated angrily, 'I said no pictures. The last thing we want is photos of a dead girl being found on a phone that is connected to us – so, put your phone away – NOW!'

After he had complied, by slipping his phone into his pocket, I continued, but with a change of tone in my voice. 'She's dead, but the next one will be taken alive and I can guarantee they will talk.'

'You kept her ID,' whispered Max when we were out of earshot of the clean-up crew.

'You don't miss much,' I answered, surprised, but remained mute as I had no intention of telling him why. The secret was that I didn't know myself.

Max and I left the private aerodrome for the drive to Dubrovnik where Monya's luxury yacht was docked and waiting to serve as our floating hotel until after the reception, when it would take us to Split and the beginning of a two-week vacation sailing around the Greek Islands. The drive took us past the seaside village of Kupari and the resort we were negotiating to buy. Turning off the highway, we drove towards it and the beach, stopping near the five derelict buildings that were abandoned hotels.

'Come on,' I said to Max, 'I want to look around.'

'Where are we?' he inquired while surveying the scene. 'It's like a ghost town! Almost surreal.'

'This is one of the reasons we came to Dubrovnik, to buy this place. It was built as a resort for the elite of the then Yugoslav army. There were once four hotels here and one grand hotel. That's it over there,' I said, pointing as we picked our way through the rubble. 'When the war broke out, the Balkans war, the army left, looting and destroying much of it. They used phosphorous bombs to systematically burn them, floor by floor. It's still beautiful is it not? Just look at the beach and the crystal-clear Adriatic Sea. What a magnificent backdrop. I love the contrast, the sweet and sour of this place. Desolation against the beauty of the sea. Violence and harmony, ugliness and splendour.'

'Is that why you want to buy it, to turn it back into a resort?'

'Yes, we intend doing that, but that's only part of the story. Look at the buildings, see how they are embedded into the slope? When the military had it, they built a maze of passages and rooms tunnelled into the hillside. That's why they blew it up before they left, to hide and seal the entrances to the chambers. The Croatian Army set up base here in 1998 and stayed until 2001, but they never found what's hidden behind. We will consolidate our cyber divisions here, relocating the Moscow office, merging it with our Dubrovnik operation. What could be better than a forgotten military complex hidden in the side of a mountain? And the cover for the operation.

A holiday resort, teaming with people coming and going. Look about you. The Adriatic Sea! When we build a private harbour to accompany the resort, we will have access to the ocean, a smugglers paradise.'

'Can you just do that? Can someone from Russia buy Croatian property that easily?'

'No.' I said and laughed. 'Monya owns a multi-billion-dollar property development company in Russia called the Edsel Group. It has a subsidiary, a Croatian-based company called Titanium, that can buy here. It has already built several residential and commercial complexes in Croatia and it will buy Kupari with Russian money, which is quite legal.'

Talking about the resort reminded me that, before long, the history here and its connection to my past, would be gone. I stopped talking and gazed around the derelict site before turning and silently staring out to sea and then surveyed the ruins once more.

'Were you here during the Balkans war?' Max asked, drawing my attention back to him.

'No, the Yugoslav army left in 1991, about the same time that you left me with my parents.'

'What is it about this place that draws you to it?'

'What do you mean?' I answered, trying to appear surprised by the question.

'People touched by war often have a place that means something to them, and not always in a good way. I don't know what happened after we left, but you were in a war zone. Zvornik, near where you lived, became synonymous with mass-murder by

Serb paramilitary groups like the White Eagles and Yellow Wasps. If my memory serves me correctly, a total of 3,936 people, were killed or went missing between 1992 and 1995, near where you were.'

'How do you know that?' I snapped while trying to hide a slight lump that had formed in the back of my throat.

'We may have left you but we never forgot you.'

For the briefest of seconds, I let Shakespeare's Lady Macbeth invade my consciousness. *Out, damned spot.*

By clenching my fists, I pushed her away but not before saying, indignantly, 'Why is it that you go to war, kill and God knows what else, but become a victor? On the submarine, Captain Andrey called you a hero of the Russian people. I do no more or no less than you and I'm a war criminal.'

I waited, wanting Max to reply, but he didn't and, for more than a minute, silence hung in the air before I felt compelled to continue, this time soberly.

'I visit this place whenever I come to Dubrovnik, though I don't like the memories it evokes. It draws me to it like a malevolent force that I can't control. The ruins remind me of another time, one of war. The burned-out shell is a monument to darker days. As I said, the contrast is alluring, a ghostly reminder of the past.'

'What happened when you went home, after we freed you from Macinec?'

I hesitated, before deciding to share some of my story. I skipped the first couple of years, saying that it was difficult to fit back into family life, and started when I ran away to join the Yellow Wasps. I recalled how I enjoyed the discipline, the rigorous exercise and how I excelled in combat training. The Yellow Wasps and my activities during the conflict, I left out. I did wonder, when I moved the story to fleeing Yugoslavia and entering Britain illegally, if Max would ask but he didn't. Instead, we moved to where we had a better view of the ocean. Surveying the waves, I pondered whether I should continue my tale and found I wanted to tell my story but was worried that it would come out wrong. No one had ever been interested, so it was a chronicle never told before. Luckily, Max seemed content and patient to wait.

'When I came to London,' I said, 'it was as an illegal immigrant. You see, I had to flee Zvornik toward the end of the war and I arrived with nowhere to stay, no friends, little money and no work. I ended up in a cheap cold and damp boarding house in Soho, sharing a room with four, sometimes five, other girls. On the trip over, I heard others say how important it would be, if you wanted to avoid deportation, to become fluent in English. Although I had basic English, that I learnt as a teenager, from the moment we landed, I set about mastering the language and softening my accent, which was predominantly Russian from having been held captive during my developmental years. Being virtually penniless, even though I picked up a few low paying cleaning jobs, I discovered that hanging around in libraries was a good place to be because they were warm in winter and cool in summer. It was there that I taught myself to read, and discovered it was fun. I could escape from reality by becoming absorbed in a book. I was a quick learner and a frequent visitor. One of the librarians introduced me to western classics and I greedily indulged myself in their covers. Although I was broke and powerless, I learned that, in British society, fun could be had by using literary references as a weapon, which only encouraged me. The girls I was staying with didn't understand and, eventually, suggested I leave. One of them, Stephanie was her name, who was also leaving, told me of a lap dancing job she had acquired at a place called the Mayfair Club. She told me that they were still hiring and suggested I pay them a visit.

'The Mayfair Club turned out to be an exclusive strip joint in London. I was given a trial as a lap dancer and, with a good teacher, picked it up quickly. The money was better than I had been getting as a cleaner, but not as good as those girls who were willing to go the whole nine yards, as the Americans would say. The club provided private booths for those clients wanting additional services and I was surprised by the number of girls who were using prostitution to pay their way through university. It was a good place to work.

'As a lap dancer, I was forbidden fruit, the honey pot, tantalising and arousing the leering and lecherous men by rubbing myself erotically close to their bodies as I could without touching them. They would push £50 notes into my knickers while fantasising that the paper was their fingers. At the same time, I would let my breasts brush once or even twice across their face. I did my job well, stirring them to uncontrolled excitement by being sexual without being sexual – yet with the promise there. When I finished, they would be willingly escorted away to one of our private booths, to release their pent-up desire and money from their wallet. My salary was linked to a conversion rate, lap dancing to private booth. Most men are weak,' I scoffed, wondering if I was shocking Max and realising that I was not, I continued, 'and fell easy prey to my entrapment. Even those who would regret it later succumbed.

'I was good at the job and it was easy money. Anyway, within twelve months or so, I had worked my way up to supervising some of the girls. Because management saw me as well-spoken, classy and able to engage in intelligent conversation, I was often asked to join the table of some of our more influential clients. This was not as a lap dancer but as a concierge to ensure the night met their expectations; organising company and other requirements they had. That's how I met Monya. He wasn't a regular but, when he was in London on business, he would use the Mayfair Club to host guests or for his own personal enjoyment. I knew him as a Russian property tycoon, although it was rumoured amongst the girls, that he was involved in the Mafia. Compared to some of the other gangsters who frequented the establishment he was perhaps more genteel, sophisticated. Whatever it was about him, he didn't come across as a thug but I knew that he was dangerous because he was always accompanied by bodyguards.

'On one of his business trips to London, he visited the club almost every night accompanied by, and entertaining, different people, some of whom I arranged for our most discreet girls to meet, all at Monya's expense of course. Two nights before he was due to return to Moscow, I was invited, through the club, to organise and attend a private gathering for six of his closest associates at the penthouse where he was staying. His private secretary came to the club before the night and I was taken shopping for a new wardrobe that I was expected to wear. I remember that day even now because I never imagined having that kind of money to spend, or standing in front of a mirror thinking and feeling how beautiful I was in a blue Versace dress and gold necklace.

'The afternoon of the function, a silver Rolls-Royce came to the club and I was chauffeured to an amazing landmark building on the banks of the Thames. The penthouse suite covered the top two floors and had a grand entrance hall that was lavishly panelled in a dark rich timber. Ahead was a living room and above was a magnificent chandelier and the landing of the floor above which was accessible by an elaborate marble stone staircase with black wrought iron railings. Marble was everywhere from the entrance hall to the kitchen and the bathrooms. And what bathrooms they were! Spas, soaking tubs and I remember this huge mirror; it was glorious. We had something similar at our club but this place was prestigious and tastefully decorated; it dripped wealth. My favourite room was the private study with its imposing curved oak desk, deep rich red leather seats and a magnificent bookcase. A personal sanctuary and I could imagine myself locked away here, lost in my reading. A rooftop garden with its unrivalled views over London complemented the penthouse.

'I arrived a few hours before the guests were due and went over the arrangements for the night with Monya, including which girls were to accompany each guest. He chatted warmly. I found him charming and he seemed to enjoy showing me around the suite. It was also the first time that I had seen him on his own as the bodyguards had been stationed outside the front door. It was, he told me, to be a very selective gathering. My girls were to add atmosphere, to be disarming, enchanting, yet unobtrusive and were to withdraw to another part of the penthouse when directed. Six girls were required, one for each of our visitors and they were to arrive an hour before the first guest. Monya wanted them to be dressed elegantly, sexy without being erotic.

'Promptly, at 7.00pm, the first of our guests for the evening arrived. He was greeted at the door by the butler and then escorted to the lounge by his consort for the evening, where Monya and I were waiting. This scene played out another five times until the gathering was complete. The wine and champagne flowed freely, as did the conversation, but the girls and I were under instructions to moderate our drinking, helped by the wine waiter who ensured that our drinks were diluted, though it appeared to our companions that we were enjoying the beverages with them. Monya played the same game.

'The dinner was exquisite, formal but relaxed, and I recall it being one of the finest meals I had ever savoured. When it was over, the chef, butler and waiting staff were each dismissed for the evening. Monya had given me the nod and I discreetly directed the girls to remain at the table, as the men retired for after-dinner drinks and business discussions. As he was preparing to leave the table, Monya said, while extending his arm for me to take, "Walk with me Claudia."

'Arm in arm and with a champagne flute in my other hand, I escorted him to join the other men. When we arrived, he directed me once more by saying, "Thank you, Claudia," and I knew that it was my turn to leave.

'The sitting room, where the men were meeting, was an extension of the grand entrance hall and I chose to walk close to the front door, to examine the chandelier, before making my way back to join the women. Despite the soft music that was playing in the background, I recognised the muffled crack-crack noise from outside of the door immediately, the unmistakable sound of bullets being fired through a silencer.

'Swerving quickly, kicking off my high heel shoes in the one motion, my movements caught the attention of Monya. "Take cover," I called as softly as I could, but with urgency in my voice, "We are about to have unwanted visitors."

"What's going on?" Monya called back, and he began to stand.

'I put a finger over my lips to indicate that I wanted him to keep quiet. "Gun shots. Get down on the floor," I mouthed while looking about for the light switch. Finding a bank of switches, I turned off everything and the room was bathed in twilight, the city glow entering through the uncurtained windows and the light from the rest of the building preventing the darkness I craved. Once through the door, I knew it would take only seconds for our assailants' eyes to adjust. Scanning about I assessed the options. Unarmed, they appeared limited. Glancing towards Monya and his companions, I could see them prostrate on the floor with no guns to be seen. No one was carrying.

'At first, I positioned myself behind where the door would open but, realising that they would use small explosives to gain entry, I moved back a few feet.

'After smashing the champagne glass on the marble tiles to create a jagged edge, I crouched down like a coiled spring, ready to pounce. The moment the first person came through the door, I would have less than a second to react if we were to have any chance of surviving.

'Bang, bang, bang!

'The explosions came in rapid succession - hinges and lock targeted and the door fell to the floor with a thud. A hooded figure dressed in black and holding a pistol burst into the room but the assailant's entry was slowed by the semi darkness. I leaped like a gazelle, thrusting the broken glass into his exposed neck, turning the bleeding and convulsing body toward the next intruder as a shield. Using the assailant's pistol, still in his hand, I discharged two shots, hitting the second assassin who dropped to the floor.

'Crack, crack!

'There came the sounds of more gunshots and I was knocked backwards. A third person, someone I hadn't noticed, was firing into the body I was using as armour. Still holding the dead person, now with the pistol in my hand, I retreated further into the room, before dropping my shield and taking cover with Monya and the others while maintaining a clear view of the entrance which was lit with the light coming from the hall.

'From my vantage point, unless we were stormed en masse, it would have been difficult for anyone to make it across the threshold alive. Whoever our stalkers were, they would know by now that we had called for backup. Their advantage was lost and I thought the attack was over but we remained hidden regardless, listening. No noises came from outside until we heard the *ding* of the lift arriving at our floor. I guessed that whoever else was out there had fled down the fire escape and pushed the lift button on their way past, as a diversion. Monya started to stand but I whispered, "Wait," and gently pushed him back to lie flat on the ground. "It may be a trap, give it another thirty seconds, I'll go and check."

'Everything was silent, so I cautiously moved from the centre to the corner of the room to improve the view I had of the corridor through the door. With the gun at the ready, I narrowed the angle between me and the gap. At the last moment and holding my breath, I stepped into the corridor, swinging to the right, the direction I couldn't see and then rapidly back to the left, ready to shoot. Except for two dead guards and the second person I'd killed, the hallway was empty. Whatever remained of the assassination team had fled.

'After that,' I said to Max, 'Monya wanted to know about my past. I left out those early years as a sex slave, starting with my paramilitary training during the war and fleeing to the UK to avoid prosecution. That led me to the Mayfair club. And that's it really. As John Wade said in 1839, the rest is history. That's how I came to be working for Monya.'

'So, you took a job,' asked Max, provocatively, 'with the very people you escaped from as a child? And, doing the same thing?'

'Sweetie,' I snapped. 'are you insinuating that I'm a child abuser? How dare you! I gave you more credit than that. Are you one of those naïve idiots who believe that 80% of those abused become abusers? You're wrong. The majority of people abused in childhood don't continue the cycle. I ended up working for the Mafia, for Monya, through fate. It had nothing to do with my childhood. It's just the way things turned out when I saved his life that night.'

Standing up, determined to end the conversation, I continued, but with the assertiveness gone from my voice. 'Come on sweetie, it's time we got going.'

I reached out my hand towards his, intent on helping this senile and weak old man to stand.

'What about Macinec?' Max said, accepting the offer of my hand.

Keeping the anger I felt absent from my voice, I said, 'They don't have children there anymore. No dark web or streaming child pornography. Child exploitation has gone to the Asians.'

'You're still trafficking in human misery. Your prostitutes are modern slaves. Oh, no physical shackles, but there are financial ones that make it impossible for them to work their way out of debt. When Monya asked you to go there, I could tell that you were uncomfortable.'

I didn't answer immediately, contemplating as we strolled towards the car. I wouldn't admit that he was right and I didn't want to talk about it. Of all the things I did, Macinec was a place I wanted to stay away from.

Instead of responding to Max, wanting to alter the direction of our conversation and restore my authority, I said, 'Olivia is searching for you!'

'Are you surprised?' he replied, content for a change in subject.

'No. It would be difficult if she were to come here.' Then, raising the game, I added, 'You do understand, that if I'm ordered to, I will kill you both!'

'Though you don't want to.'

'Yes of course. If I'm ordered to was what I stated.'

Max stopped, turned and faced me.

'That's not what I said. Even though you *don't* want to.'

'Sweetie – you and me, we're the same. If your government ordered you to, you would kill me without a moment's hesitation.' I paused for effect and exaggerated the words as I added, 'Even though you *don't* want to!'

'There's a difference!' Max replied, carefully.

'A difference to whom?' I scoffed. 'In either case, one of us is dead and then what? Do you think a dead person can see the difference, that your God will see a difference? No Max, we are remarkably similar. You think you are morally superior!'

'Claudia, I would never have been sent to kill you, unless you were a threat to many innocent people. You would dispose of Olivia and myself because we are an inconvenience.'

'Sweetie, we both follow orders.'

'Is that what happened in Yugoslavia?'

'You killed in war, just as I did.'

'Is that why you had to flee to London?'

I felt the anger welling again within me.

How dare he be so sanctimonious.

Before responding, I called up my training, aiming for calm to reduce my aggression. It didn't work and spat.

'Each of our activities, sweetie, were sanctioned by our governments. The only difference is, you were on the winning side. You, considered a hero of the Russian people. What rubbish.'

'The submarine captain, if he knew what you did, how would he describe your time with the Yellow Wasps?'

War criminal, I thought privately, but aloud I said, 'Thou shalt not kill. You're a man of the cloth, isn't that a commandment? It's not meant to be a suggestion, sweetie.'

'Sometimes we must do things for a greater good; especially when failing to act is a greater evil.'

'Sweetie, who decides what is this greater good?'

'Claudia, we know that inherently there is a natural set of principles that govern our humanity. You may fight it, but you know the difference. I can tell you do, which is why you are at war with yourself!'

At war with myself - never!

I'd had enough of the conversation and wondered how I'd allowed myself again to be dragged into his agenda.

With spite and sarcasm oozing from my lips as I spoke, I said, 'Sweetie, perhaps it's time we left for the yacht. It's been a busy day for you and you'll be wanting your afternoon nap and pills.'

'That would be lovely, and perhaps you could bring me some nice warm milk. At my age, it helps me sleep.'

***

Max

I had never seen anything like it before, let alone been on one. Claudia had said it was a luxury yacht, but that was an understatement. It must have been at least 550ft long, with stunning panoramic windows that encased each of the four levels that sat atop the deck. A helicopter sat idly on the third deck towards the stern of the boat. Towards the front – the bow— was the sleekest-looking crane I had ever seen, more architectural than a functional piece of machinery.

With its dark blue hull and glistening white superstructure, the yacht cut an impressive sight. This must have been what people describe as a super yacht and it was the largest private boat in the harbour, although it had some impressive company. If Claudia had told me that she worked for the Mafia to play with the rich and famous I might have understood as I walked up the gangway.

Claudia hadn't spoken since we left Kupari. I sensed that she was angry and I found this pleasing because it showed that I was playing with her mind and exploiting the ambiguities I hoped she was experiencing. I needed to be careful. Push, but not too hard. She was a classic case of cognitive dissonance where someone simultaneously holds two or more contradictory beliefs, ideas or values. Unless I was careful, she could restore balance by

238

eliminating the irritation, namely myself. It was however, what she said about Olivia that weighed on my mind.

Monya tolerated me because he genuinely held affection for Claudia. If Olivia arrived, that wouldn't be enough. Somehow, I needed to leave before both of us were trapped and Claudia's loyalties were tested beyond dispute. The outcome was certain, and it was not in our favour. My advantage was my age, surprisingly I'm dismissed as a threat by people, even invisible to them.

'Welcome aboard the *Lelantos,* Claudia,' said the captain who was waiting at the top of the gangway to greet us.

'Thank you, Captain,' she replied. 'This is Max and, as you know, he will be joining us for our short vacation. He can have the run of the ship but tell security he's not to leave unless I am with him. Has Linda arrived?'

'She's due later this evening. Would you like one of our staff to show Max to his room? Your master suite is ready for you.'

'Thank you. Max missed his breakfast this morning and we haven't yet had lunch. Kindly ask house staff for some light refreshment to be brought to the dining room, say in twenty minutes. Then, I would like to meet with our security head, to go over the arrangements for Saturday's party.'

'Certainly Claudia. This way Max,' said the captain, pointing.

I followed, leaving Claudia behind.

'You have a beautiful ship, she must be 550ft long,' I commented, hoping to engage the captain in conversation.

'She actually 557ft. Do you know something about ships or was that a lucky guess?'

'Ex Royal Navy, a long time ago now, but the salt never leaves the veins.'

The mention of the navy seemed to work and the captain chatted warmly, pleased to tell me about his ship and, instead of having one of his staff to show me to my cabin, he did so himself. I learned that the ship had forty staff, two swimming pools, two helipads, thirty cabins, a cinema and a mini-submarine accessible from inside the boat. This meant that it could be launched and retrieved through a hatch in the bottom of the yacht.

Arriving at the cabin, he opened the door and said, 'I hope you will find the room to your satisfaction.'

Like the rest of the boat I had seen so far, the cabin was luxurious.

'More than satisfactory, thank you Captain,' I said, pretending that this standard of comfort was normal. 'Do you mind if I take a walk and familiarise myself with your wonder vessel?'

'Not at all Max, but I suggest that you wait until after lunch, so I can advise security to expect you. We wouldn't want someone thinking you were an intruder. You will find that we take our security very seriously.'

After he left, I walked around the cabin a couple of times and unexpectedly found myself anxiously contemplating the right time for me to leave for lunch and how I was going to find where it was being served. It was a silly thought until I realised that I was really missing Olivia. My ruminations were disrupted by a knock at the door.

'Good afternoon, Max,' said the man when I opened the cabin door. 'My name is Randolph and I will be your personal valet for the duration of your stay on the *Lelantos*. Please follow me. Claudia is waiting for you in the dining room. I have also taken it upon myself to find a suitable wardrobe for your stay. It will be waiting for you upon your return. One is expected to dress for dinner, the evening meal. For Saturday's function, a dinner jacket is required attire. Max, I will ensure that the appropriate garb is laid out for you each morning. You needn't worry unnecessarily. I am here to assist with your needs and to ensure that your stay with us is a comfortable and enjoyable one. If you have any questions, I will do my best to answer them for you.'

'Perhaps you could teach me how to fly the helicopter, when the others are asleep of course?'

'Ah, Claudia told me that I might enjoy your dry sense of humour, Max. Lunch is through here,' he said, winking and then pointing into another lavish room.

'Max, do come and join me,' greeted Claudia warmly.

Well that's interesting. She didn't call me Sweetie.

For the time being, at least, we were back on more friendly terms. I decided that it was conceivable that she was enjoying the *Lelantos.* Monya had mentioned that cruising the Greek Islands was something she loved. I didn't want to antagonise her for the moment because I had other plans. Over lunch, I wanted to persuade Claudia to show me the ship and then, during the polite conversation of the tour, ask if I could accompany her on her visit to the cyber professor.

Claudia was passionate about the *Lelantos*, telling me everything during our circuit, including the submarine and the ship's missile defence system. As we walked I studied, trying to remember the layout of the yacht.

Claudia stopped and burst out laughing as she said, 'If you're working out how you're going to escape, there's little point. We have six ex-Spetsnaz soldiers on board, the Russian equivalent of the British SAS. They would take you down before you made it over the side.'

'No, no,' I replied. 'That's not what I'm considering at all. I've been trying to think of a way to ask if I might accompany you to see Professor, er – Professor—?'

'Akihiko,' she said, finishing off the sentence for me.

'Professor Akihiko,' I repeated. 'I'm expecting you to say no, but am hoping for a yes.'

Claudia laughed again, saying, 'Why not, Monya told me that I wasn't to let you out of my sight. Anyway, it's not as if you will ever be leaving us, alive that is.' This caused her to snigger and then continue in a more serious tone. 'Plus, I'm quite looking forward to seeing your face when you learn what we are doing to your beloved country. We will go tomorrow after breakfast and I might even let you eat this time.'

Pondering my next move, I turned to Claudia and said, simply, 'Thank you.'

It took her by surprise. I imagined she was expecting a retort, a continuation of our before-lunch duelling. But I had changed tactics.

CHAPTER ELEVEN

Cyber Attack

Max

After the ship tour, Claudia left me on deck. The foolish fretfulness I felt earlier had passed and I found a warm shady spot beside the pool looking out over the sea. Although the yacht carried a large crew, for the first time since my kidnapping, I had my own private space without being confined to a room. Apart from Randolph, my valet, who made the briefest of appearances to see 'If Max would like a drink, white wine perhaps,' I was left undisturbed for the entire afternoon to drift in and out of heavenly sleep, spending the time in between thinking. To start with, my mind churned over multiple scenarios, seeing Olivia, missing our granddaughter Penny, escape, death and, absurdly, being rescued by Claudia. The Mediterranean, heat and the hypnotic effect of the sun as its rays shimmered and danced across the pool and out into the Adriatic Sea made me content to rest. Tomorrow would be another day with new challenges.

'Excuse me Max.' I heard and felt a hand as it gently shook my shoulder, before repeating, 'Excuse me Max.'

Opening my eyes, I saw Randolph. He smiled.

'Sorry to disturb your rest, but it's time to prepare for dinner.'

'Have I been asleep that long?' I said in good humour. 'Good job Olivia's not here – you have no idea what trouble I would be in.'

Randolph helped me up because I had become stiff and walked slowly with me back to the cabin. On the bed was a beautifully laid out evening dinner jacket and accompanying shoes. I opened my mouth, wanting to say, *how did you know my size*, but closed it again knowing he would say *It's my job Max – to know such things.*

Dinner at Monya's mansion in Moscow had been formal but tense. This one was held with a different kind of formal. The host, Claudia, was elegantly dressed and seemed graceful as she smiled, inviting me to join them. The other guest was Linda, a woman I met briefly on the helicopter when we were fleeing Scotland and before boarding the submarine. That seemed a lifetime ago, but it was only weeks. Linda was smartly dressed and was stylish rather than elegant. Approaching the dining table, I noticed the way they looked at each other as they spoke. I doubted they were lovers but there was affection, trust even.

Linda had seen though Claudia's story of why she hadn't killed me at the farmhouse. They understood each other well, which was hazardous for me because Linda had shown little tolerance for keeping me alive.

If I could influence Linda, it might tip Claudia.

I thought that Macinec was the lever but it was unlikely that Linda knew the story. Introducing it would be a high-risk strategy. I would have to do it carefully and only if the right opportunity arose.

Maybe if Linda goes fishing, trying to find out why Claudia didn't kill me. We'll see.

'Good evening ladies and, with the risk of being accused of sexism, you both look stunning,' I said, taking a seat at the table. 'Linda, isn't it? A pleasure to see you again, this time without the sound of rotors.'

Claudia and Linda looked at each other and smiled. Were they amused or could they see through my ploy?

Dinner, the wine and company were superb. I was included in the conversation and it flowed freely. Linda and Claudia recounted stories, happily sharing past adventures and funny anecdotes with me. It reminded me that life is complex and people more-so. Here I was, a condemned man with my likely executioners, having a remarkable evening. I wondered what the night would have been like if Monya were here.

Then it happened, the opening for which I had been waiting.

Linda asked Claudia, 'What did you say to Monya – about Max?'

Before Claudia had a chance to reply, I said, 'Can I bid you fine ladies a fond good night and thank you for your wonderful company? I'm afraid it's time for this old man to consult his pillow.'

I raised myself and my creaking bones slowly from the table, pausing to speak deliberately to Linda.

'Despite everything that has happened, Claudia has always been special to Olivia and me. Do take care of her. Good night again.'

From nowhere, Randolph appeared at my side to escort me back to my cabin. When we arrived, I thanked him, but added that I was going to take a stroll about the ship before turning in.

'May I assist you, Max?' he asked.

'You're so kind,' I replied, 'thank you but, no. I enjoy a little quiet time before bed.'

***

Next morning, I awoke to find the day's outfit neatly folded and ready for me on the chair next to the writing desk in the corner of the room. Despite what Claudia wanted me to hear, I was looking forward to the day as not many outsiders were able to gain access to a cyber-criminal gang and see them in action. As we were in Dubrovnik, I imagined their headquarters would be secret, concealed somewhere within the historic old city.

Perhaps, down one of its many narrow laneways, there would be a house, maybe a shop or business, that would serve as its front. Inside, against an apparently solid wall, Claudia would push on the face of some gargoyle, or a stone with a symbol embossed on it, and that would slide back into the wall with a distinctive clunk, revealing the passage hidden behind. A lift or stairs would direct us down three or four storeys to a secret bunker where a steel door guarded the entry to the mission headquarters. I imagined Claudia staring into a retina-scanning machine that would allow her access through the door as it unlocked with a clunk.

Once inside, a control room, like the one I'd seen on the submarine, would await, with seated men and women, manning great panels of lights, switches and displays. Perhaps a vast digital map of the world would dominate the room, recording and directing their cyber-attacks in real time.

Maybe I watch too much TV these days?

My first disappointment came soon after we left the harbour, when we headed away from the old city, to pull up, ten minutes later, in front of an ordinary looking office building. Once inside, we took the lift to the fourth floor and, other than having to swipe a card to operate the lift, there was no other security. Stepping from the lift we could have been arriving at any other business. We were greeted through a reception window by a disinterested receptionist. I wondered if this was all part of an elaborate ruse, or whether this was just how it was.

After Claudia showed her ID, which was greeted with a grunt, the receptionist said, rolling her eyes, 'Use your card at the door.'

Claudia, seemingly unfazed, by the attitude, swiped her card and we entered the offices. For the first time, I saw armed guards, only two of them, and they were seated at a desk in front of another door through which we would have to pass. Despite saying good morning to Claudia, using her name without prompting, they still checked her security pass and ran a metal detector wand over both of us. Surprisingly, Claudia was unarmed.

The door was opened and I had another disappointment.

Another ordinary office!

I scanned the room, to make a mental note, to count twenty people, seated in front of computer screens, all going about their business.

A man of Asian persuasion, Japanese I thought, came scurrying towards us. He looked nervous, on edge and not pleased to see us. I guessed that this was the professor.

Unable to control my sarcasm, I turned to Claudia and said, in a quiet voice, 'I can see why you want to move. It's not one of the most secure locations I have ever visited.'

'It was for a different time,' was all she said before greeting the approaching man. 'Professor Akihiko.'

'Hello Claudia,' he answered with a little stutter and an American accent, contrary to his appearance. 'How wonderful to see you again. Come, come in.'

He shook hands with Claudia but ignoring me, pointed towards a vacant office.

'This way, this way. It's a secure room,' he continued as Claudia and I followed him until we reached the door. He stopped and, as if seeing me for the first time, said, 'Who, who's this?'

Disinterested to explain to the professor why I was accompanying her, the reply was brief. 'Professor, this is Max, one of my associates.'

He grunted uncomfortably before opening the door and, without waiting for us, chose a seat for himself at the table. We followed casually and seated ourselves across from him. With a thud, Claudia placed on the table the briefcase she had been carrying. Deliberately slowly, she opened it, removing a pile of files and a notepad. She carefully placed the bag on the floor before rifling through some of the documents, pausing occasionally to read a few lines to herself. Other than the noise of the turning papers, the room was deathly silent. The tension grew by the second.

This must be what it was like to appear before the Spanish Inquisition.

I could barely imagine the pressure Professor Akihiko was feeling.

Placing the papers neatly in front of her, Claudia said, 'You seem unsettled this morning Professor, is anything bothering you?'

'No, Claudia, everything is fine. I think you will find I have prepared well for your visit and you will be pleased with our progress. It's in the reports.'

That's interesting. He's controlling that slight stutter and no longer repeating his words.

I was sure that Claudia would have made the same observation and was curious to see how she would proceed.

'I've read your reports. The income targets are promising but we are concerned with the timeliness for the blockchain project. We will come to those. Perhaps we could start by you giving Max an overview of our operation here. I'm keen for him to hear about the WannaCry computer worm we released on Britain but leave out the details of our cybercurrencies and blockchain work. That will be a discussion for us in private.'

I could see by the way that he replied that the professor was relieved. The pressure had been lifted – for the moment.

'Max,' he began, managing a slight smile. 'I'm the head of our cyber team. We have two divisions, research and development and operations.'

He stopped abruptly and said, more to himself than us, 'No, no that won't do. That won't do at all.'

He looked down at the table while scratching his head, obviously in deep thought.

'Sorry Max, let me start again. The internet we have now is like where cars were in, say, the late 1960s; more of us were owning one and that was creating jobs, direct and indirect. Oil companies raked in the money and government took its taxes, some of which they were spending on bigger and better roads, which encouraged us to buy more cars. And so, the cycle went around. No one, business, government or citizens, cared much about safety. All they wanted were cars even though thousands were dying on our roads each year. There were no seat belts, airbags, stability controls, speed cameras, ABS braking systems and many countries had unlimited speed limits. It was a cavalier time, when business and government cared about making more cars and little else. Then, safety wasn't a priority, it was an individual's responsibility, not a business or government concern. For the individual, safety was irrelevant because it was always somebody else who was going to be injured or killed, never themselves.

'That's where the internet is now. Business and governments are forcing everybody on line. Soon, you won't be able to pay your utility bills or even interact with a government authority without doing it on line. Tradespeople won't post a bill in the mail, it will come as an invoice attached to an email, or whatever replaces electronic mail. Online shopping, all paid for online is spreading rapidly. We no longer meet people in pubs and even dating is being done through social media. News, as we know it, is changing. Printed newspapers are in decline and, with them, advertising revenue and independent investigative reporting. People are getting their news content on line, not all of it real. This is occurring, as I tried to explain, without safety – concern for the individual user.

Like before, we're being forced to drive but without speed limits, seat belts or airbags. It's an almost regulatory-free environment, ripe for exploitation, anywhere in the world. That's what we do, capitalise on the opportunity. We scam billions of dollars as people and business race down the cyber highway and, because the internet is worth trillions of dollars, nobody really cares about the billions we make. When they do, by the time someone finds a patch to one of our scams, we have invented a new one. Our forecasts project rich pickings for a good while yet.'

I couldn't prevent myself from laughing aloud, which stopped the professor in his tracks.

'Sorry,' I said, 'that's exactly how I see the internet, as if we are racing our brand new shiny sports car, hitting phenomenal speeds, but we haven't quite got around to inventing the brakes.'

Whoops! My mission is to encourage and elicit information that I can pass on when I escape, not to air my personal biases.

'Yes, that's what I just said,' interrupted the professor sounding irritated, before continuing. 'We categorise our cyber-activities into Ransomware, Scamming, Cybercurrencies and Propaganda. Most are mechanisms for making money - some are sophisticated cyber weapons, like the WannaCry worm which we used on behalf of the Kremlin to crash the British health system. It's also ransomware. You see, we sometimes work for our Russian friends for profit, but mostly we help them with propaganda, interfering and meddling in the operation of western democracies.'

'How do you do that?' I asked, hoping Claudia wouldn't prevent him from answering.

'Things like phishing attacks when we masquerade as a trustworthy entity in electronic communication like email, to obtain sensitive information, and fake news that we distribute through social media. You see we keep busy,' he said, smiling.

'The WannaCry worm?' I asked. 'My good friend Claudia is particularly keen for you to share that success with me.'

The professor thought for a moment. I doubted it was reluctance, more considering how to explain a tangled web of activities.

'When you foiled the biological attack and our extortion and blackmailing of Britain?' He said, paused and continued, 'You seem surprised, Max. I know exactly who you are. You see, we had prepared the WannaCry worm for just such a situation. When Monya ordered its release, he also told me about the famous Max and Olivia. I've put two and two together. What are the chances of a frail old Englishman sporting the same name turning up here? You have to be *the* Max.'

'Yes,' I conceded, 'and I think that's why our good Claudia is keen for me to hear what devastation you wreaked. She believes it might be good for my soul.'

'Max you're as arrogant as Monya said that you were. The WannaCry is one of my inventions. It's both a cyber weapon and ransomware. We released it to cripple the British health system just as they were trying to cope with the influx of victims from the biological attack. It locked their computerised medical records. They couldn't process people, check their medical history, access on line x-rays or pathology. We caused total chaos. When the worm locked their computers, it displayed the tell-tale ransom demand, which is where our partnership with the Kremlin comes in. They wanted to hit back at Britain with a cyber-attack and by using malicious software it's a win-win. They get the disruption and we pocket the profits as people pay to get their information back. The WannaCry, I'm not ashamed to admit, was a devastating attack and has now spread to over ninety-nine countries and compromised over 300,000 computers. It will net over sixty million dollars and that's nothing. WannaCry is just one of our ransomware worms. You're from Australia. Last year we extorted more than a billion dollars through cybercrime activities there. What's the population in Australia? Nothing, maybe twenty-two or three million. Just imagine what we are making from places like the USA, Britain, Canada, Europe and now India and even China.'

The figures he was talking about seemed extraordinary and, although I wanted to probe and maybe ask some social and moral questions, though I knew he wouldn't care, I thought it better to wait.

Instead, trying to sound impressed, hoping to learn more about the way the Mafia operated, I asked, 'Monya's syndicate, it can manage all that—worldwide?'

'No. Each member of the Brotherhood has their own dedicated areas of activity. Something like the WannaCry worm crosses all boundaries, so we pay the other members a royalty. These big initiatives have a single Brotherhood syndicate as sponsor, like the blockchain project. The other Brotherhood members contribute money to the research and development and, in return, receive a share of the profits. Not all our schemes work, so having other syndicates involved is a way of sharing the risk.'

'Some projects are too big to fail,' interjected Claudia, looking sternly towards the Professor for talking about blockchains.

He nodded, simply repeating her words a little contritely. 'Yes, some projects are too big to fail.'

This blockchain project must be massive.

I had not heard the term before Monya mentioned it in Moscow and, with Claudia now closing the conversation, I decided the subject was dead for now. Instead, I chose to probe his conscience, searching for anything that I could exploit to my advantage at another time.

'I wonder, did you also calculate the number of people who would die when you shut down the British health system?'

'No,' he replied, squirming uncomfortably before saying arrogantly, 'I assume Claudia was hoping you would feel the weight. We must see these things as they are, collateral damage in a war. For us, this is simple business economics, nothing more, and nothing less.'

Several responses, most of them fuelled by my anger, rushed around my mind but, remembering my plan not to antagonise Claudia, I settled on a different approach, which I hoped would knock the smugness out of the Professor.

'Professor, I appreciate your candour. Might I extend to you the same courtesy?'

He smiled, but I could see apprehension drifting across his face as he nodded in affirmation, unsure what I was about to say.

I stared directly into his eyes and said, 'Claudia knows!

'Knows? Knows what?' he replied, hesitantly.

'That you are compromised!'

He glanced anxiously towards Claudia before returning his gaze to me. I contemplated letting silence work its magic but, instead, chose to exploit his nervousness by upping the pressure.

'Unless you want to join me in wearing cement shoes and exploring the bottom of the harbour, now is the time to speak up.'

I paused and Claudia seemed content to wait and see how the conversation played out. From his body language, the Professor was apprehensive, perhaps frightened. If he was compromised, about now he would be thinking, *how do they know.*

After about twenty seconds, I asked again, 'Well?'

From the panic that was now written across his face, I knew that a confession was moments away.

'It's—it's the CIA. They threatened to kill me and put my son in jail. Claudia, I promise you it's not our operations. No—no, it's—it's the propaganda stuff, the fake news, our meddling in the US elections for the Kremlin.'

The Professor started rambling, trying to unload as much information as quickly as he could. I had no doubt that he was telling the truth because he was petrified. He was the type of man who would be easy to threaten, an easy target. If it weren't for sloppy tradecraft by the CIA, Monya's cyber ventures could have been severely compromised.

The Professor was still ranting when I focused my attention back towards him.

'Ironic, isn't it,' he was saying. 'When the CIA have such a dubious record of meddling in others elections. They don't know how to respond to this modern warfare, when we sabotage their activities by hacking their emails and add spin on social media to exploit their political dysfunction. Claudia,' he continued, maintaining the momentum, 'what else was I to do? They threatened me. Said that, if I tried to leave Croatia, my wife and I would be assassinated. It's my son, I fear for him. He's nothing to do with any of this. He works for a big bank in the USA. They said that the FBI would investigate him and fabricate a trail of fraud which would send him to jail for the rest of his life. I wanted to tell you Claudia, I did. But I couldn't because they're monitoring all of the phones. The office is under surveillance and they are tracking my movements. I'm trapped. I'm sorry Claudia. What was I to do?'

'What information have you given them?' asked Claudia, calmly.

'Nothing about our work. They wanted to know about the fake Facebook accounts, groups, likes and comments. They wanted me to tell them how we have automated the posting across the network and how we manipulate the algorithms to push false information around. I've given them a sample of our phony accounts, a few thousand; that's all.'

'Has your handler shown any interest in the other things we do?' asked Claudia.

It's only a matter of time. The Professor will sing like a canary at the slightest hint of a threat. He's a liability.

'No—no, I promise,' answered the professor, again shifting uncomfortably in his chair.

'Let me explain how this works, sweetie,' said Claudia, smiling, an edginess creeping into her voice. 'Once you are compromised, that is you share any information, no matter how innocuous it may seem in the grand scheme of what we do, they have you by the balls. Then, if you don't give them more when they come asking, they blackmail you, threatening to expose you. By remaining silent, Professor, you have put our operation and billions of dollars at risk.'

The colour drained from the Professor's face and I was convinced that he was aware of his impending fate. I had to bite my bottom lip to stop myself from mocking with, '*Claudia what a lovely world you live in.*'

Instead I kept my counsel. In truth part of me wanted to see how she would manage this conundrum. On the one hand, he had put their business model at risk but on the other, he was an important asset.

'Professor,' she said, apparently unfazed, tomorrow there is a party on the *Lelantos* for some local dignitaries. You and your wife will receive an invitation to attend. Once on board, we will continue with our discussions. Providing you tell me everything, we will protect you, even from the CIA. We can use the *Lelantos* to smuggle you out of Croatia. Until then, continue as if nothing has changed. Don't pack or bring anything out of the ordinary with you to the *Lelantos*, not even a photograph. We will arrange for onward passage of your things, once you are safely out of the country. Professor, whatever you do, you must not tell your wife. Tell her only that you are both expected to attend the function. We were planning on sailing for Split on Sunday. Instead, after the last guest leaves on Saturday night, we will set sail. Once we are at sea, the Dubrovnik cyber operations will be transferred to our Moscow office and the office here will be sterilised. Ordinarily, Professor, it would be a simple matter of taking you off ship with the helicopter and then flying to Moscow in our plane. Unfortunately, we have some minor mechanical problems with the jet, so you will remain with us until it's repaired. The *Lelantos* is impenetrable, I assure you.'

'Thank you, Claudia. I'm really sorry. What about my son and his family?'

'Does he know about your activities?'

'No—no, of course not, he thinks I work for a large multinational company.'

'I will have them picked up thirty minutes after we leave port and are safely at sea. These things, Professor, have a habit of working themselves out, so you needn't worry yourself. Oh, and Professor—'

I had seen Claudia do this before, in the farmhouse in Scotland, when she was counting down to when Olivia should have been killed. She looks at her watch as she speaks, putting the fear of God in you, as she tells you how much time you have left.

'Sweetie, in ten minutes, our men will be watching your son Peter and his darling wife Bella. They have two delightful children. Sammy turned eight just last week and Jade, lovely Jade; five is such a wonderful age don't you think? This not a threat, Professor, call it insurance, until you're safely on board the *Lelantos*, although I'm sure you have no intention of speaking with the CIA again. Monya likes to think of us all as family and, when one of our family is going through a grim time, we help out and sometimes even forgive. If someone were to betray the

262

Brotherhood, especially after we have been generous with our help, well that would be another matter entirely.'

'No—no Claudia, I promise our operations are safe. I'm loyal to the Brotherhood, all I ask is that you protect my family.'

'Very well then, sweetie,' said Claudia.

She stood, which indicated the meeting was over, and I noticed droplets of perspiration trickling down the side of the Professor's face.

'I look forward to seeing you tomorrow sweetie and continuing our wonderful enlightening talk.'

Claudia strutted out of the office and back to the car, twice looking back to me.

'Keep up Max.'

She was in her element: confident, in control and intimidating. I knew that this was a dangerous woman. It was risky, but the timing was right to test her identity once more. It had to be done carefully, with a little humour to help lubricate the topic, moving on, before she became angry. She slowed when we reached the car and even opened the door for me.

She is feeling good.

'Thank you,' I said as she went around the other side, ready for the drive back to the yacht.

When she got in, I fired my first volley. 'We don't make a bad team.'

She didn't reply, but smiled as she fiddled with her keys for the ignition.

'Does it bother you, when you are thinking about the hundreds of people you kill through your involvement with Monya?'

'Hundreds?' She laughed, adding, 'Enough for your government to send you to kill me, perhaps.'

'It must be getting close,' I responded, jovially, wanting to maintain an intense but light exchange. Returning to a more reflective tone for my next question, I said, 'Is that to be the legacy of Claudia?'

'Max, you're mistaken if you think I care about what other people think of me.'

'Ha,' I said in good humour. 'I'm not sure that's true. Look at the way you dress. You're always stunning, even gorgeous. And the cars you drive, the yachts you like to sail on, the private jet, they all make a statement. When you enter a room, you radiate, *I am Claudia*. You have a presence and I wondered if you want to be remembered as something more than a ruthless killer.'

'Is that how you see me?' Claudia asked with a hint of surprise in her voice.

'I see you as Lucia, but I wondered if that's not how you see yourself.' Not wanting to push things too far, I added in a jovial tone, 'Even ruthless people can change; look at Yasser Arafat, Anwar Sadat, Martin McGuinness and even Gaddafi towards the end of his life. Your legacy might yet be as a stateswoman or even peacemaker. Who knows what the future holds? One thing is for certain - it's yours for the choosing. At my age, I'm happy to choose my shoes.'

'I do love you sometimes, Max. There's just one problem with your sermon. The people you mentioned are men and in case you haven't noticed, I'm a woman.'

'We men do tend to dominate when it comes to the ruthlessness stakes,' I said, shrugging my shoulders. 'What about when whole countries change. We call them grand ladies? South Africa after the Apartheid era with its Truth and Reconciliation Commission, Germany after the holocaust and Rwanda after the genocide with its Hutu and Tutsi reconciliation?'

'I noticed,' said Claudia seriously, 'that you didn't include my country, the old Yugoslavia in your list.'

'Sadly, that's true and nor did I say my home of Australia. Both of our countries are yet to reconcile their dark past – to forgive and move forward.'

We both waited, saying nothing, but it was an introspective silence, rather than being uncomfortable.

'I was wondering if I was invited to the party. Randolph did say he had a dinner jacket for me,' I said, breaking the spell.

'Will you promise not to try and escape or cause a commotion?'

'I'm a POW; it's my duty to try and escape.'

Sternly, Claudia looked across at me and, with all humour drained from her voice replied, 'Sweetie, you're a guest and it would be unwise to test my resolve.'

CHAPTER TWELVE

The Party

Claudia

After we returned to the *Lelantos*, I left Max to find Linda.

With other things on my mind, rather than his childlike antics, I brought Linda up to speed and shared my plans for the Professor. I passed the arrangements for Saturday's party over to her and then went to ring Monya on a secure line.

The call lasted over an hour and, having discussed the Professor's lapse, we agreed that the CIA had stumbled into our operation and our main work was not yet compromised. Because of the Professor's knowledge and the development work he had done on the blockchain and cybercurrency project, he was unfortunately invaluable to us. Monya and the eleven other Brotherhood members had invested billions into his research without a return which was still two years away. If the project failed, the Brotherhood could disintegrate under the weight of a bloody and brutal gang war.

'The Professor,' said Monya, 'has to be safeguarded at all cost, because of the blockchain project, of course, but also because his loss will prove catastrophic to my empire. I will not be vulnerable like this, you understand?'

We discussed the plan to smuggle the Professor out of Croatia on board the yacht. At first, Monya was uncomfortable that the Professor had been left at the office. He asked why we had not apprehended and escorted him to the ship at the time. I explained my reasoning, which had several layers. If the CIA had been watching, and I thought that they would be, the moment we bundled the Professor into the car, they would have struck. I wanted them to believe that he was still on their leash - then, they would simply watch and, by the time they realized what was going on, we would have sailed away. I explained that I wished to maintain the Professor's continued loyalty so that he remained dedicated to our task. I told Monya how I'd used the protection of his son and family as a lever and how the Professor's later attendance at the party would secure the co-operation of his wife too.

Reluctantly accepting my reasoning, Monya sealed the fate of the cyber unit saying, 'Close it down and make sure nothing is left behind that can be used to link us to any criminal activities.'

We had business continuity plans in place for situations like this one. Moving the cyber operations was more of an inconvenience than a crisis.

Before the call ended, Monya had one more question. 'Do you think the CIA were behind the attack on the plane?'

'I wouldn't rule it out,' I answered, tentatively, before adding. 'But unlikely. It had the hallmarks of another group, a personal vendetta rather than a government hit.'

If the Professor was to be believed, and the CIA were interested in him only because of our interference in US politics, he would have been safe on board the *Lelantos*. However, because of the party, security was going to be a problematic. In preparation for the event, there would be a lot of movement on and off the yacht. Businesses would be delivering the catering, band equipment and decorations. There were going to be fireworks, the real kind.

The loading dock door in the ship's hull would be open and there would be movement of goods and people along the gangway. A complete security sweep would have to be done, once arrangements were finished. As for the party, we were expecting sixty-five guests and ten band members. That, along with our own staff, meant we were going to have a lot of people on board. With the security level at orange, we should have used metal detectors and x-ray machines, like at an airport but that was not the image Monya wanted for the party or the backdrop for the purchase discussions of Kupari. He knew that it increased our risk.

We'd discussed the options with the head of the security and Linda and I agreed that, once we had the Professor on board, and until we left the harbour, he and his wife were to remain under guard in their cabin. It had bulletproof windows and blast-proof doors, so we expected him to be safe. Along with its missile defence system, the ship bristled with the latest in electronics. Like the Chinese, we had hacked the covert system the CIA used to communicate with its operatives so we were able to monitor their secure radio communications traffic. If they were planning a covert operation against us, we would know.

Like a modern warship, we had the technology to shut down communications, but ruled this out as a pre-emptive measure. We would however monitor movements in and under the water. The party was due to end at midnight with a grand fireworks display. At Linda's suggestion, I agreed to bring this forward to 10.30pm. During the party, we wanted our guards to be discreet, present but invisible and, while Linda would wear an earpiece to be in contact with the control room, I would not. My job was to mingle and conduct the negotiations, and if all went to plan, we would be safely at sea by midnight.

The next morning, the day of the party, I saw Max briefly at breakfast. He came to join Linda and myself at a table, but when he saw that we were deep in conversation, going over the arrangements for the day, he instead said a pleasant *good morning* before leaving to eat in his room.

Two nights previously, when Max infuriated me by saying to Linda, '*Claudia has always been special to Olivia and me,*' I was faced with two choices. I could dismiss the statement as one of

Max's lies designed to cause mischief or tell Linda the truth. I am not unusual. Who amongst us shares stories of our childhood, the intimate things of our past?

Max had designed his pronouncement to create an opening and test my loyalties to Linda. Though I knew his motives, I decided to tell Linda the truth, revealing my connections to Macinec and my meeting with Olivia and Max there. She was sympathetic and understood why I disliked going back to Macinec. She asked if Monya knew and, apprehensively, I told her that he didn't. My decision to spare Max in Scotland was a mistake, she told me.

'I now understand why you didn't. You were not expecting the person in the chair to be *the* Max,' she said, 'nevertheless, you should have disposed of him before reaching Russian waters. You're putting off the inevitable. What have we always said? No loose ends. When the time comes, if you want me to, I will do it for you.'

'Thank you,' I replied. 'You're a loyal friend.'

She was my only friend.

***

The first of the guests arrived at 6.00pm to be greeted by Linda and myself, waiting at the top of the gangway. Linda was to stay with me until the Professor and his wife arrived. She would then whisk them aside and escort them to their cabin.

'They should be here by now,' I said, looking at my watch impatiently and seeing it was 6.45pm. 'Ask the control room if they have picked up any CIA communication or anything else they regard as suspicious.'

Linda took a couple of steps back to speak into her concealed microphone, while I greeted yet another arriving guest. She shook her head before joining me again.

'Don't worry Claudia, they will be here soon.'

'I hope so because it was my decision to do it this way.'

'And to trust that he hadn't already turned against us,' added Linda.

With a slight toss of the head, I replied as nonchalantly as I could, 'Let's not go there.' Then in a lighter tone, I continued, 'You couldn't say we haven't chosen an interesting career.'

'Claudia,' said Linda in a serious voice. 'The control room told me that Olivia and Inspector Axel could be on their way. We suspect that they are on one of seven cruise ships that just left Venice. They don't know which one but some are due in Split tomorrow.'

'How is that possible? How does that old biddy do it?' I said, speaking to myself rather than it being a question for Linda.

'It's worse. Olivia is suspected of blowing up the Rome railway station, shutting down the Venice rail system and sinking several vessels in the Grand Canals. She's on the international terrorist most-wanted list – everybody is looking for her.'

'I thought that Max was the bumbling fool of the two but Olivia seems to be a walking disaster area. There is no need to worry, she won't be boarding this ship.'

'Claudia,' said Linda, pausing to consider her words. 'Olivia may be a fool, and is herself no threat, but she is bringing the entire world with her. Even we won't be able to shake that kind of attention if she brings it to our doorstep. May I suggest we abandon sailing to Split and instead head for Turkey. The Professor would be safer and neither the CIA or even Olivia could touch us there. Besides, there are some beautiful islands there too.'

'Are you suggesting we run?'

'Yes.'

'Would we do this, Linda, I mean what Olivia is doing for Max if one of us were taken?'

I spoke the words involuntarily and tried to inject humour into them, to hide the weakness it betrayed in me. However, I *wanted* to hear her answer.

'Of course, not. The Brotherhood wouldn't allow it. We are different.'

I looked at my watch again and it was approaching 7.00pm. Thoughts of Olivia finding us were pushed to the back of my mind, replaced by fear. If my plan for the Professor was derailing, the consequences would be catastrophic for me.

'Linda, I need to mingle, talk with the guests and pretend to laugh at their appalling jokes. The moment they arrive, send one of your men to let me know. Linda, I agree with your suggestion. Tell the captain to make the necessary arrangements. We sail for Turkey.'

I was about to leave, when I noticed a taxi appear on the dock and decided to wait - to see who it was.

'At last!' I said aloud as the Professor and his wife walked up the gangway. Relieved, I let out an audible sigh as I said. 'They're yours now. I need to go and buy us a resort.'

When a weight is lifted from your shoulders it's surprising how it lightens the mood. I paused before joining the party-goers. It was a delightful warm spring night, the sky was clear, and the music rhythmic, inviting dancing, which many people were doing. It wasn't so loud as to stop conversation.

I launched myself into the fray, introducing myself and mixing as I apologised for Monya's absence. Towards 9.00pm I joined three men, with whom I would be discussing Kupari.

'Gentlemen, may I join you?' I asked, approaching them while lifting my champagne glass.

Chatting, flirting, laughing, using all of the tricks in my repertoire, I worked to disarm them.

'More champagne,' I called, emptying my glass for the second time.

As I had expected, the men had matched me drink for drink but, unlike them, I was using the trick Monya had taught me when we first met. The wine waiters were ensuring that my champagne had the potency of mineral water. Before the negotiations, I wanted them happy and relaxed but not drunk. That would have been counter-productive. We'd agreed to private talks at 9.30pm and it was now approaching 9.20pm and we were starting our third glass.

'Gentleman,' I said, 'may I suggest we retire to start our deliberations?'

I was about to add, *follow me*, when Linda caught my attention. 'If you wouldn't mind excusing me, I will just be a moment,' I said instead.

Maintaining a reassuring smile, I left the men to join Linda at the bow of the boat, well away from the other passengers.

'Is there a problem?'

'Half an hour ago a sensor picked up some movement in the water. We checked but drew a blank. Then ten minutes ago an alarm on one of the lower level doors activated. It could be nothing, because we have people wandering all over the yacht but I'll have security doing a deck by deck search and I thought you would want to know.'

'Sounds like you have it in hand but let's double the guard on the Professor's room, with instruction that unless I have given clearance, they are to shoot anybody who tries to enter, or gains entry. Once I've finished my meeting, I'll join you. One last thing, have you seen Max? I wouldn't want our potential intruders actually being him trying to leave us.'

He's right over there,' said Linda pointing with her eyes toward the railing.

***

Max

Pretending to be gazing over the harbour, I watched Claudia and Linda as they huddled together in an intense conversation. Turning, I scanned the deck and saw the security staff, scurrying about.

Something is unsettling them.

Claudia would be worried that if the CIA discovered her plans to smuggle the Professor out of Croatia, they might try a snatch and grab operation. This was the opportunity for which I had been waiting. Having spent the last two days ensuring that I had been seen by every guard as I wandered the ship before retiring each night, now was the time to make a break for it. I would do my best to avoid detection but at the worst, I hoped that I would be ignored. Just Max going for his nightly wander, they'd think, as they searched the boat for an intruder.

I waited until Claudia headed back towards the party before I followed at a discreet distance. The three men she'd entertained joined her and they headed inside the yacht. Glancing around, I located Linda who was busily talking into her microphone, scanning the deck and then looking over the side, obviously checking to see if anyone or anything was in the water. While she was distracted, I slipped inside, making my way through the dining room before dropping down a level and stopping outside my cabin door. Pausing, I heard approaching feet as they echoed along the corridor. There was no time to hide so, waiting until they were about to round the corner, I launched myself forward, with an old man's shuffle, and, head slightly bowed, into their path.

'Good evening,' I pronounced as if slightly shaken to meet them head on.

As I was close to my own cabin, I suspected that security staff wouldn't be alarmed.

As quickly as I could, I added, 'I'm taking a stroll, away from all of that fuss and noise outside, before turning in for the night.'

'Okay Max,' was all they said.

I waited as they continued along the hallway, then smiled when I overheard one of them speak into their radio.

'We just met Max on his nightly stroll. Don't mistake him for an intruder if he comes your way.'

Moving as stealthily as I could, it took me fifteen minutes to reach the door to the submarine bay. The decision was now or never. I knew opening it would likely trigger an alarm somewhere else in the ship, but it was a risk I had to take.

Once inside, I saw the submarine. It looked like a clear bubble in front of a solid hull with two protruding pods running forward of it, which then angled down, one on each side of the dome. From inside, the pilot would have an unobstructed view in almost every direction. On the outside of the submarine, I counted six thrusters that must control omni-directional movement. Invitingly, in the dry dock holding pen, it glistened, waiting to be stolen.

To the right, attached to an inside bulkhead of the yacht, was a large panel of buttons. Moving closer to study them, I found one button with *Flood* embossed and another, *Outer Door.*

I reasoned they flooded the dry dock and opened the bay doors to allow the submarine to leave the ship.

My finger hovered over the *flood* button, while my mind churned over the best way to execute this escape. If entering the submarine bay hadn't triggered an alarm, flooding the compartment and opening the outer doors surely would. I decided that, if I could be out in the submarine before the party guests left the yacht, it would be difficult for Claudia to give chase using the ship. I had never been in a mini-sub before so I decided to risk detection for a little longer, by familiarising myself with the controls of the submarine, before flooding the dock.

Pulling my finger away from the button, I returned to the dock only to discover that finding a door to enter the sub was a test. A quick search turned frantic after my second circle of the submarine. Stopping to regain my composure and counting to ten, I scanned the submarine. Then I saw it, a hatch on top of the clear dome. Clambering up wasn't difficult and it opened with ease. Once inside, I pulled and secured the hatch, in practice for diving, and lowered myself into the middle of the three seats.

This is getting worse.

Expecting to see instruments and controls like a plane, I was confronted instead by nothing but an unimpeded view out of the front. Looking about, I found, on the seat to my right, what appeared to be a controller from a video game. It wasn't fixed to a dashboard, but attached by a flexible cord. The whole thing could be held in one hand. Like a game controller, there were two joysticks, one on the left and the other on the right.

presumably for directional control?

In the middle was a round dial which read *Vertical Thrust*. Underneath the left joystick were two buttons, one reading *Hold Depth* and the other *Hold Heading*. Under the right joystick, another two buttons read *Push to Talk* and *Dead Man Trigger*. Above the *Thrust* dial were another four buttons, two for *Diving Tanks* and the others saying, *Vent and Blow*. Exploring a little more, I saw that, in front of me and a little above eye height, was a digital monitor, attached to the dome.

Looking at my watch, I saw that it was just after 10.00pm. The submarine controls seemed simple enough but I was conscious that I needed to hurry. In a matter of moments, security personnel could be here, searching for whoever entered or left the submarine bay. The only remaining obstacle was to find how to fire it up. Somewhere, there had to be a switch or key. I turned the controller over, flipping it around several times but could see nothing like ignition, start, on or go. I looked about the bubble, seeing nothing except the passenger seats. Time was ticking away and, glancing

279

again at my watch, I noted that it was now 10.05pm. Raising my head, I peered at the digital monitor which was a dead screen. Running my fingers over it and pushing in a few places, it suddenly came alive.

Bingo, we have power.

For a younger man, perhaps opening the hatch and hauling himself out would be easy. But at eighty-seven, it proved more challenging than entering and I was breathless by the time my feet hit the dry dock. I had to stop and rest for a minute to regain my strength. Worried, I glanced around and was amazed that I hadn't been discovered. After making it back to the master control panel and, while reaching up to press the flood button, I changed my mind.

If I haven't been discovered by now, the chances are no alarms have been triggered.

I would risk another couple of minutes of rest, to make it easier for me to scramble back into the mini-sub.

What had seemed like a clever idea, proved to be a nightmare for me as any sound sent my heart racing and the anxiety of being caught made me more breathless than trying to escape.

Bugger it!

I punched the flood button and the sound of the sea rushing in and filling the dry dock with foaming water was deafening. Everyone on the ship would surely be able to hear it. I had no choice but to hit the *Outer Door* button at the same time, hoping that the unit had a safety override that wouldn't let the door open until the dock was safely flooded.

Moving as fast as I could, I clambered back on top of the submarine, opened the hatch, and shut it behind me before lowering myself into the pilot's seat. Looking again at my watch, I saw that it was now almost 10.20, perfect timing. Outside, water had risen and was surrounding the bubble. It was time to go and I imagined security staff racing towards me. Picking up the control panel, my fingers hovered, just touching the two dive buttons. Closing my eyes, I squeezed down and pushed.

Nothing happened.

Except for the sound of the sea water filling the dock, the submarine was quiet. Opening my eyes and looking up at the digital screen, I saw a key pad was being displayed and underneath it was: '*Please enter your pin.*' My heart sank and I dropped the controller, cradling my head in my hands. I was trapped and couldn't stop Olivia.

Tap-tap-tap came the sound of somebody outside knocking on the hatch. A few seconds later, it was opened.

'Good evening Max,' said Randolph. 'Claudia asks that you might join her on deck, for the fireworks.'

CHAPTER THIRTEEN

Corfu

Olivia

'Good morning, Lady Olivia,' greeted Jean-Marc when I opened the cabin door to his knocking.

'We have docked in Corfu m'lady,' he continued as a passenger pushed hurriedly past behind him. 'People are already queuing to disembark and may I suggest, it might be wise for us to join the crowd. Unfortunately, m'lady, we don't have long if we are to be at the fortress by 9.30. I would suggest that we push in.'

'The umbrella, Jean-Marc?' I asked, miming giving one or two of the recalcitrant passengers a quick jab to hasten our exit.

'Perhaps an, *excuse me*, may suffice, m'lady!'

It's difficult to highlight any advantages, except reduced cost, of travelling on a lower deck of a cruise liner shared with the humbler members of the ship's crew. Embarking and disembarking were certainly two of those, as at the end of our corridor was the gangway. While the queue of those waiting to escape for their day's adventure, exploring the island for a whole six hours, before heading to the next port, snaked up the staircase, we simply walked from our cabin, along the corridor and, following an *excuse me* or two, we were out.

Umbrella in hand and with no casualties to report from our exit, we boarded the waiting complementary inter-port shuttle and were driven to the passenger terminal. This was the moment of truth. It was possible that, after Rome and Venice, the authorities would be checking all passengers leaving cruise ships. So far, luck had favoured the brave, and with no other option, all we could do was continue. We'd have to deal with any obstacles that materialised. If we passed through an immigration check point, it was difficult to tell, for we walked into the terminal on the dockside and straight out. No one stopped or showed us the slightest interest. We had arrived.

The walk from the harbour to the town of Corfu, was about three kilometres. Time permitting, meaning fifteen years ago, I would have enjoyed the gentle half-hour walk, but a taxi was in order today and luckily, a lengthy line awaited our selection.

It's customary to approach the first taxi in the rank. Having asked to be taken into town, we were waved away like an annoying fly at a barbecue. This unsightly scene was played out a further six times. Each cab driver was waiting for a more lucrative fare, namely a rich American wanting a four-hour guided tour of the island.

'This is going well,' I said to Jean-Marc, who wisely counselled that we try the cab at the end of the line.

An obliging taxi driver, who couldn't believe his luck at obtaining a fare into town, without losing his position in the line – last— would have driven us all of the way to the New Fortress but with time to spare, having had no delays leaving the ship, we decided the town would do.

Corfu is a tourist town but the old part is charming with its vibrant architecture, fascinating little streets and hidden alleyways. Strolling around, we found influences of a history stretching back to the eighth century BC, were everywhere. It could be seen through the unique mixture of influences from Venetian, French and Sicilian.

'It's quite surreal,' I said to Inspector Axel. 'Here we are in Corfu, a place that's so beautiful and picturesque that I'm tempted to call it magnificent. Yet, we are sought by the police and hunted by the Mafia. These two things are so incongruous.'

'As is life,' he replied.

As we continued to wander, slowly making our way towards the Fortress, my sense of being out of place became stronger. We left a narrow lane, with its Byzantine buildings, and came out onto an area of arcaded terraces and fashionable cafes, in front of which was an English cricket pitch. Not exactly what one would expect to see in Greece.

The entrance to the New Fortress was in front of the Liston, near the Corfu Esplanade, a large park area running between the old town and the bridge linking the fortress to the town. Like something from a James Bond movie, this was the perfect setting for a secret meeting, with its massive bastions, twin peaks and fortified castles and a fabulous backdrop of sky and sea.

'Have you any idea how we are meant to recognise our contact?' I asked the Inspector, which was a superfluous question as he knew no more than did I.

He humoured me anyway by saying, 'I'm sure he or she will find us, providing we are on time at 9.30.'

He looked at his watch and then smiled at me.

'Our timing is perfect. In fact, being found has been one of our problems, Lady Olivia because we tend to stick out, don't you think?'

'Jean-Marc,' I said pretending to be offended. 'You are not suggesting that I look old?'

'Not at all,' he replied. 'Distinguished and elegant.'

A polite way of saying ancient!

Max and I had been lucky. We had travelled, visiting many places, but this was my first time to Corfu. Despite a mixture of trepidation, not knowing if the contact would know the whereabouts of Max, and impatience, because 9.30am had already come and gone, we wandered the grounds stopping to admire the views, as any tourist would. Trying to blend in, which *was a little unusual* for us.

The next time I stole a glance at my watch it was almost 10.00am.

We have come a long way in our search for Max and it can't come to naught.

'Geia sou file mou,' came a warm and jovial voice from behind us, repeating it again in English. 'Hello my friends.'

I'm not sure what we were expecting but the warm welcome startled us and, for a second, neither of us knew how to respond, until I managed an unconvincing. 'Hello.'

We were greeted by a man, in his fifties, speaking beautifully clear English with an alluring, sexy Greek accent. He was casually but neatly dressed, wearing bone-coloured trousers, and a light purple long-sleeved shirt, topped off by a cream Panama hat with a black band running around it.

'Hello,' he said again, tipping his hat as he spoke. 'Sando said I was to expect you either yesterday or today and here you are. What a delight. What do you think of our beautiful fortress?' His question was rhetorical so he didn't wait for an answer and continued. 'It's an impressive sight built on top of Agios-Markos. The Venetians, who occupied Corfu from 1386 to 1864, started it in 1572, to fortify the defences because the Old Fortress was no longer enough. The original architect was the military engineer Ferrante Vitelli and it took a long time to build, being finished around 1625. The French and British completed their work, improving the construction. The building you can see before you was built by the British during their rule of the island between 1815 and 1863 and they did one hell of a job - it's still standing proud and firmly. Did you know, its official name is Saint Mark, although everybody knows it as the New Fortress? You will find the best panoramic views of Corfu from on top of the Fortress. Ah, but let me stop rambling, for you didn't come all of this way for a history lesson.

'Olivia, or is it Lady Olivia,' he continued with a chuckle. 'You have had quite an exciting trip, or so I've been told. A lot of people are searching for you, but you needn't worry. From this beautiful Fortress, I could see if you were being followed and, surprisingly, you're not.'

'Are you able to help?' I asked, ignoring his observations about the unwanted attention we had gathered along the way. I wasn't sure if I was proud or embarrassed by my notoriety.

Proud I think.

'Ah, straight to the point, I like that, Olivia. Why not, you have come such a long way to ask me about Claudia.' He paused before looking from me to the Inspector. 'You are thinking – no! Will he tell us the truth? Or maybe, why would I help you?'

'It's a fair question,' answered the Inspector. 'We wondered if you would be here. Sando could have sent us on a wild goose chase and we would have been none-the-wiser, until we turned up here.'

The man, who still hadn't told us his name, thought that the Inspector's manner of speech was funny. 'A wild-goose-chase, yes, I like that. If you will excuse another history lesson, perhaps it will help you understand and trust me.

'I had relatives, family, in Yugoslavia. They were living in a place called Zvornik during the Balkans war. Even though they weren't Muslim, nonetheless, they suffered at the hands of Ratko Mladic. Forty thousand people were forcibly expelled, ethnically cleansed the media called it, from the Zvornik district and four thousand died or went missing. After the invasion of Zvornik in 1992, many fled, but were then encouraged to return, only to find that all inhabitants had to be registered. These registrations led to arrests and deportation to concentration camps. The Zvornik massacre, as it became known, was the murder and ethnic cleansing against Bosniaks and other non-Serbs living in the Zvornik district, and was carried out by Serbian Paramilitary groups. My family were among those victims. They were removed from Zvornik and we never heard from them again. Mass graves have been uncovered since the war but my relatives were not among the bodies. One of the most feared and brutal of those paramilitaries was a division called the Yellow Wasps.

'The mention of that name, Yellow Wasps, caused terror among non-Serbians and there was no person more ruthless than a lieutenant called Claudia. Towards the end of the war she fled. No one knew where for certain, but we suspected Britain. Vojin

Vučković, the commander of the Yellow Wasps, his brother, Duško, and Ratimir, were convicted in 1996 for killing seventeen civilians but that was just the beginning. War crime trials for the Zvornik massacre continued until 2010 but Claudia was never apprehended.

'It wasn't until one of my men started working on the yacht for a Russian billionaire called Monya Mogilevick, and he mentioned the billionaire's lover Claudia, that I became suspicious. I wondered if this could be her. You see we already knew that Monya was from the Russian Mafia and this seemed the perfect place for her to turn up. We have no photographs of Claudia from that time in Zvornik, only descriptions and these are tainted by time. But from how my contact described Claudia, and from her brutal reputation in the underworld, I believe she must be the and the same Claudia that we seek. So, that's why I help you – for my family.

'Claudia is on the billionaire's luxury yacht, the *Lelantos*, but she's virtually untouchable while on board. You would need a division of elite commandos to get anywhere near her. The yacht's security guards are ex-Russian special forces and it has bulletproof glass, lasers, a missile defence system and even its own submarine. Don't underestimate Monya. He is a powerful, influential and dangerous man and the head of a group of twelve Russian Mafia syndicates, called the Brotherhood. He united the Brotherhood under his leadership ten years ago. Before that, they fought each other in bloody territorial wars. Monya was unlike others who tried to unite rival factions before. He's smarter, and instead of brutal terror tactics, he's used a franchise system, like that used in normal commerce, with him as the CEO. For their loyalty, their syndicates would net billions of dollars. The empire is run like one of his companies and the syndicates have all prospered and grown. As long as the money flows, the fealty continues. Monya has become the wealthiest and the most powerful of all the Brotherhood but that's not what makes him so dangerous.

'Over the last few years he has courted the Russian Government, or maybe the Kremlin courted him. I'm not entirely sure what he's been up to but we do know that he has some powerful and influential friends in the foreign intelligence service. Ask yourself, how many people have access to a military grade missile defence system for their own private yachts? I tell you this so that you know. If you take on Claudia, understand who and what is protecting her.'

'If it's so hopeless,' I said, 'why tell us?'

'You may have an advantage. They are expecting a whale and you are a minnow.'

I peered at the olive-skinned man for a moment, intrigued at what he'd told us.

'Do you know if Max is still alive?' I asked at last, sadness decorating my voice.

'My contacts tell me that, not only is he very much alive, but that he's on the super yacht with Claudia. They were due to arrive in Split yesterday for what was to be the start of a two-week holiday sailing the Adriatic and Greek Islands. You must understand that getting information off the boat is difficult and we must be careful because of Monya's connections with Russian Intelligence. We were taken unawares when the *Lelantos* docked here, in Corfu, this morning. The Harbour Master tells me she's sailing for Turkey later today.'

'It's in the harbour now?' I asked. 'Max is here, in Corfu?'

'Unfortunately for you, yes. The *Lelantos* will be here for another one or two hours, that's all. Not enough time I imagine, to put in place whatever plan you have. I wish that I could help you but this is neither the time nor place for me to reach Claudia. I hope your rescue succeeds. Now I'm afraid I must leave. Good luck, both of you and antio sas – goodbye.'

I'd tracked Max over three-thousand, two-hundred kilometres and he was now only ten minutes away on an impenetrable ship. Watching the man with no name walking quickly away, I stared at the historic fortress where we stood. This had been the site of many battles, a bastion, a stronghold of Corfu. It had stood for hundreds of years as a monument to great resolve and architecture. In the harbour awaiting us, a modern castle, a super yacht, packed with the latest defences, imprisoned my beloved Max. I felt so close and yet so far.

'Are you okay?' asked the Inspector, breaking into my reflections on the challenges which lay ahead of us. 'What are you planning?'

'Ah – the plan,' I said vaguely. 'The cunning plan. That will depend on what we find when we reach the dock.'

'Lady Olivia. You do have a plan,' asked the Inspector smiling.

***

The *Lelantos* was not difficult to find; it dwarfed the other private yachts in the harbour. From our vantage point, standing behind a parked car, we had an unobstructed view of the ship, while believing we had cover ourselves. Without binoculars, it was difficult to make out clearly what was happening. The gangway was down and, at the top, on either side, were what looked like two guards. People in white sailor's suits, we assumed were from the yacht, were on the dock talking with what looked like some local harbour officials. A blonde woman about the same age and stature as Claudia, was standing near the yacht's railing. I stared intently but I didn't think it was Claudia. She was joined by a man.

Is it an old man? Could it be Max?

It was difficult, no impossible, to tell from this distance but still my heart leaped. I wanted to jump up and wave, to call out and attract his attention so that I could have a better look. Apart from jumping being dangerous at my age, I knew that doing this would-

293

be folly. The element of surprise and being a harmless old lady were my only weapons.

'Stay here,' I whispered to the Inspector, though no one would have heard had I talked normally.

'What are you going to do?' he asked.

'I'm going to put up my umbrella, to keep the sun off my head and as a disguise, and then simply walk up and take a closer look. They will be expecting two of us, so I'm sure I will go quite unnoticed. I will return with the intel– isn't that what you police on a stake out call it – intel?'

'Don't you think I should go?'

'Not at all, Inspector. A strapping young man like yourself. The moment you are within even a hundred yards of the yacht, they will intercept you and shepherd you away. I'll be quite safe and will be a couple of minutes, no more.'

Without waiting for a reply, I popped open my brolly and strolled, as fast as I could, inconspicuously, towards the *Lelantos*. When I reached the sailors and harbour staff, I simply said. 'It's a beautiful morning isn't it?' While giving the umbrella a twirl in my fingers, I made it to the bottom of the gangway before the guards at the top payed me any attention. Folding my umbrella, I yelled out, as I mounted the stairs.

'Claudia I'm here!'

With resolve, I marched towards the top and a burly man with broad shoulders and six feet six if he was an inch, moved to block my way.

'Out of my way,' I called, giving him three good whacks with my brolly. 'Claudia is expecting me.'

I pushed past him and on to the deck. The other guard, the one I didn't whack, was paralysed, staring at me in the upmost disbelief.

'Go on,' I commanded in a loud voice to ensure the harbour officials could hear. 'Toot sweet now, let Claudia know that Lady Olivia Suzanne Elizabeth Huggins has arrived!'

CHAPTER FOURTEEN

Lelantos

Claudia

The security alert during the reception was caused by a faulty door sensor. The night had gone off without a hitch and our purchase of Kupari was all but guaranteed. Max's attempted escape had been a source of much entertainment. Even I, when summoned to the control room, laughed as we watched him on CCTV, particularly as he sneaked about, hiding when someone approached, thinking he was going undetected. The funniest moments had been watching him trying to climb in and out of the submarine and the look of horror on his face when he pushed the *flood button* and the sea had started rushing in. I now understood why the guards in Moscow had been in stiches watching Max riding the scooter. Once I left the control room, having ordered Max to be brought up on deck, I wasn't sure if I was embarrassed for him or in admiration for his doggedness. Whatever it was, after the fireworks display, I ordered that he be restricted to his cabin.

The last of our guests left the *Lelantos* around 11.30pm, encouraged by the engines being started. We sailed from Dubrovnik just after midnight. Security personnel did a final sweep of the yacht and, with the all-clear, I could finally relax.

The captain had advised us that the trip to Turkey would have pushed our fuel reserves, particularly if we needed to run at speed. He recommended refuelling in Corfu before continuing.

***

A commotion from outside brought me onto the deck. I was horrified with what I saw – Olivia. Somehow, she had managed to board. What was I going to do now?

'What's she doing here?' I barked at the security guards protecting the gangway, before seeing the harbour staff on the dock, watching on, intrigued.

'Olivia, sweetie,' I called aloud, changing my tactics, while approaching with my arms stretched out for a warm embrace.

Giving her a big hug, I guided her away from the prying eyes.

'You,' I commanded to one of the guards who had let her on board, 'take her down to the dining room, and,if she gives you any trouble, tie her up. And, take that stupid umbrella away from her.'

'Is Max on board?' Olivia asked before being marched away.

'Sweetie, you will be lucky if you live long enough to find out. You have no idea what you have done.'

When I had finished saying the words, I realised that my anger had been replaced by frustration.

'What are you going to do? Kill her? You know she can't stay.' said Linda who had been on deck the whole time and watched the comedy of errors unfold.

'It's a dilemma, a real dilemma,' I said. 'Ordinarily, we would just dispose of her, but if she's a wanted terrorist and is traced to us and with her Inspector Axel still at large, the authorities will want to arrest her. The harbour staff were watching us but we can't hand her over to them now, because we have the Professor and Max on board. You can be sure that they would take the opportunity to search the *Lelantos*. No, we can't kill her and we can't hand her over, not yet anyway. For the time being, unless you have a better idea, we make the run for Turkey. Our priority must be the Professor. What do you think?'

'You're right, the Professor comes first, but when you hand over Olivia, what about Max? You can be sure that they will search the boat looking for him and what about the Professor then?'

'The Professor will be gone by the time we have to deal with Olivia.'

'Not if we are intercepted between here and Turkey and now that we have Olivia on board, that's entirely possible. No Claudia, I think, as soon as we are at sea, we dispose of Max and get rid of all evidence that he was ever on board. We can just say that she was lying.'

'The Professor?' I asked, thinking that a sea intercept was a possibility.

'If it looks as if we are going to be stopped, we put him and his wife in the mini-sub and they sit on the bottom of the ocean until we have been searched and cleared to continue. At worst, the sub can take them ashore.'

'All right, Linda, we have a plan. I'll go and issue the instructions to the captain.'

'And Max?'

'We put him down, wrap the body in weights, use the helicopter to fly him off the ship and then dump the body into the sea. He will never be found. But not until we are out of sight of the land, and we'll do it nicely – kill him as painlessly as we can. You might as well take him to Olivia, so they can spend some time together before the end and I want to be the one who tells them. Max will understand and I'm sure Olivia will want to go with him. They're a couple of silly old buggers. Olivia didn't think that she was going to rescue him - she came to die with him. But that can't happen right now. Linda, guard them carefully and I will join you once I've spoken to the captain.'

I found the captain and we discussed the safest and fastest route to Turkey. He recommended that we track deeper out into the Ionian Sea, as if we were heading into the Mediterranean, before cutting back inside of Crete for the Aegean Sea. A patrol vessel or a warship could easily outrun us, so our best strategy was to avoid them. If radar picked up a vessel and it altered course in response to a manoeuvre by us, he would alert our security and myself immediately.

Before joining Linda, I met with the head of security demanding that, until we were safely at the Turkish Riviera, I wanted the submarine manned twenty-four hours a day, ready to be deployed at a minute's notice. If the Professor or his wife left their cabin, they were to be accompanied at all times, ready to be evacuated. The helicopter was to be prepared and I wanted all our CCTV recordings destroyed, especially anything featuring Max.

Corfu was one of my favourite islands and I decided that, rather than joining Linda, Max and Olivia in the dining room, I would stay on deck and watch as we pulled out of port.

I'm only putting off the inevitable, I thought as we gathered speed heading out to sea.

My mental torment started the second I hesitated and refrained from killing Max back in Scotland. *This moment was always coming.* I knew why I hadn't pulled the trigger but Max was right, ever since, I had been at war with myself, trying to make sense of my life. There was no stopping it now and most of what was about to happen was of my own doing. If I had left him behind, things would have been different, but Max's time had come to an end.

Yet, I felt stirred, even touched, by Olivia who had come all of this way to be with him at the end. It would be cruel to make her live. What an irony; sparing Olivia was going to be the most painful thing I could do to her and Max.

I feared killing Max, knowing that it would weigh heavily on me. Yet out of kindness, to ensure that it was swift and painless, it had to happen at my own hands. I lingered a moment longer, staring at the brilliant blue of the water, to where it met and mingled with the sky. In that space, I saw a frightened Lucia, with her arms stretching out before her, running.

'I knew you would come,' I said aloud.

***

Max and Olivia were sitting together, holding hands, of all things. I'm not sure if it looked odd or perfect.

Sighing loudly while shaking my head, I said, 'I should have guessed, the moment I heard you were looking for us, that you would find your way here. I spared Max because I remembered, yes, I remember both of you. But I can't help both of you now. Olivia, you are wanted for the Rome bombing, even though we both know you weren't involved. Nonetheless, because of the terrorism alert, we must hand you over. It's possible that they already know you are on board. I'm afraid, Olivia, that we can't let them find Max and you understand what that means?'

From the expression on Olivia's face, I knew that this revelation had taken her by surprise, but for Max, he was expecting it.

'Believe it or not,' I continued, 'this is not how I wished it would end. It may come as a small consolation but, I promise you Max, that your death will be quick and as painless as I can make it.'

I paused for a couple of seconds to let what I had said sink in.

'How long do I have?' asked Max looking at Olivia.

'I'm afraid we risk being intercepted at any time, so it will be as soon as we are clear of the land and any other shipping. Maybe another hour, no more.'

If either of them was planning to fight, their expressions didn't betray their intentions. Max simply tilted his head in recognition of his fate.

'We will place guards on all the exits and they will be instructed to tie you both up if you try and leave. Linda and I will give you some time to be alone, that's the best I can do.'

If these were lesser people, they would have begged, but with the stoicism you expect from the British, they remained resolute. The only thing that Max did say as we were leaving was, 'Goodbye, my Lucia,' which made me stop. When I turned, he looked deeply at Olivia, took hold of her hands and whispered, 'A thing of beauty is a joy for ever.'

'Wordsworth?' I asked.

'Keats,' he replied, now smiling at me.

'Yes, of course. Keats. *Its loveliness increases; it will never pass into nothingness,*' I said, completing his lines. Our eyes met as they did in Scotland and once more I knew it was him. It was Max who came for me all those years ago – but this time I wouldn't be safe.

I wanted to say, *Goodbye.* To say, *sorry Max*, but I stubbornly resisted and instead, Linda and I left, walking out and onto the deck. There we stood together in silence, gazing out over the water. She didn't speak nor ask any questions but I felt that she knew, perhaps understood, that, even for a person like me, this was difficult.

Another Kupari - at least this is a beautiful day to die.

The sound of the explosion and the yacht being violently lifted and thrown from bow to stern shattered the tranquillity of the moment. The engines stopped, and the instant I regained my balance, it was almost lost again when the ship dipped noticeably to the stern. For a second, Linda and I were frozen, stunned, confused and unsure what was happening. Then, through the shouts of alarm, I looked around but could see no signs of fire or damage on deck. I guessed that the explosion had come from below the waterline.

'We need to get to the bridge,' I said to Linda, ignoring members of the crew who were now appearing on deck.

Calmly, despite the chaos that was beginning to unfold around us, we made our way to the captain. He was busy issuing orders over the radio as we entered the bridge.

'She's going down,' was the first thing he said.

'Do you know what happened?'

'Torpedo, mine, or explosive device attached to the hull. Whatever it was, we have a hole in the stern. We need to abandon ship.'

'Issue the orders,' I said, 'but I want the Professor off first and well away from here before any rescuers arrive. Can we launch the helicopter?'

'No, she's tipping too quickly.'

The emergency alert sound rang out over the ship's PA system.

WOOP, WOOP, WOOP.

It was deafening and was followed by the captain's voice saying, 'All hands to your abandon ship stations.' He paused before saying three times, 'Abandon ship, abandon ship, abandon ship.'

'Who?' asked Linda.

'No idea,' I replied as we moved as quickly as we could towards the bow of the yacht in search of the Professor.

Moving about was becoming more difficult by the second. Because we were sinking stern first, the bow of the ship was beginning to point skywards at some twenty-five degrees. I was relieved to find the Professor and his wife being helped by two of our ex-special-services soldiers into a lifeboat.

'Go!' I yelled at them. 'Get him off.'

The yacht dipped farther backwards, making moving about almost impossible. Looking around, I saw several life-rafts were in the water, filled with people. The captain, whom we had seen

305

moving from one abandon ship station to another, ensuring that all of his crew were accounted for, was now holding on tightly to the rails with one hand, and speaking into his walkie talkie, as we joined him.

'The Professor,' he said, 'is in one of our high-speed dinghies and heading away from here. The rest of the crew are all accounted for and have abandoned ship. Ladies, that leaves just us.'

'Max and Olivia?'

'They didn't make it out of the dining room and, with the angle of the ship, it's impossible to get to them. I would say it's already flooded, gone under. I'm sorry but they're gone. I suggest we abandon ship ourselves.'

***

Max

The sudden explosion and the violent movement of the yacht knocked Olivia clean off her chair and onto the floor. She must have struck her head, because despite my kneeling beside her and calling, 'Olivia, Olivia,' she didn't move. The ship tipped suddenly and I found Olivia and I were sliding deeper into the ship, while the items on the tables, plates, glasses, knives, and forks, rained down upon us. When the ship tilted even farther, anything that wasn't held securely on the walls and ceiling became missiles.

'Help us!' I cried out, but the men guarding the exits had gone.

From the depths, I could hear sea water as it flooded the compartments below. Looking about, I realised that, even if I could arouse Olivia, we couldn't crawl up the slope to freedom. From where we were lying, the huge glass windows, which normally gave a magnificent view out over the front of the boat, were filled with sky. We were sinking stern first.

'Wake up my love,' I said again, and she stirred, probably because of the sea water which was beginning lap around us, rather than my voice. 'We've got to try and move, Olivia, the water's coming in.'

Opening her eyes, she somehow managed a smile and said, 'You do seem to get us into some trouble.'

'Me?' I answered. 'I was about to live out the rest of my life in the lap of luxury. Do you think you can move?'

With some help from me, she managed to stand and we rested ourselves against the rear wall, adjusting our position as the angle of the yacht increased. The water was now pooling about our feet.

'Any suggestions?' Olivia asked, unable to hide the distress in her voice.

The only response I could think of seemed wrong, but I said it anyway. 'They say drowning is a nice way to go. Anyway, anything is better than dying in that godforsaken nursing home.'

'At least we're together,' added Olivia, reaching out and taking my hand.

I could feel the seeping of the water as it climbed over our bodies. Glancing down, I saw that it had reached our knees. I was surprised how difficult it was to control the panic that was racing through my mind. I began to imagine the last minute of my life. The water would cover our faces and, even though there was little point, we would hold our breath anyway. We'd hold it until we were about to burst, with our eyes wide open, looking about in terror. Then we would take our last gasp but, instead of air, sea water would flood into our lungs.

Is there a God?

Thinking of all of the bad things I had done in my life, I wondered if Claudia had been right. If I came to knock on the Pearly Gates, what would St Peter say? *A death is a death is a death?* Or, *Sometimes, Max, we must do these things for a greater good?'* *I'm frightened.*

The bubbling sound as the water filled the dining room was briefly overshadowed by the sound of gunshots from outside. I counted fifteen shots, a short break, possibly while somebody changed a magazine, then another fifteen rounds. Whoever it was, a rescue team perhaps, was trying to smash the windows that now sat almost vertically above us.

Olivia also heard the shooting and looked up.

'It's bulletproof,' I said looking up at the window. 'Someone is trying to reach us. Even if they do get through, I have no idea how they will get to us, but maybe we should put that table in front of us, in case of falling glass.'

With the water now well and truly above our knees, moving to grab the table proved challenging. If nothing else, frantically working out a way to hide behind the table took our minds off drowning.

The dining room once again sank back into its new-found rhythm, a melody of gushing water. We huddled, hidden from the sky by our table but there were no more gunshots. Water began to lap around our waists and the thought of drowning swilled around in my mind once again.

'Have I told you that I love you?' I asked Olivia.

'Not in many, many years, Max, but I know and have always known.' She squeezed my hand with affection before saying softly, 'I'm scared Max.'

I wanted to comfort her - to say something profound so Olivia would feel safe but, '*I'm scared too*', were the only words that came to my lips.

A mighty *thud* was followed shortly after by another *thud* that was so loud I imagined the yacht exploding again. I went to peep around the table, to see what was making such a noise, but Olivia held me still, saying, 'Not yet my love.'

A second later, another colossal THUD! sent glass cascading down, hitting the walls and bouncing harmlessly off our shield.

Items dislodged or upturned that could float began bumping into us as the water continued to rise, quicker now. Discarding our cover, I saw the hook from a crane dangle through the now shattered window and bump and crash as it was slowly lowered towards us. Its route down was difficult because the descent wasn't vertical and it caught, before falling again, only to stop agonisingly close, just above us.

Stretching as high as I could, I even tried to jump, which was impossible as we were encased by water. It was just out of my reach, tantalisingly close. Dropping my arms back to my sides and into the water, I wondered what was the point. Even if we could have held it, then what? Neither Olivia nor I had the strength to haul ourselves along the cable.

Claudia appeared at the window and started the long climb down towards us as the water was reaching our chests. If it wasn't for Olivia steadying me, when the ship tilted farther towards the sky, I would have fallen over and gone under the water. The movement of the yacht was throwing Claudia violently about but she kept descending. Finally, when she reached the hook, she wrapped her legs around the cable then entwined herself in the hook, before flipping upside down and hanging towards us with her arms outstretched. I reached up, stretching towards her and our fingertips touched ever so slightly, but she was too far away.

Seeing despair ripple across her face, I smiled and said, 'I knew you would come.

With tears in her eyes she reached towards us again now screaming out in anguish. 'It's all right Lucia,' I said warmly. 'You have to let us go. We will be okay because we are together.'

Still she hung there, looking down. 'Go on,' I encouraged, 'it will be all right.'

'Max, she cried, 'a thing of beauty is a joy forever.'

I gazed back at my Lucia, smiled and said 'Wordsworth?' Reluctantly, she pulled her fingers away from mine, turned and hauled herself upright, putting both of her feet in the hook at the end of the cable. The water was now lapping just below our shoulders. It was probably survival instinct and a waste of time but we lifted our arms out of the water.

'Go on,' I called again, 'climb!'

It just missed me; a life buoy and then another, both attached to rope, as they came falling from the sky above. Linda appeared at the top, lowering something else towards Claudia.

'It's a radio,' I heard her call. 'Attach the rope holding the life buoys to the hook, and I'll operate the crane. We will bring them up, one at a time, if you radio me the instructions.' Linda then vanished again, as quickly as she had appeared.

Claudia grabbed the rope attached to one of the buoys, securing it to the hook and yelled, 'Put it on and I will help you climb out. One at a time as Linda said.'

'Go on,' I said to Olivia, 'you go first.'

'Max, my dear Max, it's not because we are in a time of equality and it's no longer women first. But if we are both to have a chance of living, you need to go. By the time Claudia comes back, climbing out is going to be harder. I might make it but you won't, my love. Put the buoy on and go. I've got the life jacket, so I will be okay. Wait for me on top.'

I knew that she was right. Olivia was the stronger of the two of us. With Olivia's help I slipped the life buoy over my head and under my arms. I felt a pulling on the rope. Claudia was climbing down it to join us in the water. Just before her feet reached my head I heard her say into the radio, 'Okay Linda, bring us up slowly.'

With a jerk, the life buoy pulled tightly against me, as if it wanted to rip my arms and head off.

Claudia dropped down to my side.

'Max, once we are clear of the water, Linda is going to move the crane and we will swing gently to the side. Together we are simply going to walk up the wall and out of the top. I'll be with you all of the way. I promise, I won't let anything happen to you.'

She wrapped one arm around the rope which hung above my head and placed her other arm around me. I could feel her immense strength, supporting and guiding me as we were dragged partially though the water and lifted skywards at the same time.

'I knew that pole dancing you did would come in handy one day,' I puffed, working with all my strength to help Claudia walk me out.

Each time I slipped, she held me as, one step after another, we inched slowly upwards. The yacht lurched again, tipping ever skywards, as if it was taking its last breath, before sinking forever below the sea.

'Come on,' I muttered to myself, 'for Olivia's sake; climb you old bugger, climb.'

Finally, we were free of the dining room and winched clean out of a massive hole in the window, a window that ran the whole width of the deck we were on.

The winching stopped.

'Wait here,' Claudia said, as she helped me out of the home-made sling to take it with her.

'Lower away,' she said into the radio and I watched as she vanished back inside the sinking boat.

It seemed to take an eternity before the cable stopped feeding out and I imagined that Claudia had reached Olivia. I waited as the boat sank farther into the ocean and sea started creeping towards me, engulfing the sides of the deck where Claudia and Olivia were locked inside. I imagined the sea was now gushing into the dining room from all sides, making it nearly impossible for them to escape. The cable remained stationary and I wondered if the power had given out, leaving Claudia and Olivia dangling helpless, waiting for their end.

'It's moving, it's moving,' I screamed aloud, as the cable began its arduous retraction.

Inch by inch it slowly came up, being matched second by second by the rising sea. Then I saw them, first Olivia and then Claudia, and they were both alive. The crane stopped and Claudia, as she had done for me, released Olivia from the harness.

'Thank you,' I said.

'It's Linda we should be thanking,' Claudia said. 'but let's get off, before the *Lelantos* goes under.'

WOOP - WOOP - WOOP

From the port side, the sound of a ships horn startled us. Pulling alongside was a grey warship or maybe it was a coast guard vessel, I couldn't tell, but, as long as it wasn't the Russians, Olivia and I would be safe. But sadly, with what I now knew about Claudia and Linda, despite what they had just done to save our lives, they would spend years behind bars, if they weren't terminated first by their own side.

People with proper harnesses and safety gear appeared and we were lifted from the sinking ship and onto the rescue vessel where Linda was waiting for us.

'This way,' said an officer with a Stars and Stripes badge emblazoned on his shoulders as we were led into a room.

'Wait here,' said the officer before leaving.

In front was a large desk with its papers neatly and meticulously sorted. A high-backed chair was facing away from us. Slowly it turned.

'Hello Claudia and Linda. Welcome to MI6,' said Stephen.

Epilogue

Max

Life is a relentless march of time. In its wake, everything is changed but still seems to remain the same. It feels like only yesterday— but also a lifetime ago— that I stood on the deck of a battleship in times of war, on the convoys to Russia, was married and raised a family. Each morning I would rise, full of anticipation, in search of adventure and excitement, but complain bitterly of having no time. As years came and went, life changed. I became a grandparent and then found retirement, or did retirement find me? Yet free time was still elusive. Finally, when the chaos slowed, old age and frailty had become my companion and time a burden.

I had taken again to checking the newspaper each morning; a ritual of my lifetime stopped only when Olivia, my wife of sixty-three years, and I, were first confined by our children to this nursing home. Was it a desire to be needed or a fantasy for a life now lost that caused me to peruse the paper in search of a secret message? Why, after all of this time would there be one? For a short period each morning, as I scanned the papers, I was transported back to those days of long ago. In that dream, my body no longer ached, my balance was steady and my mind was sharp. In that fantasy, I didn't fear the prospect of dying the slow, cruel and painful death of old age—but saw instead the resurrection of a dormant soul.

So much had changed in a little over a month. We had thrown off the chains of a nursing home, travelled halfway across the world in *Operation Underpants* to save the United Kingdom from a devastating biological attack, then criss-crossed Europe, taking on the Russian Mafia. What were they going to do with us now? Olivia and I couldn't and we wouldn't go back to die a slow, dismal, agonising death in the Australian prison, the nursing home, from which we'd escaped. After the trail of destruction, we'd left in Britain, France, Italy and Greece, neither could we remain spies, or so those governments told us. This left them with a dilemma. What to do with the famous Olivia and Max—the heroes that nobody wanted?

***

The sinking of the *Lelantos*, the super yacht owned by billionaire Russian property tycoon Monya Mogilevick, made headlines around the world. The papers said the yacht was sunk when it struck a partially submerged shipping container which ripped a large hole in its hull and that it sank in a matter of minutes. The security agencies, MI6, CIA and even Mossad denied responsibility, instead, spreading the rumour that it was the work of one of the other Russian Brotherhood syndicates in a vicious power struggle. Despite the disastrous accident, according to the newspapers, only two people, Claudia, the Russian billionaire's lover, and Linda Orr, had tragically lost their lives.

We knew this wasn't true. Claudia reverted to her real name, Lucia, and, throwing off the shackles of the past went to work for the British Secret Service, along with Linda and Inspector Axel. Not long after their recruitment, one of the world's biggest and most sophisticated cyber-crime networks was smashed. As to who really attached the explosives to the hull of the yacht, nobody knows or nobody is telling.

As for Inspector Axel's daughter Kate and husband Edward, their bodies were not found in the burnt-out ruins of the house in Horton-cum-Studley. What happened to them and whether they are alive or dead is still a matter of speculation. Olivia and I think they must be involved in something and been given a new identity. If I were younger, I would have enjoyed finding out what.

***

The authorities were still left with the problem of what to do with us. It was Olivia who proposed a solution and, on reflection, I think the idea had its genesis because she secretly enjoyed playing the part of Lady Olivia Suzanne Elizabeth Huggins. We were granted, at the expense of Her Majesty's Service, a permanent berth, luxury suite and stateroom of course, on the Queen Mary 2, sailing the seven seas. This became our new home and if we felt like it, we could leave the ship, staying in a country, until the Queen made her return to whisk us away on another grand adventure in a far-off country.

It was summer, more than a year after the sinking of the *Lelantos,* when we sailed into Dubrovnik. Perhaps rather naively, we had taken a taxi to Kupari. I had wanted to show Olivia the derelict resort, the place that had haunted and connected Claudia to her past. The old resort was as desolate and disturbing as I remembered and yet, like Claudia, I found it both moving and beautiful. Whatever development Monya's company was planning, nothing had started.

As we walked among the ruins of the burned-out hotels, I told Olivia of the secret chambers that were built into the hillside behind. We had stopped and were examining a wall within the old Grand Hotel, wondering if we could find the hidden entrance to the tunnels, when Olivia gently touched my arm.

'I think we're being followed,' she said.

The End

Disclaimer

Claudia is a work of fiction and uses actual events to supplement its story. However, these occurrences are not intended to be historically or chronologically accurate.

CPSIA information can be obtained
at www.ICGtesting.com
Printed in the USA
LVOW11s0309250817

546314LV00002B/419/P